I0517344

TAMING MARIA

by

RHEA SILVA

ISBN 9781780804590

Chapter 1

There was silence throughout the assembly hall, apart from the whack of cane meeting bare flesh and the groans of the girl being chastised that echoed under the high, fan-vaulted ceiling.

She lay face down across a narrow table placed on a low platform at the far end. This was usually reserved for announcements or awards, for morning roll-call or evening prayers. Now the victim's hair streamed over one side of the bare board, her exposed buttocks raised on the other, legs astraddle. She was of ample proportions, her flesh white and soft, with big breasts and broad hips. Her buttocks bore livid stripes laid on by an expert, placed precisely, no one stroke crossing another. A pair of muscular women stood guard, ready to pounce should she attempt to escape.

The cane was wielded by a slim, middle-aged lady dressed entirely in black. There was an aura of power about her that no one dared gainsay. Her hair was drawn back into a severe bun, concealed by a white linen cap. Still handsome, her features were set in harsh lines, her eyes snapping as she stared at her prisoner's naked posterior and the split fig of her sex jutting below, barely covered by a slight coating of floss.

'Ow! Oh!' the girl cried. 'I'm sorry, Mrs Rossiter. I won't do it again. I promise!'

'Indeed you won't, Lady Cynthia!' The cane rose and fell, leaving a further trail of scarlet marks. 'Playing with yourself after lights out! It's disgusting! I won't have such behaviour at my school. It is my bounden duty to turn my charges into gentlewomen who will be suitable brides for noblemen. Stop making so much noise. Where is your dignity?'

A further blow was too much for Cynthia's control. Her bladder failed her and urine trickled between her thighs, wetting her bunched up skirt and the floor beneath. This was not the first time the spectators had witnessed such a humiliating scene, and one of them in particular was fascinated by it, a dark skein of arousal stirring in her loins.

'She couldn't hold her water, Jane,' she whispered to her companion, her green eyes sparkling, cheeks flushed and her body thrumming with excitement.

'Oh, Maria! The poor thing,' murmured her friend, a slight girl who did not possess the other's long limbs or full breasts. She was a blue-eyed blonde, whereas Maria had fiery chestnut hair and a temperament to match.

Maria was experiencing the thrill that always shot through her when punishment was being inflicted on fellow pupils. She was not the only one, it seemed. She glanced across to where Mr Robin Claremont sat. He was a young clergyman employed to give religious instruction. The girls giggled about him, starved of male company except for the servants, groundsmen and gardeners, and these were definitely out of bounds, the class system a rigid one. Now his face was red, the skin shiny with sweat, and Maria noticed that he sat with his legs crossed, his hand resting in his lap. Concealing what? she wondered.

She knew nothing about men and had never seen one naked. She had examined the Greek statues that stood in alcoves in her aunt's London residence, but although perfect examples of the male physique, their appendage were no bigger than a little finger. Sexual matters were never discussed by her tutors. Girls were supposed to go to the marriage bed innocent virgins with no idea of what lay in store. Maria burned to find out about it and discussed the matter at great length with Jane.

She had managed to keep out of trouble during the five years spent at The Lakeside Academy for Young Ladies, situated in Surrey. This may have been due to her own cleverness or the fact that she was so well connected, but lately she had begun to daydream about having the headmistress, Mrs Rossiter, take the rod to her backside. This positive woman was feared yet adored by the majority of girls, including Maria. Masturbation fantasies featuring her filled Maria's mind when she fondled her nipples and rubbed her clitoris, bringing herself off.

And Mrs Rossiter had just said that this was a forbidden occupation. Well, Maria decided, as Cynthia continued to writhe on the table, every girl here would have to be flogged if that were truly the case. We are all at it when the chance arises, either alone or with a friend. Jane and I have often pleasured one another thus.

Thinking about it made her even hotter, her sex clenching at every blow that landed on Cynthia's plump, quivering posterior. Maria could feel juice seeping from her secret place, wetting the inside of her thighs and she longed to touch the slippery little pearl swelling between her lower lips, demanding that she massage it.

How would it be to have Mrs Rossiter do it for her? It would be worth the kiss of the rod if she would only slip a hand round Maria's mound, find her crack and fondle her nubbin. And what of Robin Claremont? He was a churchman, but they were not forbidden to marry. Maybe he would know all about her cunt. She yearned to give him the chance to prove it.

At last, Cynthia was released, almost falling as she adjusted her skirt and covered her bruised hindquarters. No one was permitted to speak with her, and the rest of the pupils trailed out, very subdued as they returned to their classrooms, with the exception of Maria who strode along rebelliously. She was constantly being lectured about walking with a boy's gait instead of moving gracefully like a genteel young lady.

The school, once a private residence set amidst rolling parklands, had become her home, and she spent eleven months of the year there, only visiting her aunt, Lady Arabella, at Christmas. On these occasions she had always been left in the care of a governess, her aunt too busy to bother with her. She was one of the leading lights of the ton - the flippant, frivolous members of smart society.

Maria could clearly remember her life as it once was, the only child of Sir Piers Granger of Burrington Manor. She had been his darling, her mother dying when she was born, and he had brought her up to ride like a man, shoot and hunt like a man and hold her own in any argument, be it physical or verbal. Her life had changed radically when he died as the result of a fall from his horse. The manor was closed, save for a skeleton staff, until she came of age, and she found herself in the care of Arabella, her mother's sister. This lady was young and married to an elderly nobleman and did not want to be burdened with an orphan, so had bundled her off to the Lakeside Academy.

There Jane Dunn had become her close friend and confidante and now, lessons over, they walked hand-in-hand. Maria wanted so much to take her to bed and there bring her to bliss, caressing her pert breasts and flawless body, and the delicate little fork that concealed the seat of pleasure, and have her do the same in return. They wandered into the garden. Spring was in the air, buds bursting and the birds engaged in frenetic activity, nesting and mating. It inspired a deep hunger in Maria, for what she did not know, only aware of an emptiness within her that cried out to be filled.

'I'm so glad we are leaving school at the same time,' Jane said, finding a stone bench and sitting on it, watching the play of sunlight over the lily-pond. Even the frogs were amorous, white spawn spreading like delicate lace over the surface.

'Not long now. Thank Heavens! I can't wait.'

'Neither can I, though Papa has arranged for me to wed the odious Right Honourable Percy Tate, a man I simple can't abide.'

'It's not fair! We are treated like chattels to be bought and sold on the marriage market, our wishes of scant concern.' Maria was voicing a grievance months old. She knew this was to be her fate, too, if her aunt decreed it. 'I've a mind to run away.'

Jane's eyes became wider. 'You wouldn't dare, would you? Where would you go? What would you do?'

Maria shrugged. She had not really thought this through. 'I don't know. Make my way to Burrington Manor, find one of the villagers to take me in, get a passage on a packet-boat going abroad, maybe dress in breeches and sign on as a cabin-boy.'

'You couldn't go to France, not with the war and all.' Jane sounded intrigued, but Maria's spirits dropped, recognising that such ambitions were unlikely to come to fruition.

She would need money to break away, and her aunt and Viscount Damien Strafford, that mysterious guardian appointed by her father, had full administration of her estates until she reached twenty-one. She often wondered about this man, having never met him. He spent most of his time overseas and her aunt was not very forthcoming, hinting vaguely that he was a busy person, far too important to pay much heed to his ward. Maria knew little about him, and assumed that he was a contemporary of her father's.

'You'll have to obey your aunt and reside in London, won't you?' Jane asked and clung to her. 'Oh, my dear friend, what shall I do without you? Bath is so far away and our country house even further.'

'You will come and stay with me.' Maria hugged her close. 'I shall write to you and ask my aunt if you can visit or perhaps your parents will invite me to the West Country.'

'And if they make me marry Piers, will you come to my wedding?' Jane was close to tears.

'Of course, and if it happens before I'm a bride, then you must tell me all about your wedding-night.'

'Will it be like the mating of animals, do you think? I've seen my mother's pet bitch being covered by a dog. How horrid!' A shudder shook Jane's slim form and Maria tightened an arm about her.

This part of the garden was secluded. No one would interrupt them and she undid the tiny mother-of-pearl buttons that fastened the front of Jane s high-waisted bodice, slipped a hand inside her chemise and started to caress the small nipples that hardened at her touch. At the same time she dropped her other hand to Jane's knee and slid her skirt up, higher and higher until she reached the crisp curls that coated her friend's pubis. Jane sighed and parted her legs a little so that Maria might slip a finger into her cleft. It felt so soft and slippery and she breathed in its oceanic scent. She wanted to taste it, and lowered her head while Jane spread herself on the bench, sliding down on her spine, making herself available for Maria's mouth.

Lost in pleasure, Maria was about to suck Jane's swollen organ to completion when she stopped abruptly, aware of a sound close by.

'What's that?' Jane whispered, sitting up sharply and buttoning her bodice; skirts once more demurely in place around her ankles.

Maria put a finger to her lips and they tiptoed in the direction of the noise. It was hardly anything, a rustle of clothing, a stifled groan. Bushes screened whoever or whatever it was, and she crept closer, Jane beside her. She approached the bushes from which the sounds emerged, and carefully parted the branches.

Robin stood with his back against the bole of a tree. He was oblivious to everything, concentrating on what he was doing, the expression on his face that of a martyred saint. From where they stood, peeping between the foliage, Jane and Maria had an uninterrupted view. Maria drew in a strangled gasp, gazing in astonishment to where Robin had unfastened the flap of his form-hugging black trousers. From this protruded an object which she instinctively recognised - it was long, thick and swarthy-skinned - a fully erect penis.

The young clergyman was stroking this appendage from base to tip, working the foreskin up and down over the bulging red helm and exclaiming under his breath as he did so. Toying with it, as if it were the most wonderful of playthings, he took his hand away, releasing it from his palm so that it sprang up, slapping against his belly, reaching almost to his waist.

'Good heavens!' Jane breathed in Maria's ear. 'What a monster! Is that the thing we women are expected to take into our bodies?'

'I'd love to try, wouldn't you?' Maria whispered, her genital area on fire, her own miniature organ drumming in response to the sight of Robin's much larger pleasure instrument.

They stared fascinated as Robin, no longer able to keep his hand away, began to rub his cock again. It jumped, swelled, the helm oozing juice and he pulled down his trousers further, exposing a fine pair of balls in their hairy sac. He weighed and caressed these in his free hand and his penis grew ever bigger in response. Maria longed to fondle them and replace his fingers with her own, feeling the silky smooth skin of his shaft, the ridge of his uncircumcised knob, the red and shiny glans.

He was groaning now, his pelvis moving uncontrollably. Maria guessed that something stupendous was about to happen, though she did not know what. Would it be like her own sensations when she brought herself to fulfilment? What form would it take with a man? Robin's cries were almost piteous and his cock leapt in his hand. He rubbed it harder, harder still, almost brutal in his quest for satisfaction. Then, suddenly, it gave a final spasm and white fluid jetted from its single eye. Once, twice, thrice it discharged until finally drained of its tribute.

The penis sagged and shrank. Robin wiped it on his handkerchief and collapsed against the tree, utterly spent, eyes closed and a peaceful smile on his face. He looked hardly more than a boy, his brown hair flopping over his forehead, his prick still resting in his hand.

'I want to do that for him,' Jane said, as they crept away. 'I think I love him. How can I tell him? Help me, Maria.'

'She'll be here in a week,' said Arabella, wife of an earl, mistress of a huge country estate, and enthusiastic hostess of many an extravagant and orgiastic party.

She was in the vault of Strafford Hall, a magnificent gloomy pile in Hampstead, on London's outskirts. It belonged to her master, Viscount Damien Strafford. Manacled to a wooden crosspiece, her arms were outstretched and her legs, too, a brace holding her knees apart, her ankles in metal cuffs chained to the lower struts. She was naked apart from straps that passed round her neck and hoisted her breasts high. The nipples were pierced with gold rings from which dangled little bells that tinkled whenever she moved. Her ribs were arched, her belly flat as a lad's, the navel embellished with a further ring supporting chains that disappeared into her delta. This was hairless, a handsome barber ordered to shave her daily.

'I'm glad to hear that. It is high time I met my old friend's daughter. We were close, you know. He saved my father's life in battle and I owed him a debt I could never repay,' Damien replied, running the leather thongs of a flogger through his long, aristocratic fingers.

'How noble, and I expect you've not forgotten that she's an heiress. Whoever marries her will come into a fortune,' Arabella reminded, as she feasted her eyes on him through the veil of honey-gold ringlets that straggled over her face.

The vault was lit by braziers set at intervals along the grey stone walls.

He was worth looking at, his black hair curling around his neck and over his brow. His broad shoulders were covered by a fine linen shirt with full, belled sleeves. Open at the throat, it displayed a tanned, darkly furred chest. He strode over to stand directly in front of her, his long legs apart, covered in black leather breeches that fitted flawlessly, outlining the bulk of his penis at the apex of his thighs, and ending in highly polished riding boots.

Arabella had taken her fill of good-looking men, but no one thrilled her like Damien. They had been lovers for ages, or rather she had been his submissive. Love did not fit into the equation. Both milked life of its bounteous pleasures, and neither gave a damn about anyone else.

'Would I forget such a detail?' he answered, a cynical smile lifting his finely chiselled mouth. 'No one else shall have her dowry, lands and possessions. We'll see to that, won't we, my sweet little slave-slut?' He emphasised this remark with a flick of the whip.

Arabella squirmed and pouted. 'More, master... give me more. You know I'll support you whatever you decide to do. Maria is an innocent, a pawn in our game. Let me help you tame her for I gather that she is wilful and likes her own way. Sir Piers spoilt the girl, I fear.'

'Leave it to me,' Damien assured her, standing closer and running the pliable, many-thonged implement between her legs. 'I shall enjoy breaking-in this wild creature. You know that nothing pleases me more than subduing a hell-cat. Take yourself, for example. Didn't you fight me, once upon a time?'

'I did, master, I admit it,' Arabella murmured, while he moved the tails backwards and forwards over her love-lips and nubbin, the leather darkened by her emissions.

'Her initiation should prove to be enjoyable.' He replaced the thongs with his fingers, tugging at the labial chains, frigging her till she yelped. 'When is she arriving? I can't wait to begin her education.'

He removed his hand, threw the flogger aside and picked up a whip. She rested against him for a second, and then he turned her on the crosspiece. This was cleverly designed to give access to its victim, back and front, according to the master's desires. Her shapely shoulders, spine and buttocks were now displayed for his amusement. She guessed that the curve of her thighs and calves, the slender ankles and high-arched feet would satisfy his aesthetic taste. He was a connoisseur of art and lovely women. He moved closer and she knew he was breathing in her scent, a combination of heady French perfume, sweat induced by passion and the female juices that betrayed her arousal.

She shuddered as he trailed his lips over the nape of her neck, and then ran his tongue around the rim of her ear. She gasped. He withdrew and was silent for a long moment. She grew restless, trying to turn her head and glimpse him, but he kept out of sight. She was in a ferment of anticipation. He had excited her, then left her frustrated. He knew so well how to do this. She hated him for it, cursed him, lusted after him, completely out of control where he was concerned. Despite her restraints she tried to rub her clitoris against a knot in the wood, her aching breasts and pierced nipples, too, the tiny bells jingling.

Concentrating on seeking satisfaction, she was taken completely off guard by the fire that shot through her backside as the whip struck. She yelled and it fell again, not on the same spot, but a little higher. No sooner had she started to assimilate the agony when that wicked strip of leather writhed like a serpent as it flew high, then became a bar of pain as it landed, controlled by Damien's hand.

She had received it many times before, and had used it, too, well versed in the dichotomy of pain/pleasure. She sobbed, tears running down her face and was not sure if she was crying with happiness, fear or sheer agony. She smiled as he caressed her skin gently, around her arse, between her legs, a finger dabbling in her dew and massaging her clit, but she was wary enough not to sink into joyful anticipation. And she did not forget the instrument of torture he held in his other hand.

It touched her, gliding along her body. She started as he pressed the tip into her crack. Wet with her dew, he inserted the tip further, and then flicked the sensitive clit head. She wriggled in an attempt to control her rising pleasure. As soon as she believed she was finding the rhythm that would lead her to bliss, he took it away. He moved, and she no longer breathed in his smell.

She felt the whip tickle between her toes, up her legs, behind her knees. He was taunting her with it, goading her into breaking down and begging. She stayed silent.

Biting pain stung her back. 'Tell me what you want,' he crooned above the hiss of the lash. It became gentle, drifting around her upper thighs. 'Shall I whip your arse? Your crack? Spin you and lash your belly, your breasts, and your mound? It's no use answering for I shall use you as I fancy. And at the moment I fancy seeing your hinds change from blush pink to hellish red. Like this!'

She heard the sound of the whip rushing through the air. She felt his power and the force of the lash raining down on her flesh again and again. Her breasts seemed to become one with the wooden cross, her whole being as nothing compared to his will. This was not new, yet whenever Damien mastered her, it was as if for the first time.

He made her seem worthless, as if she was the most debased of slaves being punished. Each blow quivered through her flesh to her loins, rousing her towards orgasm yet never quite achieving it. He was like a creature possessed, blow after blow falling on her while she entered that state where pain could hardly be distinguished from sexual pleasure. Then he stopped. She heard the clunk as the whip hit the stone flags. His hand folded round her delta, the middle digit rubbing her clit until she forgot the pain and was swept up in a mighty orgasm that broke into rainbow shards around her.

He chuckled, undid his belt and let his breeches gape. He held her bruised buttocks apart and thrust his erection into her cunt. He fucked her hard for a few strokes and then pulled out. Her battered body responded, wanting more and more of him.

He set her free, each manacle removed before he forced her down in front of him. The folds of his shirt partly concealed his upraised cock. Arabella greeted it rapturously, an acolyte kneeling before this unusual altar. Her mouth opened wide and her tongue licked the length of it, finding the weeping slit and tasting the rich salty dew of his pre-come coupled with her own wetness. She rocked there, forgetting the pain that flooded her, taking him deeper until the mushroom-shaped tip butted the back of her throat.

She choked on it, gasping, 'God, you're so big!'

This pleased him, and he used her hair as a halter to draw her closer, her face buried in linen and skin and the hairy mat coating his lower belly. She breathed in the musky odour of aroused male, mingled with the eau de Cologne with which he always doused himself. He began to ride her face and she worked to bring him to the peak, cheeks caving in as she sucked vigorously.

At that moment she loved Damien, in so far as Arabella could be said to love anyone save herself. She was proud to be the one to bring him bliss. Usually she had to share him, for he was always up for it. But just for that minute fraction of time he was hers and hers alone, that marvellous, complex, cruel yet strangely sensitive and aware man. It was supremely satisfying, making her feel like a queen, an empress, a goddess.

He groaned as she enveloped his length and girth, and she felt his knees tremble. His penis swelled to its full extent. It surged and then her mouth was filled with the warmth of the semen that flooded from him. She took it all, coughing but swallowing, greedily licking up the drops that escaped to bedew her lips.

He pulled away from her, wiped his cock in her hair and adjusted his clothing, once more in perfect control of himself. Filling two goblets with wine, he handed her one and allowed her to put on her clothes. This took a matter of moments, for she had been wearing a semi-transparent gown that offered no more concealment than a nightdress. It was the height of fashion and Arabella was always in the forefront.

They moved to a divan covered in a lavishly embroidered Oriental quilt. Damien clapped his hands and a magnificently muscled Nubian servant wearing nothing but a loincloth brought in an exquisitely chased Turkish hookah. Rose water bubbled in its bowl as Damien and Arabella drew deeply of the fragrant smoke, and then blew it upwards towards the silk tenting that draped this luxurious couch.

'Our young ward has no idea of the delights in store for her,' Arabella murmured dreamily and relaxed within the circle of Damien's arm, forgetting the stripes he had inflicted, or rather rejoicing in them, an adjunct to the sensual pleasure he always lavished on her.

Chapter 2

'I miss Maria so much,' Jane confided to her leather-bound journal, the trustee of her deepest secrets.

She was seated near the window of the dormitory in the almost deserted school. 'The coach came for her two weeks ago,' she wrote on, 'and it already seems as if she has been gone a lifetime. Papa has written to say that I shall be collected tomorrow. They will stop here on their way to London. I may be able to see Maria, perhaps even be allowed to stay with her, although I understand that we will be visiting Percy and his parents in their townhouse in Mayfair. Papa is thinking of purchasing one there, though he already owns a residence in Bath and, of course, our country seat.'

She stared into the distance, tapping her lips with the tip of the quill pen, the brass inkwell to hand, the diary she had been keeping for months lying open on the escritoire. Suddenly her attention sharpened. There in the garden below her walked Robin Claremont, upright and manly, hat beneath his arm, the sunlight glinting on his brown hair. Jane drew in a sharp breath, closed her book and locked it with the key she wore on a ribbon around her neck, and then slipped it into the valise that stood, half-packed, on her bed. This was too good an opportunity to miss. She could use saying goodbye as an excuse for addressing him. In reality, she had thought of little else since that never-to-be-forgotten day when she and Maria had caught him pleasuring himself.

This scene had haunted her and she had been unable to look at him when he was taking the class for divinity. All she could see was his lean frame resting against the tree and his hand rubbing his cock and the relaxed, sensual expression on his face after he had discharged.

Driven by the thought that they might never meet again, she lifted her skirt and fled along empty, echoing corridors, down through the hall and servants quarters to the rear. Only the caretaker and his wife remained and she had been cooking for Jane in a half-hearted manner, making it plain that she would be glad to see the back of her.

Once outside, she raced to the spot below her window where she had seen Robin. He was still there and looked up when she appeared. 'Lady Jane!' he exclaimed.

'Mr Claremont.' She stopped dead, only a few inches away from him and very conscious that the rapid rise and fall of her breasts almost made contact with the sober black coat that covered his chest...

'So, you've not left yet.'

'Tomorrow. I shall be glad, for my best friend has already gone.'

'You haven't enjoyed school?' He was obviously racking his brains for subjects of conversation that would delay her.

'No, sir, not much. I don't know what I should have done without Lady Maria.'

'I remember her. A forthright young person.'

'And you will go, too? Or are you staying here?'

'I shall be heading home to Somerset, and later taking up my new post as curate in the village of Burdock.'

This is truly terrible, Jane thought. I don't know what to say. All I can visualise is his swollen cock with milky liquid spurting from the helm - his moans - his pleasure - my crying need to touch him there.

He hesitated, making her feel suddenly much older than her years. Before, he had been a teacher and she a schoolgirl, but now the memory of him in a compromising position coupled with the realisation that she was no longer under his tutelage put them on an equal footing. She liked him; could almost say that it was more than mere liking. He appealed to her in an extraordinary way, her emotions vastly different to those she experienced when with Percy Tate. She always avoided the touch of his damp, flabby fingers whereas now, as Robin tentatively reached out, she met his hand gladly, her heart fluttering like a caged bird in her breast.

He smiled widely, surprised and pleased by her acceptance of this gesture. 'Lady Jane... I didn't dare hope... have been aware of you for months. What more can I say? I'm a clergyman with modest expectations, though well connected. My uncle is a magistrate. He occupies a seat in the House of Lords, but you must have many much more suitable gentlemen begging your father's permission to court you.'

'I have one and am almost promised to him, but I find him displeasing and shall try to dissuade my parents from encouraging his advances.' The words gushed from Jane's lips. It was a wonderful relief to be able to speak to him so frankly; something she had never before achieved with anyone expect Maria.

'Oh, Jane... if I may? Is it possible that you could somehow introduce me to your Papa and put in a good word for me? I'm certain that my uncle's name might influence your father in my favour.'

'The coach will stop at the main door while my luggage is being loaded. Be in the hall, offering to assist and I'm certain that I can present you to them. My mother has a penchant for the clergy. She will be impressed.'

'Then that's settled!' He smiled rapturously. 'And you are in agreement, my dear young lady? You don't find me too repulsive?'

Jane was blushing, her heart beating so fast that it made her breasts tremble. Her nipples chafed against the lace trim of her chemise, the sensation shooting down to her loins, labia thickening, her bud rising, fluid dampening her floss. The school was empty of students and teachers. They had all left, including the formidable Mrs Rossiter. The sudden thought struck Jane that they could slip up to the dormitory unobserved and use one of the narrow beds for their first coupling. It was so outrageous a concept that she shook and Robin felt that tremble pass through her fingers into his.

'Jane!' he exclaimed softly, and his mouth came closer, hovering over hers.

'Oh, Robin!' she replied on a sob.

'Darling angel.'

Inexperienced at kissing, his nose bumped hers, but she had learned the art with Maria and angled her lips, puckering up to take his. At first it was a chaste kiss, their mouths remaining modestly sealed, but this wasn't enough for Jane. She wanted to experience what she had felt for her girl friend, opening up and finding Robin's tongue, tangling with it in a dance of desire. His breath was fresh and he quickly followed her lead, giving her so much pleasure that she collapsed into his arms, careless of anyone seeing them.

He was conscious though; his prospects of advancement would be hampered if it was reported that he had been seen toying with one of the pupils. He reluctantly withdrew from her, straightening up and saying, 'We must find somewhere private. Dare I ask you to accompany me to my room?'

This was indeed an unusual request and no doubt he knew the rules whereby it was customary for a young lady to be chaperoned at all times and never, under any circumstances, be alone with a man. Her reputation would be ruined if this happened, yet his impetuosity thrilled her; it was as if he could not help himself. Common sense said no, but a new, bold persona urged Jane to take the plunge. Instinct recognised that Robin was no philanderer who would seduce and then abandon her.

In a short while they had traversed the upper floors, passing no one on the way, and at last reaching the seclusion of a medium sized apartment in the west wing where he had lived for eighteen months. Clear of clutter and practical it contained a desk, a tallboy, a fireplace, two chairs and a wash-stand. A four-poster bed took pride of place, its width promising much.

They kissed again, unable to refrain from touching, cleaving together, needing to be as close as was humanly possible; one mind, one flesh. Now Jane understood the meaning of the marriage vows - *Forsaking all others - till death us do part - with my body I thee worship...*

For the first time ever she realised this could be a wonderful commitment - with the right man. I shall tell Maria, she promised herself.

Then all sensible thought fled. Robin caught her to him and to her joy she felt the pressure of the long bough of his penis. It bored against her belly, hard and hot, and she was not afraid, knowing what it looked like.

'Jane! Oh, my dear, I shouldn't have brought you here. It's too tempting. I don't know if I can control myself,' he muttered, his face buried in the softness of her neck, his breath tickling her ear, causing a flurry of sweet sensations.

She was not sure that she wanted him to exert control, though dire warnings issued by her governesses rang in her ears. 'No man respects a girl who gives in to his lustful desires. You'll end up on the stage if you are too free with your favours, no better than you should be!'

Then there was the matter of pregnancy. More than one of the maid-servants in her father's household had been thrown on to the streets when confessing to being with child. There was no provision for a woman who conceived out of wedlock. If the father deserted her, and nine times out of ten he did, and her relatives cast her out and the parish refused to support her, then she was doomed to a life of begging or prostitution to feed herself and her bastard.

Jane had not heard of it happening among her own class, but then an arranged marriage would go ahead, the date simply brought forward a little, titles, property and religion of prime importance. But if she found herself in the family way by a humble clergyman? What then? I can't, her mind screamed, but I want him, her wayward flesh argued.

Despite her reservations she found herself lying on the bed with Robin beside her. It felt so natural, his arms holding her, his mouth against hers, his body part covering her. Even the new sensation of his jaw was a novelty, slightly rasping although he was close-shaved. She was accustomed to Maria's smooth cheek. Being with a man was altogether different - his embrace was harsher, his kisses rougher, his whole attitude one of dominance. It made Jane feel puny and of no account against the force of his passion.

His hand closed over one of her breasts. At first he seemed content just to cup it, but then his fingers began to move, tracing over the pert swell of the nipple. It rose towards him like the hopeful nose of a household pet, begging to be caressed. He bowed his head and she felt his hot breath warming the eager teat, then the delirious sensation of him sucking it through the muslin. Encouraged by her moans of pleasure he unbuttoned her bodice, exposing the pink rosebud and licking it.

Jane could feel her resolutions melting like snow in sunlight. He was so hesitant and shy, almost afraid to touch her, as if she was made of spun-glass that might shatter. Wanting to reassure him, she wound her arms round his neck and ground her pelvis against his thigh. He started, trembled and his prick became larger and harder, wanting release. She dropped her hand down, groping for the trouser closure.

His own clamped over her searching fingers. 'No,' he begged, in a tumult of indecision. 'No... I mean, oh, yes... can you really want to handle my manhood?'

'I do,' she urged, then bowed her head. 'I must confess that I have already seen it. Maria and I were hiding behind the bushes and watched you bring yourself relief.'

'You did? And you weren't shocked?' He released her hand, permitting her fingers free rein in their exploration of his person.

'I was excited,' she murmured, finding the flap that was buttoned each side of his waist, releasing it and unfolding the square of material to below his crotch.

His cock was hidden by his shirt, but she lifted this away and freed the sturdy phallus from its confinement. It felt every bit as good as she had imagined - so warm and heavy and needy. Greatly daring, Jane followed the dictates of nature and lowered her head so that her mouth engulfed it, taking in the length and girth until it prodded her throat.

Robin lay there transfixed. It was as if his wildest fantasy had been fulfilled, transporting him to heaven. 'Jane, Jane...' he whispered, with a catch in his voice. 'This is the first time a woman has touched me, let alone done what you're doing. There were whores haunting the taverns in Oxford where I

13

attended university, and some of the other fellows used them, but I was studying religion and didn't think it right. A few of the students practiced sodomy, but this, too, I avoided. I never dreamed... never even hoped that a genteel young lady would want to do this to me. Where did you learn?'

She freed her mouth and looked up at him, replying, 'Like you, I'm still a virgin. I've made love with Maria, caressed and fondled her and she me. We've rubbed each other's nubbins and brought on that heady sensation and the wonderful rush of relief, but neither of us have ever been with a man.'

'My dearest, what you did with her is supposed to be sinful and, as a man of the cloth, I should condemn you for it, but oh, God forgive me, I can't find anything wrong in that innocent exploration. It was but preparing you for the delights you would find with your husbands, in the fullness of time. Ah, that's it! Go on, darling, nibble round my foreskin. Play with my cods! Oh, I can't hold on much longer! Stop for a moment and let me see your cunny. Show me how to pleasure you as Maria did.'

Jane raised her skirts higher and higher. It was all very well displaying her treasures to Maria, but a different matter entirely to show them to Robin. It was embarrassing, yet strangely enjoyable. She was proud of her fair, curly bush and neat fork, considering the whole area much tidier than a man's equivalent - the clubbed penis and ugly balls. For the first time in her life she was glad to be female, suddenly aware of their superiority, and not only in the sexual arena. They were clever, cunning, wily and manipulative. Men thought themselves to be in charge, but they were merely putty in the hands of a skilful woman.

She held her labial lips apart with delicate fingertips, permitting Robin to see her greatest asset - her clitoris. Dear little pinnacle of joy, so sensitive and discreet. It throbbed, sending shafts of pleasure through every part of her body, always happy to oblige again and again.

He stared down at it, puzzled. 'But I thought... imagined... gathered from what my fellow students said, that a girl needed a man inside her to bring her off. What is this that resembles a pink pearl lying within your folds?'

'My bud, my little button,' she said, shivering with delight as he tentatively touched it. 'I don't know a great deal about it, but this is where we obtain our joy. I've no idea how the male thingy feels as I've never had one in me. I daren't. I don't want to have a baby.'

'Indeed not.' Robin could not stop touching her, wetting his fingers with her copious juice and applying it to every nook and cranny, even dipping down to anoint the tight moue of her anus. 'I won't let this happen. I only want to caress you a little, to hold you in my arms and make tender love to you.'

He undressed her very carefully and she helped him for he was unskilled with buttons and lacing. It did not take long for her to disrobe. She wore nothing but a puff-sleeved dress made of thin material worn over a single petticoat and a chemise. Only the very daring and avant-garde wore drawers as they were considered to be a scandalously masculine garment.

When she was completely nude, Robin worshipped her beauty as an artist

14

will adore the perfect female form. 'Now I know why God created Eve,' he whispered.

He was naked, too, impressing her with his broad chest and shoulders and narrow waist, his sleek hips and long legs. Somehow his cock did not seem so absurd now that he was as nature intended, a prime example of young, virile maleness. She could almost find it beautiful, was glad to stroke it, her fingers responding to the softness of the skin that covered the stem as she admired the crimson glans rising from the flared ridge and the dew seeping from its single eye.

His touch on her delta was inexpert and she guided his fingers. 'Gently, gently... don't rub it so hard. Make it wetter... that's right... softly, softly, leave the tip for a moment and stroke either side. Can you feel it swelling? Oh, oh... now back to the head. Harder! Harder!'

She could no longer wait, his unskilled fingers following her instructions, getting into the swing of it until she forgot who she was and where, only knowing that she was climbing to the peak, reaching that point of no return, overwhelmed with a blinding ecstasy that robbed her of consciousness for a second.

The next thing she knew was urging him on top of her, taking his prick between her thighs and rubbing herself up and down on it till he, too, cried out as he came, spattering her belly with his emission and then collapsing.

So, we didn't have complete intercourse, she mused, running her fingers through Robin's hair as he dozed beside her. There was no actual carnal knowledge and no fear of a baby, but oh, it was so enjoyable nonetheless, and she made notes in her head in order to relate every aspect to Maria.

'She's a stunner! I've never seen such a lovely girl,' Damien observed as he stared down.

Unaware of his scrutiny, Maria was romping in the garden with Arabella's miniature spaniel, Poppy. The tiny creature was as much a fashion accessory as her fan, or the young black page in his turban and colourful livery.

'I'm glad you like her.' Arabella nestled back against Damien as they stood in the window recess. His breath lightly fanned her ear and she could feel the baton of his sex pressing into her, the material forming hardly any barrier between their bodies.

'I do indeed. It was worth staying away until she matured. A most pleasant surprise.'

'I did tell you that she was growing into a beauty.' Arabella caught her breath as his hands encompassed her breasts and his lips continued cruising around that sensitive spot at the back of her neck.

'I can't wait to indoctrinate her into our ways,' he murmured, thumbs revolving on her nipples. 'She doesn't know I'm here?'

'No. You wanted to introduce yourself in your own time, didn't you?'

'That's right. If she is biddable, and I'm sure I can make her so, then I will marry her. She is an heiress with a vast fortune and I wouldn't like to see it squandered by some spendthrift rake.'

'As her guardian you will have the last word,' Arabella reminded, standing like a statue as he raised her skirt, parted her buttocks and inserted his erection into her. She moaned and eased herself down on it.

He kept his eyes riveted on Maria while he mounted her aunt, and the lust that drove him had little to do with Arabella. It was fired by his ambition to own both the girl and her money.

Armitage House, town residence of the Earl of Westwood and his wife, Lady Arabella, was situated in a half-moon terrace of elegant houses close to Hyde Park. They were much sought-after, a stone's throw from the city, within easy reach of shops and theatres, the Palace, and the seat of Government, the Houses of Parliament,

The park was the largest of those green, tree-shaded areas that brought a breath of the countryside to London, reminding the occupants of how it had once been. Originally a port on the River Thames, it had gradually absorbed the surrounding villages until it became a powerful city.

Among many other entertainments, Maria was taken to this popular venue by her aunt. In daylight it was a meeting place for the rich who liked to enjoy refreshments at small cafes, to gossip and preen and stroll, showing off the latest fashions while their coachmen waited in a space reserved for their ornate vehicles.

'At night,' Arabella told Maria, 'it acquires a different aspect, the haunt of thieves and harlots, vagrants and villains and is certainly out of bounds to genteel young ladies. You must never even consider coming here.'

As part of her introduction to the high life, Arabella had taken her riding in Rotten Row. They sat side-saddle, their skirts trailing down across their mounts' withers, the wind pressing their hat veils against their faces and elegant gentlemen cantering alongside. Arabella flirted with them outrageously. Maria was beginning to get her measure. It seemed that she did what she liked, indulged by her elderly husband. He did not object if she entertained gentlemen in the privacy of her boudoir, and followed his own inclinations in the company of common women, maidservants, shop-girls and the like.

Maria kept her mouth shut and her ears open, absorbing the nuances of this unconventional household. Arabella had given him a legitimate heir, in the shape of little James, and it appeared that should she have any more children he was quite prepared to accept them as his own even if they were of some other man's spawning.

Although she had only been in London for a short while, Maria was already causing a stir. Eighteen years old and an heiress. The world was her oyster. Doors had opened for her and she found herself accepted. Her aunt was taking an interest in her, no longer handing her over to governesses, although there was a chaperone. Mrs Sarah Jenkins, a portly widow, had been engaged for the post. She fussed over her charge, but had an eye for any attractive footman or other male member of staff who might be disposed towards her. Maria had deduced that it would not be difficult to twist her round her little finger and probably get away with murder. She had a maidservant called Emily who was pretty and pert, but she missed Jane dreadfully and, so far, they had not met up.

One morning they went to take the air in the park. The earl's coach had deposited them and now waited in the carriage rank. It was midday and warm. Children accompanied by nursemaids were running around the pond and feeding bread to the ducks. Girls fresh from finishing schools were walking with their duennas while their mothers chatted to cronies, the latest court scandals on everyone's tongue, the goings-on of the heir to the throne, George, Prince of Wales and his numerous mistresses. Maria had not yet had the honour of being presented to His Highness.

Attended by her entourage, Arabella, wearing floating white, held up an unfurled parasol to fend off the sun's rays. 'One must preserve a pale complexion at all times,' she instructed Maria as they walked along a tree-lined avenue. 'It is essential that one isn't confused with a gypsy or, heaven forefend, a working woman!'

Mrs Jenkins was in tow, and Arabella's personal maid, Kitty Ford. The page-boy, Ali, brought up the rear, with Poppy on a scarlet lead attached to a bejewelled collar. They reached Rotten Row, that meeting place for equestrian fanatics, where gallant men rode noble beasts, much admired by their ladies. There was a high-perch phaeton race in progress and people stood aside to let Arabella through. Maria found it exhilarating, the two vehicles flashing round the course, hooves thudding on the turf and iron-bound wheels rumbling. Light, high carriages, fast and dangerous, each was drawn by a pair of sweating horses. The spectators yelled with excitement, a collection of quarrelsome young bloods who were obsessed with gambling. They had put money on the outcome.

'Will you look at them?' Arabella said scathingly. 'They are a conceited bunch, racketing around London as if they own each stick and stone.'

'Who are they?' Maria was intrigued, for several were smiling and bowing as they caught her eye.

'Blue-blooded sons of the nobility, who care for nothing but the cut of their jackets. They drink and whore and are usually deep in debt with their tailors and fellow gamblers.' Arabella sounded unusually stern as she added, 'Beware of them, Maria, for if they haven't already succeeded in netting a rich wife, then they are on the lookout for one. Keep them at arm's length, my dear, for the word is already out that you are a "fortune".'

'That's not very nice,' Maria protested, turning her back on them, too absorbed in the race to pay them much heed.

'They aren't very nice. I'm warning you. Leave any prospective suitors to myself or your guardian.'

'When shall I meet him, this mysterious man who is in charge of my affairs?'

Sometimes Maria longed for her twenty-first birthday when she would be allowed to manage her own estate.

'Very soon, my love.' And Arabella tapped her lightly on the cheek with her closed fan.

'I'd like to race like that,' Maria cried, as the phaetons thundered towards them, one gaining on the other. She longed to feel the reins under her gloved hands and experience the speed and exhilaration and receive the adulation of the crowd.

'And why not, my darling? You are a splendid horsewoman. Your father trained you well and this would be a novelty and rouse much interest... a female taking part,' Arabella agreed, a thoughtful look in her eyes. 'I know of one person who would be overjoyed to accept such a challenge.'

This was intriguing and, 'Who is it?' Maria asked eagerly.

'That's a secret. You'll meet him on the appointed day and not before. Doesn't this make it all the more thrilling? Do you want me to act as go-between and arrange matters?'

Maria's challenge had been accepted by this unknown adversary. It was fascinating and her pulse was beating fast when she arrived at Rotten Row on the morning of the race. A groom drove the high phaeton and she sat beside him. It was a splendid vehicle, its green varnish gleaming, picked put with gold lines. It was pulled by a pair of matching greys, fierce-eyed and spirited, with flowing manes and tails. Arabella had said airily that she had the equipage on loan from a friend. Sarah Jenkins, all of a flurry because they had left the house so early, was driven in an open-topped gig, somewhat mollified because the coachman was young, personable and flirtatious.

Maria had been practicing daily, and the groom had shown her how to steer the fine sporting vehicle and the best way of handling the horses. It had proved more difficult than she had at first thought, but her early training with her father proved vital and she had not forgotten any of it.

Under Arabella's guidance and with the help of a fiercely expensive tailor, she had elected to wear a scarlet jacket cut like a man's, military in style. With it was a long straight skirt of matching fabric slit to the waist on one side and worn over close-fitting breeks and riding boots. The only time breeches were acceptable was as part of a lady's riding habit, but even so Maria's outfit was daring enough to cause a ripple among the spectators as she took the driver's seat. The groom jumped down and held the horses' heads. They snorted and tossed their manes, fidgeting nervously, flight animals ready to bolt.

Arabella had arrived in her chaise, and was waiting for her at the start line where the Master of Ceremonies was ready to drop his kerchief, signalling the off. She was escorted by half a dozen personable fops, all agog to meet Maria, their jaded appetites titillated at the notion of a woman racing against a man. This would set a trend, and they loved novelty, gambling lavishly on the outcome.

Maria paid them little attention. She was concentrating, gentling her nervous team, speaking softly to them, their twitching ears convincing her that they could hear her and were soothed. Then Arabella reached up and touched her hand, bringing her back to reality and saying, 'There he is, my dear. There's your adversary.'

She was pointing to the right and Maria followed her direction. Her challenger was standing by the heads of an ebony team, his dark blue phaeton gleaming. The group of admirers around him were laughing at some remark he had just made. She feared it concerned herself for they were looking her way.

It was impossible to drag her eyes from him, for he was a tall, striking man, splendidly attired. His figure was shown to full advantage with the coat cut away in front and the wide lapels folded back. His tight white breeches were so high in the rise that they disappeared under his beige waistcoat, his torso and legs displayed in an unbroken line that ended in polished black top boots with brown leather trim. Maria's eyes kept returning to the fullness in his crotch, his cock pressed against his left inner thigh, emphasised by the close fitting buckskins.

He was extremely handsome, a stiff collar and black stock wound several times round his neck, framing his patrician features. He was bare-headed, his curly-brimmed topper in his hand, and his black hair fell about his ears and neck and over his brow. But it was his eyes that captivated her, even from that distance; their power and persuasiveness. Were they grey or icy blue? He was too far away to tell, but there was a ruthless slant to his mouth that made her weak at the knees.

This was the man she would ride against! The task ahead seemed almost impossible. Then their eyes met and she read something in them that stiffened her resolve. He was mocking her, challenging her, certain that she would fail and make him the conqueror. Damn him, she thought, fury welling up. I'll show the arrogant bastard! Who the hell does he think he is? But this was really of no consequence against her desire to prove herself to him and end up in his arms and in his bed, kissed by that arrogant mouth, possessed by that strong body.

She guided the phaeton with a light touch on the reins, and a roar went up from the crowd as her opponent took his place on his lofty perch. Now they were much closer and she was piqued because he did not look at her, staring straight ahead. Grooms attended the horses, checking that they were on the starting line. The atmosphere was tense. Silence fell, all holding their breath, everything so quiet that even the singing of the birds was an interruption. The cloudless blue sky stretched above them, a glorious English summer, but Maria was in no fit state to appreciate it, only aware of the straight track before her and the man beside her.

'Don't let her beat you, sir!' shouted a lad from among the throng. 'Can't have a woman thinking she's as good as us!'

Laughter welled up and Maria's rival nodded solemnly in the speaker's direction. The crowd hushed again as the Master of Ceremonies lifted his white handkerchief. It flashed momentarily, and then dropped.

Maria forgot everything except the reins in her hands and the team in front. Freed from restraint, they shot ahead. The phaeton rocked and bounced as it gathered speed, gravel flying from beneath hooves and wheels, the scenery a blur of colour. She had no time to see what was happening to her challenger. Her greys were not yet at full stretch; she was keeping a little in reserve. Both vehicles reached the end of the avenue, neck and neck, spraying grit as they turned. They teetered precariously and then Maria's vehicle shot forward in a sudden burst of speed, rearing towards the other, her team plunging madly.

He swerved. She crossed his path. He wheeled, and she heard him curse. He was a pace behind her now. She set her teeth grimly, determined to keep her advantage, but he let out his team, little by little, a master horseman. He edged closer to her, gained on and passed her. He cast her a glance in which she read triumph. Infuriated, she was almost on her feet. Ahead lay the turn and both took it at reckless speed. They tore down the stretch that marked the end of the second lap. Four more to go, and they took three without either gaining advantage, two perfectly matched contenders. The spectators were wild with enthusiasm, betting furiously, Maria's performance causing a change of heart among many. They began to applaud her.

The tension mounted as the dust-splattered phaetons went into the final round. He was half a length ahead, his team full-out, their ebony backs white with foam, responding as he shouted encouragement. Maria's greys were pounding behind him, ears and tails flat, nostrils dilated and sweat creaming their hides. Now they were shoulder to shoulder with the blacks. The spinning wheels grated as they touched for a jarring second, and then broke free as they took the home stretch, galloping together.

Suddenly his whip cracked and Maria felt a burning sensations as it struck her shoulder. A fractional blow that could have been intended for his team, but he was too skilful for that and she knew it was meant for her. Surprise mingled with fury that he would have dared and yet, deep down, she thrilled at the kiss of the lash. His blacks reached the finishing post just in front of her greys. They slewed to a halt and the crowd shouted and cheered.

The groom was there to take the horses and Maria leapt down nimbly, though her shoulder still stung and she intended to take her opponent to task. She took off her hat, shook out her hair and peeled off her gloves in rapid succession, too annoyed to pay much attention to the group of beaux who quickly surrounded her, all smiling and congratulatory. Arabella was with them.

'Darling, you did very well,' she enthused.

Maria refused to be mollified. 'He beat me!' she snapped, humiliated by her defeat. 'Not only that, he caught me with his whip and I'm sure it was deliberate.'

'Ah, maybe. Come and meet him.'

'Must I? I'm hot and sweaty and in need of a change of clothing.' Maria had never been more reluctant, yet her curiosity about him was boundless.

Arabella slipped an arm through hers, saying as they walked towards the group gathered round the winner, 'I'm sure he won't object to this.'

They reached him and Maria found herself coming under the scrutiny of ice-blue eyes set in the most handsome face she had ever seen. Every resolve to complain about his use of the whip melted away. Longing filled her as he reached out his hand, took hers and, bowing, placed a kiss on the back of it. His lips seemed to scorch her skin.

'You did well,' he said, in a deep voice the cadences of which seemed to ripple along her nerves and connect with her sex. 'A worthy contender in every way.'

Arabella stepped forward, smiling and saying, 'Maria, meet your guardian, Viscount Damien Strafford.'

Chapter 3

Just for a moment Maria lost her grip on reality. The stranger who had just bested her before a crowd and had had the nerve to take his whip to her, was none other than her legal guardian.

She had expected him to be at least as old as her father, but this was a man in his prime, not yet thirty perhaps, virile and handsome, with fierce eyes and an arrogant manner. A far cry from anything she had visualised, even in her wildest dreams.

It was a second before she remembered to dip into a curtsy, daring to glance up and stammer, 'I had no idea...'

'That was how I wished it to be. We organised it very well, your aunt and I. Don't you agree?' His tone was light and he retained possession of her hand for a fraction longer than was necessary. In his eyes she read volumes - appraisal - interest - a challenge.

She rose to her full height, spine stiff, chin tilted at a stubborn angle. 'I do not agree, sir. It was a cruel trick to play. Could you not have introduced yourself to me first?'

His black brows swooped down in a frown and his eyes were like Arctic ice. 'You presume too much. You are in my hands until you are of a responsible age, and will do as I say, even in such paltry matters as this.'

'You're not my father!' she stormed, filled with indignation. 'You can't tell me what to do.'

'Indeed and I can, young lady. You are my ward and as such must regard me as having the authority of a parent.'

'That's not fair!' she ranted, glaring at him and then at Arabella.

'Very little in life is fair, as you will discover as you go on,' he observed cynically.

'You deuced lucky dog, Damien!' one of his raffish companions exclaimed, digging him in the ribs. 'Damme, I wish I had a ward half as pretty.'

This caused raucous merriment, each beau striving to outdo the other in witty remarks. Damien stared at the first speaker coldly. 'You will respect her, sir, or have me to answer to. If I take offence and call you out you may choose your weapon, pistol or rapier. As you are probably aware, I'm an expert with both.'

This silenced any further comment and he offered his left arm to Maria, who placed hesitant fingertips on it and permitted him to escort her to his cabriole. A groom unfolded the iron step, and she lifted her skirt, giving a glimpse of those immodest breeches as she entered the well-sprung vehicle. Damien cocked an eye at them but said nothing. Arabella was already seated, while Kitty and Sarah travelled in the gig, along with Damien's manservant.

'Will you partake of luncheon with us?' Arabella asked, pressing against Damien as they occupied the seat opposite Maria.

'Thank you, I'd like to,' he replied, glancing at her in a way that indicated a long-standing friendship. 'I want to look through Maria's wardrobe and ascertain that she has everything required by a young lady entering society. I hope she isn't entertaining the idea of this latest notion for wearing a damp petticoat beneath the dress to make it cling to the legs, or even adopt pantaloons under a diaphanous skirt.'

'I can assure you that I have spent hours with her at the dressmakers and milliners, and her clothing is most suitable for her station.' Arabella fluttered her long eyelashes at him, making no secret of her admiration.

'I take your word for it, but will check to make sure. Giddy girls can be disobedient and wilful and I'll have none of this.' He stared straight at Maria with a piercing look that seemed to dart down her spine and connect with her loins. 'As you know, Arabella, I'm holding a soiree at Strafford Hall tonight. I would like you both to attend.'

'I'm looking forward to it; your gatherings are always so stimulating,' Arabella answered, slanting him a meaningful glance.

Maria's cheeks were hot. He made her feel most uncomfortable. She was terribly aware of his masculinity and power, not only of body but of will. No one could gainsay him, least of all someone like herself who was new to the games played between adults. The place where his whip had caught her burned and she could not stop thinking about it, remembering the savage look on his face, the heat and sweat of the contest and the humiliation of losing. She had never before felt her strength draining away in a man's presence, but this was the sensation that swept her, even in the calmness of the carriage trotting sedately through the park.

She envied Arabella seated so close to him. Her thigh, thinly covered by a silk skirt, was pressed against his. As she leaned towards him her breasts rose, two firm alabaster globes bare almost to the nipples at the edge of her low bodice. Maria sensed their intimacy and envied it, yet knew he was trouble and she would be wise to steer clear, although there was something about the dangerous man that was irresistible.

When he addressed her directly his tone was more one of command than request. 'You'll come to my party, Maria.'

'Yes, sir. Thank you for inviting me,' she replied, though despising her weakness. Why could she not have feigned a headache or weariness? Would it have been of any use? Or would he have insisted anyway? She feared the latter would be the case.

When she arrived at Armitage House it was to find Jane waiting for her. They were in each other's' arms in a second, with Jane exclaiming breathlessly, 'At last we are together! Mama left me here just now. The butler said you would be back by lunchtime.'

'How long can you stay?' Maria held her at arm's length, examining her face intently. 'She will be collecting me shortly.'

'Are you in London for long?'

'For a while. Mama is visiting her dressmaker and milliner and also attending the opera. I hoped to see you before this, but it hasn't been possible I've so much to tell you.' Jane's eyes were sparkling and there seemed to be a new confidence and maturity about her.

'Maria, you are forgetting your manners,' Arabella chided, coming up to them. 'You've not yet presented your friend to the viscount and myself.'

'I apologise,' Maria said, and drew Jane forward. 'Lady Jane Dunn, my dear friend from school. Jane, this is my aunt, Lady Arabella, Countess of Westwood, and my guardian, Viscount Damien Strafford.'

Jane curtsied low and then gazed at them shyly. 'I hope I'm not intruding,' she said nervously. 'I so much wanted to see Maria and promise not to be a nuisance. I am in the care of my chaperone, Miss Bailey.' She pointed to a plain woman in black who was standing in the background.

'Welcome, Jane. We are about to partake of luncheon. Won't you join us?' Arabella said graciously. 'It will be a pleasure to have the company of two such charming damsels. You can tell us about school. Maria has rarely spoken of it. But first, I suggest you go with her to her room for she must change out of her riding clothes.'

Sarah was ordered to look after Miss Bailey. She took her to the housekeeper's quarters where duennas, who were not exactly servants nor yet members of the family, took their meals and mingled with this doyen of the female staff, and the butler who was in charge of everything else, including the wine-cellar.

At last Maria and Jane were alone, dancing round the beautiful bedroom with its floral wallpaper, Persian rugs and rosewood furniture. Then they collapsed on the ornate four-poster, laughing joyously. 'Oh, it's so good to see you!' Maria exclaimed.

'You, too. I've missed you!'

Maria got up and stripped away her jacket and the shirt she wore beneath, then the skirt and breeches, wearing only her knee-length chemise as Jane helped her tug off her boots, unfasten her garters and peel down her white stockings. Maria went to the washstand and poured water from the jug into a basin, soaping her hands and face and underarms, getting rid of the sweat induced by her ordeal.

Jane, watching her, clasped her hands against her breasts, gave a tremulous smile and with eyes shining like stars said, 'I'm in love!'

'What? Who? Tell all,' Maria demanded, taking up the towel and drying herself, then sitting on the bed and tucking her bare legs under her, careless of ruffling the lacy quilt.

'You'll never believe it!'

'Don't tease, Jane! Tell me at once!' Maria's blood was already running hot, unable to think of anyone save her guardian.

'It's Robin... Robin Claremont.'

'The clergyman?' Maria was astonished. Her closest friend and that rather solemn young man? It was almost beyond belief, and yet hadn't she fancied him herself, as had most of the other pupils?

Jane sat with her arms clasped around her hunched knees, a rapturous expression on her face. 'We declared our love the day before I left. He's gone home and I'm with my parents so it makes it awfully difficult to have any contact. He can't even write to me, for Agatha Bailey has eyes like a hawk, so I was wondering if he could send letters here, perhaps. I did meet him very briefly in Bath one afternoon but it was terribly risky. However, he told me he was coming to London to study so maybe we can arrange a meeting while I'm here, especially if Mama lets me stay with you. He gave me his address. He has lodgings with fellow students for a while, before he takes up a post as curate.'

'Isn't it possible that he might see your parents and tell them how he feels about you?' This seemed a sensible approach, though Maria knew all too well the restrictions put upon girls of their class.

'He did meet them when I was leaving the school, and Mama liked him, but he's not titled or wealthy enough to be taken seriously as a suitor.' Tears welled up in Jane's eyes and she turned to Maria. 'Oh, I love him so much, and we've made love...'

'What? You've lost your virginity?' Maria was both envious and appalled.

'No, no... not exactly, but I did give him the ultimate pleasure and he caressed me like you have done, so I feel already committed to him.'

'Was it good, better than when we've pleasured one another?' Maria was filled with curiosity, wanting to know every detail.

'It was wonderful. I can't begin to describe what it is like to be held by a man so strong and passionate... and to fondle his thingy to feel it throb and spurt.'

Jane sat there as if transfixed by memories.

'I think I understand,' Maria said slowly. 'Of course, I've not yet experienced it, but today I felt such strong feelings towards my guardian, meeting him for the first time under unusual circumstances. I can imagine what you are telling me.'

Jane sat quietly while Maria recounted the race, the wagers, the shame of

24

being defeated and the strange thrill when she had tasted Damien's whip. 'He is very handsome, but there's something frightening about him,' Jane said.

'Don't you see? That's part of his charm. One could never be certain what he was going to do. He could be angry or loving, fierce or gentle. He's an enigma and I'm certain there's something going on between him and my aunt.'

'But she's married!' Jane was genuinely shocked.

'That doesn't seem to stop her encouraging other men,' Maria responded. 'This is a liberal household, Jane, and I've been invited to a party at the viscount's house tonight. If we can persuade your mother to let you stay with me, then you can come too.'

'I'd like to do that, but nothing can take Robin's place. Oh, what are we to do?'

'We'll think of something. My maid, Emily, is very resourceful and likes to deceive Mrs Jenkins, if she can. I'm sure she'll help us.' But Jane continued to look so miserable that Maria took her in her arms to comfort her. She rocked her as if she was a baby, but soon that maternal feeling changed.

She kissed Jane's lips tenderly, and they parted slightly, the tip of her pink tongue meeting that of her friend's. They had played like this together so often that it came as second nature to both. Jane relaxed, and her hands came up to caress Maria's breasts. It felt wonderful, and the tension that had been building within Maria ever since meeting Damien now demanded relief. She sighed and lifted her tingling nipples towards Jane's fingers in an ardent quest for further pleasure. Her chemise was loose-fitting and slipped from her shoulders and uncovered her to the waist. Jane did not hesitate to take advantage of this, admiring Maria's beautiful assets, kissing and fondling them.

They pressed their bodies even closer, and Maria found Jane's smaller breasts, baring them to her touch. As they lay back among the pillows she whispered, 'Tell me about Robin's manhood. Did it grow big for you as it did when we watched him playing with it?'

'Oh, yes, even bigger.'

'What was it like to touch?' Maria asked, feeling Jane going limp beneath her hands as she pushed her skirt up to her waist and worked her hand past her flat stomach and started to comb through the curly fair hair that covered her mound.

'Incredibly smooth and silky,' Jane gasped, her hips rising to meet Maria's touch.

'And hard?'

'As a lance... reaching to his navel...'

Jane began to return Maria's favour, diving a hand under her short chemise and inserting her middle finger into her damp cleft, rubbing the labial wings and exciting the stiff nodule at their crown.

'Was it as good as this?' Maria asked, hardly able to speak.

'Almost, though perhaps not quite as good,' Jane averred, repeating that enticing friction, while Maria bent to suck one of her friend's nipples into her mouth, lapping at it with the tip of her tongue.

'Let us try to come off together,' Maria freed her lips to suggest, and her fingers rubbed each side of Jane's pleasure nubbin, making it slippery wet with her juices, while Jane did the same for her.

Delight raised Maria to the heights and she continued to rouse Jane, even though she reached the pinnacle, dying a little as she plunged down from the peak, her body shuddering. Jane gave a strangled cry and Maria opened her with gentle fingers, pressing into her virgin hole and finding an obstruction.

'You didn't lie, my dear. You still have your maidenhead.'

'I wouldn't lie to you,' Jane insisted, wrapping her legs around Maria as they lay in abandonment on the crumpled quilt, still caressing, still rejoicing in one another's flesh.

Then, without any warning, the door opened. Damien stood there, backed by the chaperones.

There was a startled pause before he said, with an amused twist to his lips, 'Ah, I see that you two young ladies are... resting.'

Maria recovered her aplomb first, straightening her chemise and reaching for her dressing robe that lay at the foot of the bed. 'Indeed yes, sir. I have had an exhausting morning. Now, if you will be good enough to leave I shall ask Jenkins to attend me while I change.'

Her coolness astonished her. She didn't even blush, but Jane was considerably rattled, swinging her legs over the side of the mattress hurriedly, head hanging down and scarlet in the face. Maria took one look at her guardian and realised he found the situation arousing. His lips twitched and he could not hide a smile, and his eyes went from one girl to the other in a speculative manner.

He had changed from riding attire and was now wearing beige breeches cut so tight that they outlined his phallus. Hessian boots rose to his knees, and he had on a dark blue velvet cut-away jacket over a double-breasted waistcoat. Lace showed at his cuffs and gold fobs glittered from a watch-chain, while a diamond pin flashed amidst the frills of his shirt-front. His hair was ruffled in the latest 'Brutus' style, falling across his brow and curling about his neck like that of a Roman emperor. He was the epitome of a very fine gentleman of leisure, wealth and impeccable taste.

'I have seen your Mama,' he said to Jane. 'And she is perfectly agreeable to you staying here with Maria. A valise will be sent round containing articles you may need, and another for Bailey who will, naturally, accompany you.'

Jane almost jumped for joy, forgetting her embarrassment. 'Thank you, sir.'

'Jenkins, conduct Lady Jane and her chaperone to guestrooms, while I take a look through the armoire,' he ordered, in complete command of the situation.

The duennas and Jane curtseyed and took themselves off, and he paced towards the wardrobe, flung it open and perused the contents. It contained everything a lady of fashion might require; hats, bonnets, wraps and shawls, dresses in a variety of pastel shades as well as white. There were drawers containing delicate chemises and petticoats and stockings, and shelves holding pumps and shoes, Grecian sandals and riding boots. He rifled through it then stood back, apparently satisfied.

'Clothe yourself in suitable apparel for luncheon and tonight I shall expect you to look even more beautiful,' he said. 'But now I want you to strip.'

'What?' Maria was flabbergasted. 'How can you say such a thing?'

It was bad enough that she was alone with him, though his position of authority made this acceptable, but his suggestion was outrageous. He smiled and seated himself in a wing-chair, elegant and perfectly relaxed, one knee crossed over the other. He did not take his eyes from her.

'I wish to ensure that you are flawless,' he said, touching the silver top of his black Malacca walking cane to his lips. 'Am I not about to enter you on the marriage market? Why, even slaves at auction are put on the block for the prospective buyers to examine.'

This infuriated her so much that she stood before him, arms akimbo, glaring down into his face and shouting, 'I'm not a slave! And I shall marry whoever I please!'

'I think not,' he said, shaking his head solemnly, hands clasped around the cane. 'You have a duty towards your name and estates, and must bear this in mind when you take a husband. Not just any chancer shall have you, but a man of refinement and taste. Now, stop arguing and get undressed.'

She was wearing nothing except her shift under her over-robe, and held this to her as if it was a suit of armour, protecting her from his gaze. 'No,' she said mulishly.

He moved so quickly it took her off guard. He leapt up, wrested the robe from her, seized the hem of the chemise and pulled it off over her head. She gasped, and so did he. It was as if one was as surprised as the other, he by her peerless beauty and she by the shock and sexual thrill that raced through her.

'Don't hide your treasures from me,' he said huskily, as she placed an arm across her breasts and a hand over her mound.

'You should not see me thus, sir,' she quavered, cheeks flushed and her whole body trembling.

He stepped closer and she caught the pungent odour of his hair pomade coupled with that of shaving soap and the personal smell of him. It was a potent brew and she could not stop swaying towards him. He held her for a second, closing a hand over her bare breast and holding it. A spasm of voluptuous pleasure shot through her, entering her womb and making her wet. She was astonished at the effect this had on her. Every vestige of reason seemed to desert her and she wanted to pull him down into the depths of the bed and encourage him to have his wicked way with her.

'So young and fresh,' he murmured, his thumb stroking her nipple. 'Would that such innocence might last forever, but it never does. Soon you will be as wanton as the rest of the jill-flirts.'

'You will make me so, sir, if you don't let me go at once!' she grated, eyes on his mobile mouth, longing to feel it close over hers. 'It is your duty to safeguard, not corrupt me.'

He did not relinquish his hold, and she was certain he could hear the loud thumping of her heart. He dropped a hand down and cradled her pubis, one finger opening her cleft and caressing her bud. She was wet from her encounter with Jane and the way he had aroused her.

'You were exciting each other, weren't you?' he muttered, and she could feel his erection pushing against his breeches.

'No, sir.'

'There's no need to lie to me,' he continued. 'Though it may be necessary to chastise you for it. Would you enjoy that?'

'Being beaten? No, sir. I've watched it happen at school but was always glad it wasn't me being punished.' She backed away from him, her clitoris tingling from his touch.

He laughed lightly and then lifted a finger to his nostrils, inhaling her fragrance that lingered there. 'I don't think you are being quite truthful. You felt my whip during the race. Did the blow excite you?'

'Of course not!' She voiced indignation because he had hit upon the truth and she was ashamed of such confused feelings.

He laughed again. 'So adamant! What is it Shakespeare says in his great play Hamlet? "The lady doth protest too much, methinks".'

'You imagine that you're so clever and superior, don't you?' she hissed, beside herself with annoyance because he disturbed her so much. 'Well you won't get the better of me, my lord viscount. Leave me alone before I scream for help.'

'Do you really believe that anyone would answer?' Despite his tight smile he seemed annoyed and she was glad to have riled him.

'Oh, so you have them all in the palm of your hand, have you?' she challenged. 'You forget that this is the earl's house.'

'I forget nothing.' He was so much in control of himself that she yearned to strike him across his handsome face, to break his cool reserve, to really get to him and have him lose his temper. 'You are simply a saucy chit who has never been shown her boundaries, like a filly that needs breaking.'

'Nothing you can do will break my spirit! I'd rather die!' Now she had gone beyond reasoning, fists bunched ready to defend herself against attack.

'Your father should have used his crop on you.' Damien's eyes glittered with rage. '"Spare the rod and spoil the child" applies to you in full measure.'

She squared up to him, naked as she was, a wild-haired, wild-eyed harpy waiting to take on all-comers. 'Leave my father out of this! He was kindness itself. I loved him and I miss him. I don't want you ordering me about! Go away!'

For answer he grabbed her, taking her completely off-guard. Before she knew it she was stretched out over his knees, face down, hair dangling towards the carpet. She yelled, kicked and struggled but to no avail. He was far stronger than her and equally determined. She knew she must present a lewd spectacle with her bare bottom in the air. Helplessness swept over her.

'Let me go! You can't do this to me!' she cried, very aware of his hard thighs beneath her belly and his hard penis pressing into her side. 'How dare you? I'll tell Arabella.'

'Tell who the hell you like. but it won't stop me. You need a thorough spanking, wench, and I'm the man to do it.'

She lay there, wriggling and spluttering, then shot forward as his first blow hit her with resounding force. Her buttocks went numb, followed by a rush of fire as the flesh came to life. He struck her a second time, before she could recover from the first.

'Oh! Ouch! Stop it! No more...' she protested. Ignoring her, he administered four further blows in rapid succession. Maria let rip, calling him every vile name she could think of, but he continued in that painful punishment till tears ran across her face and dripped to the floor and she begged for mercy.

'Shut up!' he commanded, increasing the pressure of his palm connecting with her sore hinds, adding to the rose-red hue.

'You bastard!' she shrieked.

This outburst did nothing but add to her pain. She jerked as he hit her again, and then he drove a hand between her legs, finding her throbbing bud and massaging it rapidly. Desire added to her torment, but he withdrew that tantalising frottage, adding further stinging slaps to her red backside.

She bucked and threshed without avail, unable to escape his firm hold. His erection was like a solid staff behind those restricting breeches and the very fact that he was excited made her ache with unsatisfied passion. It was on the tip of her tongue to beg, not for release of her person, but for him to continue rubbing between her legs until she exploded into climax. But her pride refused to allow this. What right had he to treat her thus? She used her knuckles to pummel his leg.

With an oath he tumbled her from his lap unceremoniously, standing over her as she crouched there. 'Behave yourself, Maria, do as I tell you and we shall get on well enough,' he said crisply.

She raised her tear-filled eyes and was surprised by the expression on his face. He had enjoyed disciplining her! There was no shadow of doubt. It was betrayed not only in the way he was looking down at her, but in the symbol of arousal that still tented his breeches. Her guardian lusted after her and she did not know whether to be glad or sorry.

'Go to your aunt before the party and she will advise you on your attire,' he ordered briskly, then stalked to the door and left the room.

Chapter 4

Maria was in a state of shock. It was not so much what Damien had done that was so upsetting, but her own reaction to it. Her bottom stung and, squirming around and staring at it in the mirror, she could see the imprint of his palm. To her horror she found she was becoming excited, dampness bedewing her pubic floss.

The marks were a tell-tale sign of her humiliation and she was careful to keep the area covered as much as possible when, shortly after his departure, Arabella came to her, saying, 'Let me help you choose something to wear tonight. Your guardian wants to be proud of you, my dear. This is an important occasion. You will be meeting some of his friends and taking your place in society.'

Maria wondered if Arabella knew what had happened, as Sarah and Emily prepared her. She and Damien seemed thick as thieves. Was this how aunts and guardians usually acted towards their charges? She found it hard to believe, but had no yardstick by which to measure their behaviour. Sarah seemed enraptured by Arabella, positively fawning as she obeyed her instructions, but Emily was her usual pert self, following orders but bowing her head to no one. Jane was in her own room, being groomed by her chaperone, helped by her personal maid, Abigail. Everyone seemed to be in a froth of excitement, but the anticipation had been tarnished for Maria, and it was all due to Damien.

When her attendants had finished she stared at herself in the pier-glass, flattered by the transformation, yet uneasy. She wore so little, but knew it was the mode to appear in public half-naked. She had been taken to Arabella's tailor who was providing her with a complete new wardrobe. Whilst busy with tape measure and marking chalk he had explained, 'The French Revolution left its mark even over here. Clothing was made simple so that one could pretend to be a peasant, a milkmaid, anything but an aristocrat. Now Napoleon's wife, Josephine, has set her seal on these fashions and we, the couturiers, follow suit. Although at war with that country, whatever appears in Paris is quickly copied by us.'

This was the first time Maria had been so exposed. The gown was pure white; but had a low neck and short sleeves and the high waistline emphasised her breasts, even though girded by a girlish pink satin sash. The skirt was cut a little fuller than of yore, with pleats at the back. She wore one petticoat beneath the dress and this was equally transparent. Her legs were bare and her feet, too, toes showing in thong sandals, following the vogue for anything Neo-Classical.

Her hair was swept high at the crown, with wispy ringlets falling at her nape and about her ears. Her jewellery was minimal, drop pearls in her lobes and a single string around her neck, the whole effect turning her into a legendary nymph. Emily took up a chiffon scarf and draped it around Maria's shoulders.

Arabella stood back and viewed her, nodding her approval. 'Hold your head up, my dear. Your fame has spread since the race. Everyone who is anyone is clamouring to meet you. Several spirited young ladies are begging their fathers to permit them to drive high-perch phaetons.'

Maria had not realised that she had caused such a stir, and this made her all the more apprehensive. The guests would be staring at her and making comments. She was tempted to feign a headache and take to her bed in order to avoid such a confrontation.

Arabella left for her own apartment and later reappeared looking like a goddess from Mount Olympus. Jane wore more modest attire, though her bodice was as revealing as Maria's and the material of her dress almost as thin, but sleeves to the wrists concealed her arms and she had on white stockings, her feet encased in flat-heeled black shoes laced around the ankle.

Maria envied her aunt who was looking radiant, her eyes shining at the prospect of another party. If only she had some of her confidence! They walked out into the dusk and a groom opened the carriage door, unfolded the iron step and helped his mistress and her companions to enter. Others aided the duennas and maids to take their places in a less ornate vehicle.

'It should be an august assembly,' Arabella said, glancing across at Maria and Jane who were seated opposite. The driver cracked his whip, the horses leaned into the straps and the vehicle swayed into motion. 'I simply adore dancing, and Viscount Damien always employs the very best musicians.'

'Where is the earl?' Maria had noted his absence, but then he and Arabella were seldom together and it was a wonder that she had managed to conceive his son, little Jamie.

'He has been called to a meeting with the Prime Minister. Oh, this tedious war! It's been going on for ages and prevents one from visiting Paris,' she answered tartly, and it was apparent that she did not miss her husband and was probably looking forward to dallying with the beaux. Despise them though she might, she seemed to find them irresistible.

Maria sat there with burning buttocks, hating herself for being aroused at the thought of seeing Damien. They were transported to Strafford Hall, an ancient grey stone building that had once been a monastery. Now its gloomy exterior was lit by flares. Maria was aware of the law that decreed the outside of every house should be illuminated at night to discourage burglaries. The crime rate in London was high, even though watchmen armed with muskets were employed and the punishment for those apprehended was public hanging.

Arabella's coaches pulled up on the gravel, joining others engaged in disgorging passengers. Flunkies in plush red coats, white knee-breeches and powdered wigs ushered them inside. Maids attired in black taffeta skirts, tight bodices, aprons and frilly mob-caps, conducted the ladies to a room where they could leave their cloaks and perform last minute titivations.

Maria was impressed by the grandeur of Damien's residence. The saloon was of magnificent proportions and decor, and there were other rooms where guests could enjoy the gaming tables or billiards or whatever took their fancy, and these were only the ones on display. Arabella's hints and sly smiles intimated that there were private places where certain of those present were encouraged to take their pleasure in whatever form they desired. Maria could only guess what these might be.

She held Jane's hand and followed Arabella into the main room. They were accompanied by their chaperones who then took their places among others on couches placed each side of the double doors. She was sure that Sarah's attention would soon stray. Her liking for men often worked in Maria's favour and she took full advantage of it. Jane had inferred that the tight-lipped, sour-faced Agatha Bailey liked nothing better than to take her cane to female posteriors, and the maids lived in fear of her.

'She's like Mrs Rossiter,' Jane had added. 'Gets heated when she's wielding the rod. I've never seen any of the manservants giving her the eye and the dislike seems to be mutual.'

The saloon was already full, and Maria wondered if she should have worn fancy dress, though sure that Arabella would have instructed her if this was necessary. There were men attired as cardinals, pirates, sultans and troubadours, but the light also flashed on medals pinned to military uniforms and orders crossing the chests of sober-suited dignitaries. The women were garbed in gorgeous gowns, their hair topped by diamond tiaras, but some had decided on exotic costumes, appearing as harem beauties, Spanish dancers, queens from history and even Orientals. Whatever they had elected to wear had been designed to show off their figures to full advantage.

Maria drank it in, the gaps in her education closing by the second. Is this how the gentry comported themselves, those people who associated with Prince George? Was he as unconventional? There were so many questions that needed answers and she was fully occupied with Jane, who was moping because she could not be with Robin.

As Maria advanced her fears became reality as she met stares and knowing smiles, saw ladies whispering behind their fans and gentlemen looking her up and down as if she was a prize filly for sale. Arabella was pressed for introductions and Maria besieged by bowing men, and women pretending to be admiring, their animosity thinly disguised. She stiffened her backbone and accepted their congratulations, though fearing that very few were sincere.

A string quartet played background music. Footmen hovered, bearing silver salvers of champagne and canapes. Maria searched for one face only, but her relief was mixed with disappointment when she realised that Damien was not yet there. Then her attention was caught by a late arrival who strolled in from the direction of the hall. He stopped, raised the quizzing-glass that hung on a ribbon round his neck, and studied her through it. 'Who is that?' she exclaimed indignantly. 'He seems exceedingly rude, a supercilious dandy if ever there was one.'

Arabella laughed and steered her towards him, saying, 'Ah, darling, after your guardian he is the most sought-after man in London. He's rich, a friend to the Prince of Wales and privy to affairs of State. His name is Lord Charles Bradley. I'll introduce you.' People made way for her and she greeted him informally. 'Charles, what a surprise to find you here.'

He bowed and kissed her hand. 'Lady Arabella. It's been some time since we last met.'

'Too long, sir. You've been neglecting me.' She tapped his chest reprovingly with her gloved fingers.

'Lay the blame on that tetchy fellow, Viscount Damien.'

'Have you two fallen out again? Tut, tut! Come, meet my niece, Lady Maria.

She's the viscount's ward. And this is her friend, Lady Jane.'

He looked at Maria and a spark passed between them. She felt it like a bolt in her heart. There was no doubt that he was attractive. Curly hair holding the rich sheen of mahogany framed a narrow face with high cheekbones. His smile was infectious, and his hazel eyes twinkled with impish humour. Tall and slim, he carried himself well and was dressed with extreme elegance.

A bottle-green jacket fitted his shoulders without a flaw, short at the waist in front, flaring into coattails behind. His white breeches displayed the strength of his legs, ending in gleaming boots. The frills on his shirtfront were spotless, as was the stiff collar that reached his sideburns. Ornate fobs dangled from a gold chain that spanned his embroidered waistcoat. Maria subjected his crotch to a fleeting glance. If the bulge there was anything to go by then he was very well-endowed.

'Ladies, I am charmed to meet you,' he said, but his glance lingered on Maria.

'How did you come to be invited?' Arabella leaned towards him and her cleavage deepened, those alabaster breasts bare almost to the nipples. 'I thought you and Damien disliked one another?'

He smiled a little ruefully, and shrugged. 'We do... or we did. A mere trifle, I assure you. An issue concerning a wager, nothing more. Will you reserve a dance for me later?' Though he addressed her aunt, Maria knew he was asking her.

Jane, who never missed a trick, whispered, 'You've made a conquest there.'

'Don't be silly,' Maria hissed crossly, thinking, if only I had met him before Damien. How is it that he manages to blight everything in my life and succeeds in blinding me to other men?

It was not dancing time yet. Supper was served in the dining-room, linked to the saloon by cedar wood doors that were now folded back. 'May I escort you?' Charles extended an arm to Arabella.

Hundreds of candles blazed in the chandeliers that hung from the ceiling where bosomy goddesses frolicked with shepherds against an Arcadian background. These paintings were set between swathes of lavishly gilded plaster garlands. No expense had been spared to transform the monastic setting into one as secular and extravagant as a king's palace.

'My guardian must be exceedingly wealthy,' Maria observed, wondering which delicacy to try first. There was much to choose from; salads and salmon, wafer-thin slices of beef and ham, cold chicken, a variety of cheeses, butter fresh from the dairy, crusty bread from the bakery, pyramids of fruit, delicious syllabubs and concoctions made from ice-cream.

Glass scintillated and silver cutlery gleamed. 'Prinny would enjoy this feast,' Charles remarked, flicking out a lace-edged handkerchief and dabbing his lips.

'Prinny?' Maria was puzzled.

'Prince George. He loves food almost as much as fucking.' He said this as casually as if he was discussing the weather.

Maria did not even blush. Let this popinjay try to embarrass her. He would find he had met his match. She was determined not to let him get the upper hand. She ignored him, filling a plate and carrying it to a couch where Jane sat, picking at the food.

'What's the matter now?' Maria was finding her friend's unhappiness hard to endure.

'I'm missing Robin so much. It's torment to know he is but a few miles away.'

'Stop fretting. Emily is a resourceful girl and walking out with Tranter, one of the grooms. I'm sure that if you write a letter to Robin I can get it delivered. Tranter will wait for a reply and we can arrange a tryst.'

'How wonderful! Oh, I can't thank you enough!'

'We shall have to be careful. The viscount would be furious were he to find out.' Maria knew she would be held responsible and her spanked flesh tingled.

She dispatched Jane to the library where pen, ink and paper could be found and then ordered Emily to attend her in the cloakroom. Arabella was too engrossed with Charles and the dilettantes who clustered around to notice her disappearance.

Maria succeeded in giving Sarah the slip. The duenna was getting tipsy, encouraging the attentions of a strapping flunky who was supplying her with champagne. Maria hoped that she would forget her duties and have nothing on her mind but fornication.

Jane handed her the note and she passed it on to Emily who slipped out to the coach, found Tranter and gave him his orders. There would be time for him to borrow a horse from the stable, find his way to Robin's lodgings and complete the business before the event concluded. Not only would he be rewarded by more of Emily's bounteous favours, but half a guinea as well. Maria and Jane returned to the party.

Damien observed his guests through a cunning invention that appeared to be a gold-framed Venetian mirror in the saloon, but was in reality a window giving a clear view to anyone on the other side of the wall. He stood in a narrow corridor that separated him from those he had invited; one of the secret places that honey-combed Strafford Hall. A cynical smile lifted his lips as he mentally saluted those old monks who had known a thing or two about spying.

This aroused him, his cock rising within the slim-fitting pale grey trousers that were part of his evening attire. His guests were already inebriated, losing their inhibitions and behaving like the indulged, licentious individuals that existed beneath their polite exteriors. Not all, of course. He was duty bound to invite a few stuffy, influential people who would uphold his reputation when others reviled him. He had many enemies, but then who didn't in those troubled times? There was an unpleasant rumour circulating that his wealth was partly due to his dabbling in politics, his loyalty to the Crown suspect. None of this had ever been proved. He was too cunning for that. He smiled and inserted a hand down the front of his trousers, finding his erection and caressing it.

Soon those of a virtuous disposition would take part in the minuet, whilst other, more adventurous spirits would accompany him to the vault. He knew who they would be - a bishop, a duke, a magistrate, a Member of Parliament and the like. Whilst the women would have countesses and ladies-in-waiting among their number, to say nothing of well-bred brides and blue-blooded virgins, actresses and high-class prostitutes.

We are all the same under the skin, no better than rutting animals, he decided, and not for the first time Maria's image swam into his ken, and his cock jerked in his fist. Chastising her had been the most exciting thing he had done for a long time. He had every intention of marrying her, transferring her money to his bank and her lands, properties and every other part of her estate into the hands of his lawyers. He could father two or three children on her and then, if she became troublesome, have her diagnosed as insane and incarcerated in a lunatic asylum for the rest of her days. This was a common practice among those of their class.

The feeling was mounting in his balls as he handled his penis. He had time to spare and could jerk off before performing his duties as host. He opened his trousers and drew out the proof of masculinity of which he was so proud. The notion of thrusting it into Maria's virgin hole almost tipped him over the edge. He slowed down, avoiding the helm, but keeping up a slow, steady frottage on the dark-skinned, vein-knotted stem, careful not to slide his foreskin up and over that all too sensitive head. Pre-come was dribbling from the single eye. Passion began to take over, the urge to ejaculate uncontrollable. Nothing mattered but that divine sensation when he spurted. He was a heartbeat away, no more, when the rush suddenly slowed as he saw the man standing talking with Maria.

His spunk retreated, his balls slackened and his penis drooped. 'Charles Bradbury! Damn him!' Damien growled. 'That bloody upstart! How dare he approach her! Jesus Christ, I'll call him out!'

'It is exceedingly hot in here,' Maria remarked, stirring the air with her fan and wondering how Tranter was getting on.

By now couples were dancing, a colourful collection going through the steps of minuet and gavotte that they had learned in childhood, when they were being prepared to take part in events like this. Her toes tapped but she did not want to dance with anyone except Damien, and he was still absent. Charles smiled at her and said, 'Shall we take a stroll in the conservatory? I promise you that I'm not such a bad fellow, and respectful of maidenly virtue.'

Maria could not be sure if he was mocking her but, bored and restless, permitted him to escort her. Sarah should have followed, but she was nowhere to be seen, probably in some secluded nook with the flunkey, getting up to all sorts of ribaldry. 'I wish I was a commoner.' The words popped out of Maria's mouth without thought.

'And why, pray, is that?' Charles stood back, so that she might precede him into the luscious tropical area.

'They have so much more fun than we do. What with finishing school when we were ordered around by dames and then residing with relatives who expect us to be as chaste as nuns. We have no freedom and it is driving me insane.'

They paused by a pool where a pair of swans floated majestically, stirring the water-lilies. The fronds of palms imported from the East brushed the glass cupola, and exotic perfume breathed out from white flowers with orange stamens reminiscent of phalli. Others trailed from baskets or occupied jardinières - - vines, orchids and other plants imported from hot climates.

Maria and Charles were not the only ones seeking seclusion. Couples lingered in the shadows, or leaned against stone balustrades or sat entwined on benches. There were no chaperones, which indicated that the women were either married, widows or, like Maria, downright disobedient. Charles stood with her, gazing into the darkness that stretched away into the distance. She was lost for words, wondering why she had put herself in this position. It was indiscreet to say the least. He moved and she jumped nervously. All he did was draw a sliver snuff-box from a pocket, open it, take a pinch, balanced a tiny dune at the base of his thumb and lift it to each nostril in turn, sniffing appreciatively.

'I saw you race,' he said, replacing the box.

'You did?'

'I put money on the outcome, backing Damien.'

'You had no faith in a woman winning. That was short-sighted of you.' This annoyed her and she wanted to go back to the saloon.

'I shan't make that mistake again. You were superb. Did you know you were challenging your guardian?'

'I had never met him before.'

'Strange. Had he not taken an interest in you?' Charles slanted her a glance, and she was very aware of his shoulder touching hers, velvet against bare skin.

'Lady Arabella tells me he is away a lot. She was the one who had cared for me, sending me to school and letting me visit her sometimes.'

'You are an heiress?'

'So I'm told. I would like to go home to Burrington Manor and take command, but they say I must wait until I'm twenty-one or find a husband to manage my estate. I don't want to do this. I'd like to marry for love, not because it is convenient.'

'Hmm, this only happens among the working class, and even then the parents often have a say in the matter. No doubt things will change eventually. It seems that you have ideas ahead of your time.'

It was pleasant to be holding a conversation with a man as if they were on a par intellectually. All too often Maria had endured being patronised, but Charles was not like that. She'd never had a brother, and felt that had she been so fortunate he might have been something like Charles. Then, honest to the point of brutality, she scolded herself. It was not a fraternal relationship she wanted with him, but a full-blown sexual one.

He moved a step closer and desire speared her. If she had entertained impure thoughts when at the finishing school, then these had increased tenfold since coming to London. She longed for Charles to kiss her so she could test her own response and compare his mouth to Damien's.

'Were I your guardian I'd not let you out of my sight,' he said, speaking low. 'You are too beautiful, Lady Maria.'

'He trusts me,' she replied, though not sure if this was true.

'Then the man's a fool!' There was mockery and a trace of anger in his voice.

'Are you suggesting that I'm a strumpet?' It aroused her to argue with him, the air sizzling between them.

He chuckled. 'That's not very nice coming from the lips of a genteel young lady. Do you know what a strumpet is?'

'Of course, do you think I'm a complete ignoramus?' She did not want to talk or explain herself or do other than be folded in his arms, pressed to that broad chest and caressed by those strong hands. If Damien had abandoned her, then there was no reason why she should not flirt with another man. She owed him nothing. The tender skin of her backside still remembered his harsh handling and, though ragingly indignant at his treatment, she quivered and burned. Would Charles seek to chastise her? The idea made her nipples peak and sent ripples down her spine into her womb. I'm bad, she thought, really bad. Maybe I do have the makings of a strumpet.

The moon was rising, filling the garden with blue radiance. Bats swooped from the bell-tower and barn owls were engaged in hooting and hunting. Maria wanted to remain like this for ever, and nestled into him as he drew her close, not caring if he was testing her morals. He did not take unfair advantage, simply stood there, holding her, then raised one of her hands to his lips and kissed each finger, one by one.

She felt laughter sweeping through him as he murmured, 'You shouldn't be allowed out. Much too potent for the male race. Are you aware of the effect you're having on me?'

She was fully aware, recognising the hard bulge distorting the front of his breeches. Unable to control herself she moved sensually, rubbing herself against it. He bent and kissed her, their mouths opening and their tongues meeting while his hands clasped her buttocks, making them make contact with his cock, using small, firm thrusts.

His kiss was different to Damien's, as commanding, but more sensitive to her feelings. It was lovely, but lacked that spice of danger associated with her guardian. His hand wandered to her breast and his touch turned her insides to jelly. He toyed with her nipples and the pleasure shot down to her clitoris. He employed both tongue and fingers to give her the utmost pleasure, so skilled that she became jealous of those fortunate women who had been the recipients of his lovemaking before her.

He lifted her skirt, cruising up her thigh and finding the downy fork between. Maria drew in a sharp breath as he landed unerringly on her crack, parted it and found her nubbin. She was not sure about this intimate caress. It was too soon.

She hardly knew him. Above all she did not want him to think she was a trollop. As if sensitive to her feelings he concentrated on stroking her lower belly, brushing across the curly triangle, wooing her gently as if she was a nervous filly. It was most persuasive.

Then like a lightning strike that comes without warning, Damien was there, swinging Charles round to face him. 'What the devil are you doing here, Bradley? And get your dirty hands off my ward!'

'You invited me, sir.' Charles could not have been more composed. Maria's skirt slithered into place and it was as if he had never touched her.

'I did? When was this?' Damien looked as if he wanted to strike him.

'At White's Club last week. Don't you remember, or were you too cup-shorten?' It was plain to see that these gentlemen loathed one another.

'Are you suggesting I can't hold my liquor?' Damien's face was hard, his eyes flinty.

'Nothing of the sort, sir. But I tell you plain, you did invite me.'

'Are you calling me a liar?'

'I wouldn't dream of it, but my horse has better manners than you, even if he does piss in the street.' Charles's sarcasm coiled round the conservatory. He turned to bow to Maria. 'It has been a pleasure meeting you. Now I'll take my leave.'

'You're not welcome here at any time.' Damien stepped to her side, glaring at Charles.

'That is patently obvious. I bid you farewell.' With that he walked away, head high.

Damien rounded on Maria. His hand shot out, gripping her arm painfully. 'As for you, hussy!' he stormed. 'How dare you linger about with him?'

'Lady Arabella introduced us,' she protested, tugging herself free.

'Then I shall take her to task. And as for you, it is high time I taught you a few more lessons.'

Chapter 5

Charles left Strafford Hall without a backward glance. He clapped on his low-crowned topper and shrugged his shoulders into a triple-capped overcoat, then addressed his manservant, 'Bates, fetch the horses.'

Riding from Hampstead across the heath to his own lodgings, he brooded on everything that had happened that night, dwelling particularly on Maria. That such a desirable beauty should be in the care of Viscount Damien stuck in his craw.

Reaching his house he dismounted and entered, Bates taking the horses to the stables at the rear. Charles lived alone, creature comforts provided by his housekeeper, Mrs Pritchard, and his sexual requirements met by a number of whores from Madame Flora's brothel and, more recently, by his new mistress,

Sally Wyatt. He had an estate in the country, though visited it rarely, leaving the management in the capable hands of his agent. He had come to the capital to study art, frustrated because students could no longer attend the academies in Paris.

Having been an officer in the army, he now served his country in a less conspicuous manner, working underground in order to apprehend spies working for the French Government. On the surface he appeared to be a dabbler in painting who caroused with other young bucks, living a carefree existence. In reality he met informers and double agents, using taverns and bawdy houses in order to carry out his investigations. One of his principal suspects was Damien. In his role as a dandy whose only apparent interest was in gambling, drinking and rogering the artists' models who posed nude for him, he had attempted to socialise with him, but the antipathy between them made this impossible. As yet there was not a shred of evidence, but Charles was certain the viscount was up to something.

He lit a candle and made his way to the main bedroom. Mrs Pritchard occupied a more humble apartment in the attic. Bates slept across the corridor to his master, doubling as valet and sidekick. Cleaners came in daily and soiled linen was farmed out to washerwomen. Food was delivered from the pie shops, bakers and dairies. London abounded in eating houses, all within a stone's throw of dwellings. Only the wealthy kept well-maintained kitchens and employed cooks when residing in town.

'Ah, there you are, Charlie. I thought you'd be later than this.' Sally Wyatt spoke from the depths of the tester-bed. 'Old Mother Pritchard let me in. You'll have to give me a key, you know. Can't keep knocking her up, though I think she had a fellow with her. Dirty slut!'

The housekeeper's love-life was of no interest to Charles, but jumping into bed with the delectable Sally was. He placed his candle next to the one already burning on the nightstand, unbuttoned his shirt and took it off. She lazily walked her fingers down his chest, tracing round the wine-dark nipples and following the scrawl of hair that spread to his navel and disappeared into the waistband of his breeches.

'Did I ask you here tonight?' he asked, feigning annoyance. 'Supposing I'd met the love-of-my-life at the soiree and wanted to bring her back?'

'Charlie, you wouldn't have done that, would you? Don't I satisfy you... like this?' She unbuttoned his fly. 'And this?' Her hand reached in and withdrew his already swollen cock.

He responded, accustomed to the attention of women be they commoners or duchesses. They had always found him attractive. Although Maria filled his mind's eye Sally was there in the flesh, with her knowing hands and those luscious lips eager to suckle his helm and her mouth hungry to take the length and girth of him.

She sat him down on the bed, backed towards him, whipped up her kirtle and straddled one of his legs. She tugged off his boot and then did the same to the other. Her buttocks were rounded and generous, the darkness between inviting exploration. She was a shop assistant and he had met her whilst visiting his tailor at The Royal Exchange. She had made no secret of the fact that she was looking for a gentleman to keep her. Charles did not want such an arrangement, but he was generous, helping her out financially. He knew she was keen to better herself and did not expect her to hang around for long.

His boots were removed, but he remained seated on the side of the bed, legs open and penis erect. She backed up against him. He reached round and fondled her breasts, the nipples hard as cherry stones as she arched her spine and moaned her pleasure. Now her cleft was brushing his cock. She was very wet and he spread some of that moisture around her anus and over his weapon, readying it for penetration. He was poised to enter her darkest, most secret place. He had taken his pleasure there many times. It was a safe haven for his sperm with no likelihood of conception. The sensation was intense, that tight channel offering extreme delight.

Sally was ready, willing and able and there was no earthly reason why Charles should not enjoy her. Though Maria's lovely face floated in his memory he was a realist, accepting the fact that wooing her would be fraught with difficulties and dangers. At the precise moment when he was poised to thrust his dick past Sally's anal ring, every sensible thought fled and he was fired with primordial desire. Her spread buttocks were the gateway to paradise and she wriggled as the tip of his cock nudged into her.

She squealed, and his hand slipped round to cradle her mound, his middle digit stroking her clitoris. She cried out again, body in rippling motion against that tantalising finger, pressing back to receive more of his shaft within her. Her rectum muscles were tighter than those of her vagina, making him work. He pressed harder, guiding his prick until it was sufficiently buried. Then he started a pumping movement, the extreme narrowness of her passage causing discomfort as well as pleasure. It added to the enjoyment of this way of taking.

Sally was moaning and rubbing her bud on his finger, while her hips strained up to meet his embedded cock. Charles was lost in a world of sensation when nothing mattered but release. Her inner muscles clenched round his penis and chafed the helm. She was as desperate for relief as he, forgetting discomfort in the drive towards ecstasy. The solid bed shook with their efforts. Both were sweating and panting. Then Charles felt the overwhelming sensation that raced through his whole body, concentrating in his genitals and bursting forth in a torrent of semen. Sally gasped and shuddered, her contractions gripping his cock and wringing out the last drops of spunk.

'Oh, Charlie, I love you,' she whispered.

Maria did not give Damien the satisfaction of knowing that she was weak-kneed with fear. He marched her through the saloon where couples were dancing, and across the floor of the gaming room. Those engrossed in cards did not even look up. There was no sign of Arabella, and the crowd appeared to have thinned out, those that remained still eating and drinking, gambling and flirting. She looked for Jane, but she was engaged with her chaperone and Maria could only hope that Emily and Tranter had carried out their instructions.

Without pause Damien propelled her into the library and through a low doorway leading to a staircase that wound down. She pulled back. 'Where are you taking me? You have no right. I was talking with Sir Charles Bradley...'

'That in itself deserves punishment.' His face was grim in the light of lamps reflected on white-washed walls. 'The man's an upstart, an opportunist who cares for naught but his own advancement.'

'What's he done? Lady Arabella seems friendly towards him.'

'I've told you that she will be reprimanded. Keep your nose out of business concerning your elders and betters.'

He walked her briskly along a passage until they reached a sturdy oak door. He opened it, and Maria found herself in a long low vault built into the foundations of the house. Light from flambeaux and glowing braziers shone on some of the guests from the soiree, dressed in outlandish costumes and performing weird practices, most of which were concentrated on the genitalia. Maria stared at the racks of implements. Bull whips jostled paddles, tawses nudged floggers, manacles gleamed menacingly, handcuffs and ankle chains had a burnished sheen.

A whipping post stood close to a vaulting horse where a person could be stretched, facedown, vulnerable backside presented to whoever desired to abuse it. Next to it was a bench complete with straps, and having holes at strategic places so that breasts and cunts, pricks and arseholes were available for touching while the victim was tethered helplessly.

There was a stage to the rear with a backdrop representing a landscape. It was bordered by crimson velvet curtains and had footlights consisting of candles floating in metal holders in a long trough of water, as in a real theatre. Arabella occupied a throne-like chair in the centre, her legs hooked over the arms. A naked man with glistening dark skin knelt before her, slurping at her crotch. Two others of magnificent physique stood on either side, playing with her breasts. She held their cocks, eyes closed in ecstasy as she approached her crisis. Nude and voluptuous, she represented Venus taking her pleasure. The crowd who had gathered to watch applauded as she suddenly yelped, caught up in a sexual paroxysm.

'What a woman!' Damien exclaimed, dragging Maria forward.

'I thought you were angry with her.' She was acutely embarrassed.

'Of course I am, but this makes it all the more exciting. I'll punish her and she will revel in it.'

'I don't understand.'

'I should hope not! I am the one to educate you.' His arm was around her shoulders, clamping her to his side, and his fingers were in constant motion, caressing her skin. It made her melt with desire, yet resembled bondage from which she could not break free.

'Where's Jane? I want to go home.'

'Jane has already departed with her duenna. You will return when I give permission. Do you understand?'

'No, I don't. Why are you treating me thus? And where is Sarah?'

'Your chaperone is neglecting her duty, otherwise engaged with one of my footmen.'

Maria hoped that Emily and Tranter had been able to contact Jane and pass on information concerning Robin. To that end she was willing to yield to her guardian's wishes, providing they were within the bounds of reason.

What these were she was not quite sure. Though unable to trust him, he was a fascinating unknown quantity, and all that was wild within her responded to his challenge.

Her aunt displaying herself so wantonly was a revelation. She had guessed her to be immoral, but was astonished that, married to an earl and the mother of his heir, she was behaving like a harlot. This was a strange world in which she now found herself, where things generally unspoken of existed. Members of the higher echelon Damien's guests might be, but their mating habits were those of the farmyard.

He urged Maria forward, his fingers circling her wrist in an iron grip. The crowd parted to let him through, then returned to their pursuit of pleasure. He stood before the stage, looking up at Arabella. Disconcerted by his steely gaze she grabbed a crop, using it mercilessly on her three lovers, then rose, pulling a cloak about her nakedness.

'Well, Damien, did you enjoy the show?' she challenged, returning his stare imperiously.

He mounted the steps at one side of the stage, hauling Maria with him. 'I always like to watch you degrading yourself,' he said, in a voice hard enough to cut through steel. 'It might even make my prick rise to see Charles Bradley arse-fucking you.'

She did not flinch, outfacing him. 'What has that to do with anything?'

'Did you invite him?'

Maria could feel the rage burning through him. What had Charles done to anger him so much? Arabella tossed her curling hair and looked down her aristocratic nose. 'No, Damien, you did. Take more water with it when you're out on the town. He said you were drunk.'

'He lies! You lust after him, and for that you deserve to be flogged.'

Damien propelled Maria towards a post on the left. It was equipped with rings and chains. Before she realised his intention she felt the coldness of manacles around both wrists and the pinch as he snapped them shut. She was fastened to the post like a prize heifer on sale at market. Unable to break free she watched as people shifted towards the stage. Damien seized Arabella and made her bend from the waist and grip her ankles, her cloak flung aside, her hair streaming over her face, her buttocks and cleft exposed, shaven pudenda pierced by glittering gold rings.

'Damn you!' she spluttered. 'I'll have you for this!'

He leaned towards her and murmured in her ear. 'You love it. I'll wager you'll come off like a rocket.'

To Maria's surprise the feisty lady submitted, and Damien picked up the crop she had dropped in the struggle and raised it high before bringing it down across her backside. The hush that had preceded this was broken by the resounding impact of leather on flesh. The audience murmured and rustled, hands searching for cocks or cunts, breasts and anuses. They were aroused by the kind of performance they were accustomed to witnessing at Strafford Hall.

Arabella bucked under the whip but remained in position, taking her punishment, her alabaster skin turning pink, then red as Damien continued to thrash her. Maria's hindquarters stung in sympathy, and a strange feeling of envy pervaded her. She wanted his hard palm spanking her as he had done before, her clitoris throbbing and her nipples peaking.

Damien applied himself to his task enthusiastically. He took off his coat and rolled up his shirt-sleeves for greater freedom of movement. Arabella's posterior was larded with crimson stripes, some laid on separately, others crisscrossing one another. The back of her thighs, too, received the lash. She bucked at each blow, agony and desire appearing to rack her in equal measure.

Maria, helpless in her bonds, caught the excitement. It was like a fever in her blood. She wanted Damien to turn his attention to her. He could beat her, hurt her, and do anything - as long as he fucked her in the end. She was fascinated, wondering if Arabella would lose control of her bladder and urinate like a mare in a field, as girls at school had done under Mrs Rossiter's cane.

Arabella was made of sterner stuff it seemed, and her groans changed, becoming wails. 'Fuck me! Fuck me, Damien!' she pleaded, and the spectators applauded.

'You really want me to do that?' He paused, whip half-raised, a sardonic smile curving his lips.

'Yes, yes... you know full well I do!' She made to straighten up, but his hand at the back of her neck pushed her down again.

'Then you must grovel... beg... debase yourself and swear to have no further contact with Charles Bradley.' Damien pushed the whip handle between her bottom cheeks, and then worked it into both orifices in turn. The leather was slippery with her lustful dew.

'Yes, master... yes! Anything you say,' she cried, and he opened his trousers, presenting his fully erect cock to the cheering crowd before driving it into her.

'That's it, viscount, give her one, the saucy trollop!' shouted a grey-haired man in a sober suit and dog-collar. He was fingering the testicles of a simpering youth wearing a gown.

'Go to it, Damien!' urged another, his prick buried to the hilt in a leggy nymphet's vagina.

'Stop it, sir. This isn't fair or just,' Maria shouted above the uproar, tugging at her restraints, which simply became tighter.

He paused, now linked with Arabella, who glared at Maria between strands of her unbound hair. 'Be quiet, girl,' she ordered. 'Don't interfere. You know nothing!'

'Would you like to take her place?' Damien asked blandly. 'That can be arranged.'

This silenced her protests and she watched as the perverted pair completed their gross act, with Arabella shrieking like an alley cat on heat and Damien grunting and pumping his way to release. A storm of cheering arose as he withdrew from her and she straightened up.

They took a bow like professional actors and were greeted by a chorus of, 'Encore! Encore!'

'You want more entertainment, my friends?' he shouted, holding up his hand for silence. 'Very well. I can show you a virgin. Yes, hard to believe though it may be, she really is unsullied. You wouldn't get a dose of Cupid's Measles through fucking her. You may touch her, but that is all. Should any man attempt penetration, I'll chop off his balls.'

He undid Maria's bonds and guided her towards another device on the floor below the stage. The audience made way for them, standing back to reveal a chair. It looked ordinary enough, until Maria saw there was a hole where the seat should have been. Ignoring her protests, Damien undid her bodice and lifted her skirt high, then forced her into the chair. Her hands were chained to the arms, her thighs splayed, ankles fastened to the front legs and a blindfold tied over her eyes. Then the contraption was lifted by pulleys until it swung just above the floor. She feared she would fall and the cold air drifted round her exposed pussy. There was no way she could protect it.

She was reduced to touch, smell and hearing, feeling hands moving over her, tweaking her nipples and fondling her breasts, while her anus and labia were explored from below. She did not want to yield to the pleasure that made her wet as her clitoris was stroked, rubbed and played with, but there was no way she could control herself. Was it Damien who reached under the chair and handled her so familiarly? Could it be another man or a woman? Old, young, it did not matter. All she felt was the tremendous need for orgasm that those unknown fingers were arousing in her.

'Oh, oh...' she wailed plaintively.

The hands were suddenly withdrawn and pain shot through her as a lash landed across her bare thighs. The pain was appalling, gaining in ferocity, running through her to connect with her loins. She tugged at the chains, but this only added to her torment, harsh metal digging into her.

'Disobedient slut!' she heard Damien say, and the whip slashed across her again. 'You think to defy me? Well think again, Lady Maria!'

This time she was more prepared, feeling the air move and the lash hiss as it passed through it. She absorbed the pain, biting her lower lip until the blood ran. Tears welled up, wetting the blindfold, but she was stubbornly resolved that he was not getting the better of her. She hated him, was in agony because of him, yet had never felt more alive!

'I bow the knee to no man,' she declared defiantly. The covering was torn from her eyes and she stared into his furious face a few inches from her own.

'Oh, but you will, my dear. You'll be subservient to your husband.'

'My husband? You? Never!' She spat at him, the gob landing on his cheek.

'Aren't you going to breech her maidenhead?' shouted one of his cronies. 'Go on, viscount. Show us her virgin blood.'

He ignored this advice, wiped away her spittle with the back of his hand, his expression almost one of respect as he said, 'Is there nothing you fear, Maria?'

She did not reply. It suited her to have him believe that. They exchanged a long look charged with meaning, and then he released her, gave her time to rearrange her clothing and took her upstairs. As they stood in the hall while a servant was sent to summons Sarah, he raised one of her hands to his lips. 'This isn't over between us.'

'I know,' she answered, regretful when the chaperone arrived, looking hot and flustered and extremely guilty.

'You will be my wife one day.'

'You can always hope, sir,' she shot back, but inside she was reluctant to leave him, dominating master though he was.

Every inch of her body seemed to have its own particular smart, increasing as the numbness wore off and pain gained complete ascendance. She had the urge to be a slave receiving punishment all over again, her body tingling, her cunt wet with arousal. It was a paradox she failed to comprehend. All she knew was a longing to be taken into Damien's arms, comforted, petted and having him make violent love to her. At the same time she would have liked to see him stretched out dead at her feet.

'Did Tranter deliver your note?' Maria asked as she entered Jane's room. Sarah and Agatha had retired for the night and the girls were alone.

Jane was sitting up in bed, looking angelic in a white nightgown, buttoned to the neck and having long sleeves. Her eyes were shining and her smile wide. 'He did. He found Robin's lodgings and he was there! Can you believe our good fortune? He wrote to me and suggested that we meet in a tavern tomorrow night! He mentions one close to where he lives. Can this be arranged? Can we slip away? You must come with me. Oh, it's so exciting and I want to see him so much!'

'Calm down, dearest,' Maria said, her smile matching Jane's. 'You'll give yourself an apoplexy.'

She, too, was attired for bed, and she had succeeded in disrobing without Sarah seeing Damien's brand upon her thighs. The marks would fade after a while, but just for now she lifted her robe and displayed them.

Jane's eyes widened. 'Good gracious! Who did that to you?'

'It was Damien.' Maria found she was proud of her welts, lust warming her belly every time she ran her fingers over them. 'He was cross with me for talking to Charles Bradley. He took me to his dungeons where Lady Arabella was also punished. There was a crowd there, and oh, what a crowd! I've never seen people fornicating like that!'

'Fornicating? In front of everyone?' Jane was fully alert now, sitting up, her hands clasped to her breasts. 'I wish I'd been there.'

'I don't think you'd like it. And as for being beaten? Well, if it was anyone other than Damien...'

'You're sweet on him, aren't you?' Jane accused, but she was smiling mischievously.

'There's something about him. I don't know what it is, but I'm drawn to him even though I want to fight him every inch of the way.'

Jane looked puzzled. 'Is it love? I feel nothing but tender regard for Robin. I want to cherish him and I'm certain that he feels the same about me. Do you enjoy Damien inflicting pain on you?'

'I can't explain, but obviously Lady Arabella experienced the same intense sensations for she reached fulfilment and so did he.'

Jane leaned back against the lace-edged pillows. 'How could they do that in public?'

'It seems that some people like to be watched.'

'Your aunt keeps some very strange company. We mustn't let my Mama know about it or I'll be forbidden to see you and you're the only one who can bring Robin and me together. You will help me, won't you?'

She looked so woe-be-gone that Maria climbed into bed beside her, drew the covers over them and snuggled down, being careful of her aching thighs. 'Of course I will. Tomorrow we'll lay careful plans, but just for now, let's sleep.'

Jane nestled her head on Maria's shoulder. The familiar feel of her so close reminded Maria of heated nights they had spent together under the covers in a narrow dormitory bed. It was almost second nature to slip a hand into the button fastening of Jane's nightgown and caress the swell of her breasts, crowned by rosebud nipples that stiffened at her touch.

Maria's own teats tingled and she needed the same treatment. She had been aroused by Damien and left unsatisfied. Now she could take her pleasure with her dear friend. A simple, uncomplicated exchange of caresses that would bring them both satisfaction. What more could a girl want than the closeness and intimacy of a trusted female companion? Yet there was more, much more and both knew it. It still lay before them, like uncharted territory, the blaze that could be ignited between man and woman. Jane had almost but not quite achieved this yet, and she received Maria's lovemaking wholeheartedly, returning every gentle touch.

Desire made Maria moan, and she forgot her soreness, gripping Jane's thigh between hers, their nightdresses riding up as she ground her pubis against it, her clit burning for relief. Jane responded eagerly, whispering, 'Oh, it's been so long since I was with Robin. I need you to make love to me.'

She freed herself momentarily, sat up and pulled the gown over her head.

Maria gazed at her admiringly. She was so perfect, small bones, tight muscles, and beautiful little breasts. Her fair curls tumbled over her shoulders and her red mouth was parted in eager anticipation. Below the curve of her belly her mound was exposed, covered in blonde floss. Maria stripped too, and then returned to fondling Jane's nipples that rose from pinkish-brown areolas.

She breathed in her own perfume wafting from her delta, the oceanic odour of sex, a rich, potent brew. And Jane's too, lighter, like jasmine with an underlying hint of verbena. She pressed a thumb into Jane's passage and met an obstruction. Robin had not yet entered her. Maria, too, retained her hymen. She spread wetness over Jane's labial wings and concentrated on the little nub of flesh that was the seat of pleasure. Lowering her head so that her tongue might follow the path of her fingers, she relished her friend's delta, examining every fold. The tip of her tongue licked slowly across the wet, sensitive area.

Jane clung to her, eyes closed, pushing her pubis up to get closer and closer to the source of bliss. Maria fastened her lips around Jane's clitoris, sucking strongly, feeling it throb and carrying on relentlessly till Jane convulsed and moaned, swept up in orgasm.

They collapsed, laughing in each other's arms, then Maria said, 'My turn now,' and Jane combed her fingers through the russet curls that crowned Maria's pubis.

'You really want it?' she teased, bending her head and licking Maria's nipples.

'You know how much... go on... do it for me. Kiss me there.' Maria lay on her back and spread her legs, careless of Damien's marks.

With a hand each side of her groin she spread her sex even wider, the twin wings, the reddish gash, the hardness of her organ that resembled a pink gem. Jane could not resist, bending across her and using her tongue skilfully on that small, demanding organ. Maria was so aroused it took only a few strokes to bring her to climax. She moaned and clawed at Jane's shoulders as she reached the pinnacle and was then plunged down as the convulsions faded.

In that moment when she hovered between consummation and the little death, a face appeared before her mind's eye; a dark, sardonic face. A further ripple took her and she was filled with longing, though unable to fathom why she wanted her cruel, mocking guardian.

Chapter 6

The next evening Maria and Jane tried on the garments Emily had borrowed from Tranter. 'It reminds me of when we acted in plays at school and sometimes had to take masculine roles. I enjoyed that,' Maria said.

'I always hoped I'd be passed over,' Jane replied. 'I was never comfortable pretending to be a boy. What on earth would Miss Bailey and Mrs Jenkins say?'

'They aren't to know. We're thought to be spending a quiet time together in my room, reading Shakespeare's sonnets.'

Maria was a few inches taller than Jane, looking much more the part of a lad. She had already tied her hair back in a queue, and now turned her attention to the problem of her breasts. She bound them with a wide cotton scarf, flattening their curves. She put on cloth breeches and a jacket and wound a stock around her throat, then posed in front of the pier-glass, pleased with the effect. She assumed the cheeky air of the groom whose clothes she now wore, hat pushed to the back of her head, hands thrust deep in her pockets, strutting around and whistling.

Jane was having trouble getting rid of the awkwardness she experienced wearing breeches. She pushed her hair into a jelly-bag cap and tried to stride instead of mincing.

Tranter was slight of build and his clothes fitted them well. Emily had bullied him into loaning his best suits. These were of plain material and simple cut. There was nothing dandyish about them. His boots were too large, so they settled for ones Maria used when riding.

They left the house by the servants' entrance, their escape engineered by Emily. Their destination was The Temple, an area designated to students studying law, where Robin was staying with friends. Tranter planned to accompany them.

'How are we to get into the house later?' Maria whispered to Emily as she let them out of the back door.

'Don't fret, milady. I'll wait in the stables. Mrs Jenkins is going out this evening, all of a twitter she is, dolling herself up, meeting that footman again, and I've made sure that Miss Bailey has a bottle of gin to hand. She'll sleep the time away.'

'You're a treasure.' Maria hugged her.

'I'm only doing my duty, keeping your secrets, helping all I can. Ain't that what ladies' maids have always done?'

They understood each other very well. Both knew Emily would benefit; it was one of the perks of her position, but Maria was confident she was genuine and loyal to a fault. It was a comfort to have someone like her.

The moon hung over the rooftops, a thin thing giving little light, but the stars made up for this. Tranter led them through the garden into a lane that connected with the main thoroughfare. There he hailed a hackney carriage and gave the driver the address of The Three Tuns, an inn popular with scholars, working men and apprentices. The traffic was thick, the cobbles spattered with mud, horse dung and rubbish. Chairmen in blue kersey coats, black knee-breeches, white stockings, buckled shoes and large cocked hats, conveyed passengers in hired sedans. They were jostled by crested, privately owned vehicles. Rowdy bucks clattered through the streets in their phaetons and others, driving elegant barouches, escorted ladies to balls or the theatres.

The cabby dropped Maria and Jane close to their destination. Tranter paid him and followed them at a distance. Emily had ordered him not to let them out of his sight.

'How do you feel?' Jane asked nervously, as they joined the pedestrians who were on their way home or going out for the evening.

'I like it.' Maria swaggered along. 'Such freedom! How much better than trailing a skirt. No wonder men go off adventuring. I wish I was wearing a sword and had a real cock. Emily wanted me to pad my crotch in order to complete the illusion, but I wouldn't.'

'How do men manage with such an awkward appendage?' Jane wondered aloud.

'The same as we do our breasts, I suppose.'

'Anyway, you know it's no longer fashionable to wear a sword,' Jane reminded. 'Even when it was only gentlemen had the right, and we're supposed to be servants, aren't we? Oh dear, why did we venture on such a hazardous undertaking?'

'It's for you, and the fostering of your love affair.' Maria was revelling in the adventure. 'It's better than spending a boring evening playing backgammon with Mrs Jenkins who always cheats but denies it vigorously. Oh, look, we've just passed a group of people and they didn't give us a second glance, fully convinced that we are lads.'

Jane was not much comforted, pausing as they reached the alleyway that led to the inn. 'How can I let Robin know we're here? Supposing he's been delayed? What shall we do?'

'Courage, comrade. Didn't he say in his letter that he would meet you? Anyway, it's too late to do anything about it now. Come on!' and Maria dived ahead of her, brimming with confidence.

They had no difficulty in locating the tavern owing to the noise. It was filled to capacity. The door stood open, light streaming out, shadows passing and repassing across it. The smell was pungent; hops and grape, candlewax and tobacco, overlaid by roast beef and cabbage, for this was also an eating-house. Maria and Jane hesitated for a moment, then stepped over the threshold.

The tap-room was wide and long, with a low, oak-beamed ceiling blackened by more than a century of smoke from the open fire, human breath and the fumes from clay-pipes. The floor was rush-strewn, soaking up spittle and slops. Wooden settles and chairs stood at trestle tables whose surfaces were knife-scarred and bore the rings left by tankards. The bar occupied the whole of one wall and pewter mugs hung from hooks behind it, with glasses and wine bottles on shelves.

It was crowded, the clientele mixed. Labourers rubbed shoulders with students, businessmen huddled in corners discussing the latest news from the Stock Exchange, and travellers broke their journeys. A noisy party were drinking the health of a man who was to be married next day and gamesters, intent on play, crouched over dice and cards. Hard-faced serving wenches moved among the customers, slapping aside hands that wanted to squeeze breasts or dive up under skirts. They were well able to defend themselves, their language that of the gutter.

49

Other females swanned about, flaunting gaudy feathered hats and showing bosoms naked to the nipples, selling their bodies to anyone who would pay. Young and not so young, they were strident harpies who did not hesitate to show what they had on offer, whisking up their petticoats and displaying their hairy or denuded pudendum and buxom arses. Their presence galvanised the men into boasting about the length, width and power of their pricks. The atmosphere became more heated. Several of the whores went outside with customers, returning after a short time seeking the next punter. They charged for their favours - nothing was for free.

An old man started to scrape a tune on a fiddle. The tipsy crowd sang along and one of the harlots danced, mouthing bawdy lyrics, kicking her legs high and exciting the men even more.

Lord, what are we doing here? Maria thought. She and Jane had taken part in many a hare-brained prank at school, but never anything as risky as this. Supposing they bumped into someone they knew? Friends of her guardian for example, though it was unlikely that they would be seen dead in a place like this, but one never knew. After their behaviour in the vault, anything was possible.

She weaved through the throng to the bar, Jane close behind her. The host, a large bewhiskered man with a beet-red face, grinned at her. 'What can I do for you, laddie?'

'Two pints of cider, landlord.' She pitched her voice several octaves lower.

The fermented apple juice appeared and Maria handed over coins, then they made their way to an empty table and sat there, sipping their drinks and watching the brazen antics of the whores. It was an education. 'That's the way to handle men,' Maria said. 'Play the bastards at their own game. Make them beg for it, controlled by their pricks and rendered cunt-struck.'

Jane, still labouring under the illusion of being in love, was in a ferment of worry, repeating over and over, 'Where's Robin?'

The uproar increased as the ale flowed. Maria could feel her head swimming. The cider was strong and slipped over the tongue pleasantly, deceptively smooth but with a kick like a mule. She was not used to it; sherry or wine were her only alcoholic beverages, and then in moderation.

'Perhaps we should order something to eat,' she suggested, hoping to sober up and calm Jane.

'I couldn't touch a morsel, really. He'll come. I know he'll come.'

A man staggered against their table, slopping their drinks and sending hot wax flying from the candle. 'What the devil...?' Maria shouted, staring at him fiercely and starting to understand why drink made one so aggressive.

A full-blown row was breaking out. The gamblers were arguing with the stag-party, strong words and insults being exchanged. A table was overturned with the clash of broken glass. The serving-girls shrieked. The whores cursed. The landlord sent the pot-boy to fetch the constables. Maria looked across and saw Robin pushing his way towards them.

'Jane!' he shouted, then reached her and swept her into his arms. 'Oh, Jane!'

'Be careful,' Maria warned, as he released her and slid along the bench. 'We're supposed to be lads. You don't want this lot getting the idea that you're looking for a bum-boy.'

'All right, and your disguise is perfect, but I should know Jane anywhere.' He laced his fingers with hers under the table and she stared at him, starry-eyed.

Oh, damn! Maria thought. This was going to be tricky. Those two would give the game away for sure. Everyone would guess they were lovers.

'You must be discreet,' she said urgently. 'I don't want to get into a fight where I have to explain that Jane and I are women. This would be exceedingly awkward and we could be manhandled and possibly raped. I don't expect for a moment that the whores would help us. They'd probably find it funny and accuse us of poaching on their preserves or something equally ridiculous.'

'I'll take care of you.' He was so bedazzled by the object of his desire that it bore out Maria's opinion of the rutting male.

The cider had reached its target and she needed to relieve her bladder. This was a contingency for which she had not planned. 'I need the privy,' she said, and stood up.

'In the yard at the back.' Robin jerked a thumb in that direction, but he was not really attending, staring into Jane's eyes.

Maria had seen Tranter come in. He was standing near the door, pint mug in his hand, watching her, though pretending not to. She nodded slightly, and then went outside. The yard was dark, but she made out the bulk of the privy. It stank, a wooden structure containing buckets for the relief of nature. When full these would be emptied into the open sewer that ran down the centre of the road outside.

She shuddered. There was no way she was going to use one of those. By the state of the ground, it was apparent that many of the male clients simply stood against the wall to rid themselves of water. Women were hardly catered for, but not many decent ones frequented pubic houses, only 'ladies of the night'.

A whore was servicing her client. She had him with his back to the fence, her legs locked round his waist while he supported her under the buttocks. He was groaning as she rode him, moving her hips, his cock embedded within her. It was impossible to see clearly in the gloom, but Maria was intrigued by the sight of a woman busily employed in the world's oldest profession. Her stomach churned at the idea of taking that gross unwashed person's most intimate part into her own body. Women must be desperate to do it, she thought. Hungry children, bills to be paid, a family to support. They weren't like the trollops she had seen in Damien's vault, highly-paid and sometimes highly-born sluts who did it for fun.

Her bladder was demanding to be emptied, so she went to what appeared to be a woodshed, lowered her breeches and squatted. This was carried out with all speed. Not only was she fearful of being discovered, but there was the question of Robin and Jane and what to do about them. I shall never fall in love, she decided, while adjusting her clothes. It takes away one's power and turns one into a spineless ninny, dependant on the whims and fancies of another.

She stepped from the shed straight into the arms of a man who was passing. 'I'm sorry, sir,' he said, and she recognised his voice instantly.

It was Charles Bradley. Guilt, shame and annoyance chased through her. How unfortunate that he should patronise the tavern at the same time as her. Fate played some diabolical tricks, concerned with nothing but her own amusement.

'No harm done,' she muttered, blessing the darkness.

At that moment a couple came out of the door and a shaft of light fell across Maria's face. She heard Charles's intake of breath and knew she had been recognised. Hold hard there,' he said, a thread of laughter running through his voice. 'Don't I know you, sir? Or is it madam?'

Maria tried to pull away, but he held her arm firmly. 'I don't think so,' she muttered.

He was not to be put off, and walked her closer to the light. 'Stab me to the vitals, if it ain't Lady Maria! I'd know that mouth anywhere,' he said, and his grip softened, his smile amused. 'So, milady, what are you doing here at this time of night? Meeting a lover, perhaps? Does your guardian know?'

She shook off his hand. 'This is nothing to do with you, my lord.' But all the time she was remembering how he had kissed her, caressed her breasts and fondled her cunny.

'Maybe not, but this is a rough place and you are taking risks. It must be for a worthy cause, and a lover seems the obvious choice.'

'Not my lover. I'm helping my friend, Lady Jane. She's in love with the clergyman who used to teach at our school. He's a fine person but not wealthy enough to ask her parents if he may woo her. They are forced to meet in secret.'

'I see, and where are they now?'

'In the tap-room. Tranter is looking to our welfare. He's one of Lady Arabella's grooms.'

'Will you permit me to offer my assistance?'

Despite her stubbornness that was insisting she could manage alone, she was thankful he had come along, and not only for safety's sake. Once again she was conscious of his attraction, irresistibly drawn to him. It was hard not to press closer. She wanted to touch him, to stroke his face and wind her fingers in his hair. Damien had introduced her to passion, and she would never be the same again.

They walked back together, and Jane's eyes widened with alarm when she saw Charles. 'Don't worry,' Maria said as she took the place beside her. 'He is a friend and will help us.'

His presence brought comfort, although she was not sure if she could trust him, she had to admit that she needed a man to protect her. Though this was a sign of weakness the tavern was a threatening place, the men quarrelsome, belligerent and argumentative. Amidst the racket going on around them she tried to assess Charles, his motives and sincerity. Impressions fixed in her mind from their last encounter came back and were reiterated. A lean man, with a thin, handsome face, hazel eyes under long lashes and peaked brows over which fell strands of brown hair. He carried an air of authority that marked him as well born.

As then, he was smartly dressed, but now wore serviceable attire, as if he was out and about on business, not pleasure. He nodded to Jane, acknowledging that they had met, and she introduced him to Robin. A glance across the room showed Maria that Tranter was still there.

'It's getting too dangerous to stay,' Charles said. 'The constables will be here any minute and we must get away, for they may arrest us along with the others and we'll have to spend the night in a lock-up. Not the happiest of experiences, I can assure you.'

He headed for the entrance, and the others followed. On the way he nodded to Tranter who fell in behind. In a short time they were walking towards a more salubrious area where the streets were cleaner and the houses more imposing. 'I live down that way,' Robin said, arm in arm with Jane. 'I was hoping you might visit me there, dearest.'

'But I'm supposed to take you home, ladies,' protested Tranter. 'Emily will give me an ear-bashing and refuse all favours if I leave you.'

'Don't worry, my good fellow.' It seemed natural that Charles should take command. 'Get a cab back and tell Emily, whoever that may be...'

'My maid,' Maria interjected.

'Well, tell her I will see that they are driven home in my own coach.'

'And you are, sir?'

'Lord Charles Bradley, acquainted with Lady Maria's guardian.' To add weight to his words he produced a gold coin from his pocket and flipped it across to Tranter. 'Here's the fare, and something for your trouble.'

'Thank you, my lord. Your secret is safe with me.' Tranter touched his hat and made off into the darkness. 'I live in River Street at number ten,' Robin said, his arm round Jane. 'It's not far from here.'

'I know it. Be ready in an hour, Lady Jane. It's not long, I know, but you need to be at Armitage House before your absence is discovered.'

The couple hurried off, and Charles turned to Maria. 'You'll come inside? I can offer you a drink and we need to talk.'

She had little to lose, having thrown respectability and caution to the winds. Every part of her reckless nature was urging her to go with him. She trusted him, too, far more than she did the viscount. She nodded and they walked to his front door. The house had been built in the reign of Queen Anne, detached and surrounded by garden. Charles produced a key and let them into the hall. This was illuminated by candlesticks in holders on the walls between landscape paintings, and the floor was tiled in black and white, like a giant chessboard.

Maria tiptoed, exchanging amused glances with him. 'My housekeeper is abed upstairs,' he murmured, and indicated a door on the right. 'Let's go into my study.'

He lit a candle from one in the hall and applied it to a branched stick on a wide desk, then went round igniting others. The atmosphere was warm and friendly, the walls lined with books and a fire smouldering on the hearth. Charles stirred it with a brass poker and added more coal, then said, 'I must leave you for a moment and find my man, Bates, and tell him to prepare the carriage. I shan't be long.'

Maria settled on the couch drawn close to the fire. She took off her hat and jacket and freed her hair. It tumbled about her shoulders like a fiery cloud. There was no need for caution now and she took off her shirt and unbound her breasts, then slipped the garment on again, leaving some of the buttons undone.

Her sensible self wondered what she was doing in his house, but her desires knew precisely why she had come. It was time she experienced what intercourse meant. Damien had partly shown her, but left the act incomplete. She did not want to wait any longer, and disliked his arrogant assumption that he would win her and become her legal lord and master. She had never liked anyone telling her what to do.

Charles stood in the doorway. He walked to the table where a decanter and glasses stood. Filling two, he joined her on the couch. 'Let us not waste time,' he said, after draining his. 'We both know that we shall be lovers, so why beat about the bush?'

'I'm a virgin, and the viscount swears that he will make me his wife.'

'Do you love him?'

'No, but I find him intriguing.'

'He's after your fortune. He will do anything for money. Not that I'm suggesting this is all there is to it. You are extremely beautiful and he appreciates beauty almost as much as he does power.'

'You seem to be well acquainted with him.'

'We were friends long ago at university, but went in different directions later. He's away overseas a great deal, so I understand.'

'Lady Arabella told me, and I had never seen him until the race.'

'I am aware of this. I shall never forget you in that phaeton, looking like a young charioteer. I determined to meet you. That's the main reason why I attended his soiree, and I've not forgotten our encounter in the conservatory. What do you suppose would have happened had we not been interrupted?'

'I can't say, sir,' she blurted out, heat rushing through her.

He was so close she could not gather her wits. She could smell him, a musky, male odour overlaid with perfumed pomade. His arm was resting along the back of her shoulders and it was so easy to slide down a little and rest her head on his chest. She could hear the steady beat of his heart and allowed herself to sink into him.

'You make a lovely boy.' He dropped his hand to her crotch and laughed. Maria's cheeks were hot and she resented his amusement as he continued, 'Breeches suit you, showing your delectable bottom. If you were really a lad I might turn to sodomy.' His eyes were bright and his mouth eager as it closed on hers.

She could not help but respond, her tongue tangling with his, her breasts lifting under the shirt, straining to be caressed. He undid the buttons and spread the front wide, admiring and touching each in turn. This time she knew there was no turning back. This time she would lose her virginity.

It was as if she had spoken and Charles heard her. He lost some of his control, becoming almost harsh in his handling of her. 'Lie back, Maria,' he whispered, kneeling beside the couch so that she might stretch full length. 'Let me pleasure you. I shall be honoured to be your first lover.'

He opened her shirt fully and kissed her lobes, her neck and then her breasts. She felt his hands at her waistband, tugging at her breeches and she raised her hips a little so that they slid away from her. Now she wore nothing but shirt and hose. Charles sat back and admired her, then kissed her belly and combed through her mound, inserting a finger into her. She gasped at the joy of feeling him spreading open her labia and finding her pleasure bud.

He moved to lie across her and she felt his erect penis push against her. Her hand reached down to fondle its wet head and long hard stem. He was harsh now, less controlled. She had suspected that he might be a forceful lover and wanted it. She was dappled by firelight and candle glow but he noticed the bruises on her thighs.

'Who did this? Was it the viscount?' he demanded angrily.

'He punished me last night. In the vault, with some of his guests watching, and Lady Arabella too. He was angry because I had spoken with you. He tied me up, let his friends make free with me and whipped me.' The memory was adding to her excitement.

It seemed to stir Charles too, though he expressed fury. 'That perverted bastard! It was ever his way... submission, chastisement, bending women to his will.'

'He didn't take me, or satisfy me. But I know he'll try again. He wants me to be his slave and has already put me across his knee and spanked me.'

'Like this?' Before she realised his intention he sat up and pulled her across his lap, his naked penis like a bough between them. She felt his palm striking her buttocks, not too hard but enough to rouse those feelings deep within her that rejoiced in being treated in this way.

His blows fell swiftly, like summer rain, hard enough to send sparks shooting through her, but not so severe that they counteracted pleasure with pain. It was stimulating, underlining his strength and passion, making her feel feminine and weak and vulnerable, although she was all too aware that she was neither of these. Kneeling over her he turned her so that she faced him.

'I shall not force you. Tell me you want this.'

'I do... I think I do...' she stammered, dazzled by his beauty.

He nodded, left her and stripped, then stood before her, his naked body that of an athlete, muscular and tanned by exposure to the sun. His waist was slim, his belly flat and his cock rose up from its wiry thatch, straight as a lance, the bulbous glans shiny and red. He let her take her fill of looking, guessing that the masculine organ was an unfamiliar curiosity. He took it in his hand and it grew bigger as he stretched the foreskin over the helm and back again. The penis jerked as if having a life of its own. He lifted it and showed Maria his balls. They hung like two ripe fruits in their wrinkled sac.

Maria gaped, not knowing whether to be impressed or repulsed. Could she ever take a thing that big into her untried channel?

As if reading her mind Charles knelt across her and his mouth met hers while his fingers slipped across her clitoris, bringing it to the peak but not to completion. He lifted her legs up and around his waist and she felt his cock-tip moving between her labial lips. Using a hand as a guide he rubbed the helm over her nubbin, and then continued to stimulate it with his fingers as his phallus found the entrance to her vagina and lingered there for a moment.

Maria tightened her legs around him and buried her hands in his hair, dragging him closer. This was the moment for which she had been longing yet dreading; the invasion of her virginity, the sacrifice of her maidenhead. She would never be the same again.

He took his weight on his rigid arms, and then thrust slowly. 'Ow... ooh!' she protested as her hymen resisted this invasion. He stopped, partly within her. His hand came down between them and he massaged her clitoris. The need to come blotted out any discomfort and, still frigging her bud, he thrust slowly forward, and then with a fierce jerk, sheathed himself inside her.

Maria moaned with pain and shock. Charles remained still, buried in her virgin hole. Master of the erotic art that he was, he continued to stroke the rigid nubbin, rousing her to intense pleasure, making her forget the discomfort of his prick, that large object forcing its way inside her.

'Hold the base of my cock,' he told her. 'Let me pleasure you before I thrust in deeper. I don't want to hurt you and can tell that I'm ploughing untilled soil.'

She whimpered her need as his clever finger brought her higher and higher till orgasm burst within her. Then Charles gave in to his lust, penetrating her fully, withdrawing and entering again and again. She could feel his pubic bone grazing her throbbing clitoris and his balls slapping against her perineum. Heaving beneath him, urging him to push deeper and harder, her nails dug into his back like the claws of a wild cat in season.

His hips pumped, her wet passage receiving him with greater ease and he lost control, crushing her beneath him as he frenziedly sought relief. They rolled from the couch to the floor and this gave him greater purchase. He drove into her brutally and she felt his cock chafing her bud at every stroke, the sensation rushing through her, building and building to another orgasmic explosion. She cried out as she came again. Charles gave another savage thrust followed by a deep bark of satisfaction, flooding her with his seed.

They collapsed on the carpet then, smiling into each other's eyes, came back from the paradise of sensual pleasure to harsh reality. 'I must take you home, sweetheart,' he said, kissing the tip of her nose.

'It this the end? Shall we meet again?' She despised herself for asking, wanting to appear ice-cool, as if losing her virginity was an everyday event.

Charles looked down at her. He was already dressing, shirt and breeches on, transforming him once more into a gentleman, not a god of love. 'That's rather up to you,' he said, with his quirky smile. 'How strong are you and how much do you obey your guardian?'

'He has control of my money for another three years.' She began to realise just how much Damien was in charge and how hopeless it was to fight him.

Charles stood in front of the mirror, adjusting his cravat and combing his fingers through his hair. 'You could talk to your aunt. I know Arabella quite well and she's not an unreasonable person.'

'He has a hold over her. She seems to enjoy him being cruel to her.'

'They are of the same persuasion.' Charles's eyes were angry. Maria hoped he never looked at her like that. 'We can meet secretly for the time being, if you wish, and see what transpires.'

'Perhaps he'll go off to the West Indies again. He has sugar plantations there.' She, too, had dressed, but had not bothered to tie back her hair or bind her breasts.

Charles shrugged. 'Who knows? He seems to be a law unto himself.'

His tone made her uneasy. 'You know something about him, don't you? What is it? Tell me.'

He tapped the side of his nose mysteriously, still smiling. 'No, my dear.'

'Oh, Charles! Don't tease!' Her arms were round him and he clipped her waist, hugging her, his mouth hovering just above hers.

The door crashed open. 'Well, well!' said a scornful female voice. 'What's all this, Charlie? Are you buggering boys now?'

He turned, his arm still holding Maria. 'Good evening, Sally,' he said calmly. 'I wasn't expecting you.'

'So I see,' she retorted, her eyes going over Maria, scalpel sharp. 'I've got a key, remember?' He ignored her, gathering up his hat and Maria's and guiding her out of the door. 'Where are you off to?' Sally demanded, arms akimbo.

'I'm taking my friend home, and I don't want to find you here when I get back. Understand?'

'Oh, hoity-toity!' Sally mocked. 'Your friend, is it? We'll see about that.'

Charles stood to one side, his stance insisting that she went down the hall before him. 'Get out, Sally, and don't come back until I send for you. Give me the key.' He held out his hand and, with a curse, she dropped it into his open palm.

'Right!' Sally glared at him and then at Maria. 'You won't get rid of me that easily, and as for you... boy, girl or whatever you are, you haven't seen the last of me!'

Chapter 7

Robin used his key to gain entrance to one of a row of three-storied houses. A lantern mitigated the gloom of the hall, and he was about to lead Jane up the narrow staircase when a door opened and a man was silhouetted there.

'Come in, Robin,' he boomed, his voice loud and cheery. 'No sneaking off to your room until you've joined us in a bumper of ale. Ah, I see you're not alone. Bring your friend in too.'

'Thanks, Will,' Robin said reluctantly, and his hand tightened on Jane's.

She found herself in an untidy parlour, where a black iron kettle hung on a trivet over an open fire and several equally untidy young men lounged on broken-down couches and in sagging armchairs. One sat at the table, books spread out before him, head in his hands as he carried on studying, oblivious of the general banter, coarse jokes and laughter.

'Good evening, Robin,' shouted a ginger-haired individual, waving his tankard. 'We're holding a debate on Socrates. Was he or was he not a pederast?'

'And this is going to help you to get through your examination on Greek philosophers?' Robin took this in his stride and Jane's admiration for him mounted. 'I shouldn't think his sexual persuasion will make an iota of difference to your marks, Johnny.'

'Don't be so damned pedantic,' Johnny retorted, but still in a joking vein. 'It's blatantly obvious, my boy, that you'll come to naught and eke out your existence as a curate in some rural backwater.'

'This suits me very well,' Robin said, and Jane was acutely uncomfortable, certain that they would see through her disguise. She could not refuse when a mug was put in her hand, but found the ale too strong.

Johnny toasted her, and then put his tankard down. 'Who's your friend, Robin? Are you fond of choirboys? If I didn't know you better, I say you've brought one home for private tuition.'

Every eye turned to Jane. Even the scholar at the table glanced her way. There was a hush, then Robin cleared his throat and said, 'This is not a boy, sirs. Let me introduce Jane. We love one another, but I should not be considered wealthy or influential enough for her father to give us his blessing. We have to meet in secret and tonight she dressed in a groom's clothing and met me at The Three Tuns.'

This statement was greeted by whistles, cheers and stamping feet. To them it was great fun and not in the least scandalous. Students were a law unto themselves, neither fish nor fowl and, apart from paying lip service to their tutors, they lived very much as they liked. They were scions of great families who had been given the choice of the army, the church, or university. A humbly-born youth rarely had the opportunity to join their exalted ranks, though occasionally a nobleman pulled strings in order to have his bastard son educated.

'Well, Robin, if this is true, then why are you wasting time down here? Get upstairs and make the most of it,' advised Johnny, grinning at Jane. 'Have no fear. Our lips will be sealed and no one shall be any the wiser.'

'Thank you,' she whispered, fingers locked in Robin's.

'I hope you aren't thinking that impropriety is about to take place,' Robin blurted.

Further hoots and disbelief greeted this statement. 'I should hope not!' said Will, the twinkle in his eyes belying the sternness of his tone. 'Whatever next? We live a monastic life here, don't we, boys?'

'Pure as the driven slush!' agreed a portly youth who was kneeling by the fire. He held a coal shovel flat above the flames with a meat pie heating on its surface. 'We never invite whores back here.'

'Never!' they lied in unison.

'Can't often afford 'em,' cut in Johnny. 'It's usually a tuppenny fuck against a wall. You're fortunate, Robin, my lad.'

'I can assure you...'

'Fie, don't perjure your immortal soul. Go away and do it, man. Give the poor lass what she craves.'

Jane left the room in a welter of shame, but Robin gave her no chance to reconsider, whisking her up the stairs to his room under the eaves. It was cold, and he lit the candle and drew the threadbare curtains. Taking her hands in his he chafed them between his own to warm them.

'I'm sorry this is such a poor abode, but it's all I can manage at the moment. My lot will be improved when I take up my position in Burdock in the autumn. I shall be living with the vicar and his family in the manse.'

'That will make it all the more difficult for us to see each other,' she mourned, clinging to him, wanting to stay like that for all eternity.

'It's not too far from Bath, and your parents visit there to take the waters.' he pointed out, and held her closer. They stood together under the sloping ceiling, oblivious to the cheerlessness of their surroundings.

They could hear his fellow lodgers shouting and laughing below, but they posed no threat. There was nothing to stop them making love and they sank on to his bed together. Jane was eager yet fearful, as she had been on that first occasion of intimacy. But now the fear was much less and the desire greater. She lay back, wide legged, blessing the freedom of breeches, wanting to have him take them off for her. But for now it was enough to be able to feast her eyes on his face.

He bent over her, and his loosened hair brushed her temples. She could see the line of his cheekbone and finely shaped brows. She slid her hands under his coat and let her fingers stray across his chest, feeling the muscles under the linen shirt. He gasped, and his pupils were dilated with passion in the candlelight.

'We should stop,' he muttered, even as he found her breasts under the mannish attire. She was glad she had not found it necessary to bind them, like the full-bosomed Maria.

'I don't want to stop,' she whispered, invading his mouth with her tongue.

He pulled away to whisper, 'We shouldn't... it's a sin. You might get with child.'

For a second she wished he was a more impetuous lover, but knew it was only his concern for her that made him careful. A wayward part of her urged that she break down his resolve, proving her power over him. 'We haven't long before Maria comes for me. Let's undress and go to bed,' she urged.

No man worth his salt could have refused such an invitation, and Robin was no saint. They started to take off their clothes. She was naked first, suddenly shy, clasping her arms about her breasts and pulling the bedclothes over her. Robin, too, was self-conscious about his body, hiding his genitals as he climbed in beside her.

'It would be like this if we were married,' she said, cuddling his shoulder. 'Every night we'd spend together. Just you and me, alone. I want that, Robin. I don't like the idea of doing it with Percy, and that's what my family are planning. Can't we elope?'

'You must be patient, sweetheart.' He made it all the more difficult to do this, seizing her hand and kissing each finger, the knuckles, the nails, and the inside of her wrist. It set her on fire.

She wriggled down under the sheet and grasped his erect cock. She had dreamed of doing this again, even thought of it when Jane was caressing her. The reality was even more wonderful than she had remembered.

He moaned at her touch. 'Oh, darling, I need you so much. I have used your sweet image to fire my imagination as I satisfied myself, losing my seed, but never really stilling my craving. I love you, Jane. There, I've confessed it. Now you can make or break me.'

'Robin, my dearest! I feel the same about you. I shall die if we can't marry. I'll speak to my father or maybe Lady Arabella. She is much admired and respected by all.'

'And if not?' He was fast losing control, rolling his thumbs over her nipples and then pinching the needy points. Thrusting herself up to meet his touch, Jane was aching with desire.

'Then it's Gretna Green,' she murmured, unable to concentrate on anything except her body's demands.

He propped himself up on one elbow and looked down at her. 'We'll do it, darling, even if it means I have to leave the church. I can work at other things... as a college lecturer or private tutor to an important family.'

His voice trailed off and his hand cruised over her belly and mound and thighs. She parted them, opening herself to him. He sat back, looking at her, his hands still cruising over her. 'I could gaze at you forever,' he said, unsteadily. 'You are more beautiful than any work of art. I want you... but must give you the greatest pleasure. I'm not skilled at lovemaking.'

'I showed you what to do last time.' She took his hand and placed it on her mound. 'My love-bud is my most sensitive part. Remember?'

This time she was bolder, teaching him how to go down on her, open her cleft with his fingers and lick her till she peaked. Coming in a sunburst of pleasure, her instinct was to draw him into her, welcoming his penis, wanting it to clench herself around in her final orgasmic spasms. He needed no urging, inserting his glans, meeting the obstruction of her virginity and pushing against it.

'I'm sorry, darling, am I hurting you?' he gasped, unable to stop the urge to thrust deeper.

'Yes... no... it's all right... go on!' she squealed, tolerating the pain as her untried love-channel yielded to his invasion.

'Dear love... oh, my dearest,' he gasped, his movements quickening.

Jane flung her arms round his neck and her legs about his body, forgetful of everything in the desperate need to get closer and closer to him. His penis felt huge, and she feared it would split her asunder, but it became more bearable as their mutual fluids eased the path.

'I love you,' she whispered, her face buried in his hair. 'Oh, God, I'm going to come. I can't hold back.'

She felt him pulsing within her, then he suddenly pulled out and spilled his semen on her belly. It was wet and sticky, rapidly cooling, but to her it was a sign that he cared so much for her that her safety was of paramount importance. He was avoiding planting a baby in her womb.

'Oh, Robin, that was wonderful,' she murmured, languid in the aftermath of pleasure.

He was drowsy now, snuggling into her, wanting to sleep, but their peace was rudely shattered by Will banging on the door and shouting, 'There's a man here. Says he's come to take Jane home. He called her "Lady Jane". Is this true, or a joke?'

Robin did not answer; instead he struggled into his breeches, then said, 'Tell him we'll be only a moment.' Jane had already leapt from the bed and was almost ready. She took one last look round at the room where she had lost her virginity and then accompanied Robin and Will downstairs.

'I've done it!' Maria said, keeping her voice low.

'So have I,' Jane whispered, as Emily hustled them up the backstairs to the corridors that led from the servants' quarters.

Though Maria knew Emily would be lenient if she heard what was being said, she would undoubtedly scold them and issue dire warnings about the consequences. Wise in such matters, she never seemed to get caught out. no matter how many men she enjoyed. Maria sighed with relief when safely ensconced in her bedroom, with Jane in the one next to it. Emily attended both of them for Sarah had not yet returned and Agatha was asleep.

'This is our secret, milady,' Emily warned as she snuffed the candles, all save one that was on the nightstand. 'Tranter told me what took place and we should both be dismissed if it came out.'

'Our secret,' Maria repeated, tucking the quilt under her chin, imagining that sleep would be impossible, her brain whirling with recollections of everything that had transpired between her and Charles, but within minutes she was lost in oblivion.

Shopping was a favourite occupation for a lady. Arabella and her ward and Jane were driven to the heartland of London's commercial centre, The Royal Exchange. Arabella knew every milliner and tailor in the area, a valued customer who spent her husband's money lavishly.

She had brought along her son, James, and his nurse. He was approaching the time when he would no longer wear dresses, but be attired in miniature versions of masculine breeches, jackets, waistcoats and hats. Arabella was light-minded and immoral but a devoted mother. She doted on the child and let him have his way on every issue, to the despair of the nurse who had reared him since birth and had to put up with his tantrums.

It was no longer popular for dressmakers to flaunt a French name although, despite the war, Parisians were still reputed to be the most fashionable people in the world. Instead the exponents of the art were known simply as tailors and modistes, using their own less flamboyant titles. Nonetheless, the trade had been influenced by the influx of designers who had escaped the Revolution and settled in England several years before. It was the most famous of these, Madame Descartes, who Arabella patronised.

The shop was in a cobbled square. It was double-fronted, and had bow windows with dimpled glass panes. Green painted, flower-filled tubs flanked the doors. It breathed elegance, exclusivity and expense. Arabella swept in, followed by her entourage. Madame Descartes herself came to greet this important client.

'Your ladyship, such a great honour,' she gushed in the fascinating accent she had never lost.

She was petite. Her black ringlets were topped by a gauze turban brandishing a peacock feather. Her gown incorporated the latest innovations. High-waisted still, and of diaphanous white fabric, the skirt was wider at the hem. A tight, long-sleeved jacket completed the ensemble. Madame was in her thirties but maintained her charm. Her dark eyes were shrewd as they assessed Maria and Jane, seeking to establish an even deeper rapport with them, so that they would be her customers for all time.

'I need an evening gown,' Arabella pronounced. 'The earl and I are invited to a ball at the Prince of Wales's residence.'

'It will be a pleasure, my lady.' Though never for a moment obsequious, Madame's attitude was a nice balance between equality and reverence.

James, bored, started to whine. Quick as a flash Madame had one of her underlings bring toys to amuse him, and then dispatched him to be measured by the tailor for his manly attire, accompanied by his nurse. Madame and Arabella went into a huddle over styles and material for the ball-gown and Maria and Jane sat on a couch and thumbed through drawings of the latest vogues. But even as they did so they were whispering about their experiences of the night before, though both looked so innocent that no one would have guessed they were no longer virgins.

'I want to do it again and again.' Jane was all pink cheeks and wide eyes.

'So do I.' Maria had the smug look of a cat that has been at the cream.

'When can we arrange it?'

'All you have to do is get messages to Robin's lodgings. It is more difficult for me.' Maria was almost resentful. Being in love hurt, she decided, and almost wished she was not in that delirious state of confusion.

The showroom was delightfully decorated in pink, with swags and gilt, mirrors and changing cubicles. There were shelves holding bales of fabrics, and stands displaying elegant hats, creations of lace, straw and velvet, trimmed with artificial flowers, ribbons and feathers. Maria scarcely heeded it, every nerve in her body and each drop of her blood aching for Charles. How could she endure waiting until he sent to her? This is what he had said as they kissed when reaching Armitage House. She had clung to him in the dark after they left the coach, and she could still smell the night air and his hair, and taste his mouth on hers. It made her wet between the legs and caused mayhem in her loins and nipples.

Arabella disturbed her daydreams. 'I want you to put on one of Madame's latest offerings. I may decide to take you with me to the ball. Go along, girl, follow Madame's assistant. Not you, Jane; there are some hats for you to try, if you can afford them from your allowance.'

A reluctant Maria was led to a cubicle where she found several charming dresses on hangers. There was something about the assistant that was familiar and the girl was staring at her too hard. Maria found this disconcerting, having the uneasy feeling that she had seen her somewhere before. Then the penny dropped. It was the woman Charles had called Sally, when she found them together in his house. This could spell disaster, though Maria could not be certain if Sally had taken her for a girl or a boy.

'Leave me,' she said, with an imperious wave. 'I can manage alone.'

Sally curtsied, saying with a sneering kind of mock servility, 'Call if you need me, milady.'

She knows! Maria was certain of it, and the consequences boded ill.

In no mood for trying on clothes she was alarmed to think that Sally might betray her. She slipped out of her garments and stood naked in front of the long mirror. The marks left by Damien had faded, though a faint trace remained. It was as if Charles had obliterated them. With eyes half closed she lifted her breasts, thumbs rotating on the pink crests, her belly clenching as she recalled the feel of his fingers on her most private places. And that moment when he had ruptured her hymen! She could not resist inserting a finger into her crack, finding her clitoris and massaging it. She parted her legs a little, standing there in white stockings fastened above the knee and black shoes with spindle heels.

This was how Damien saw her, squinting through a hole in the back wall of the cubicle. He had an arrangement with Madame; golden guineas in exchange for playing Peeping Tom. The idea that he was staring at women's treasures without them being aware gave him an instant erection. It was an extension of his feelings of power. They were helpless to stop him, in total ignorance of his hidden presence. They felt free to scratch themselves, eye their bodies in the mirror, jiggle their breasts, drop a hand down to their slits, part the hairy wings and toy with their buds, even bring about orgasm and no one would be any the wiser - with the exception of Damien.

Arabella had been party to this morning's game, telling him she was taking Maria to see Madame. He had made sure his coach was parked out of sight and had occupied his hiding place. Jane did not interest him much. She was if anything too ingenuous. There was a hidden naughtiness about Maria that he longed to tap, convinced that once opened, her sexuality would reach full bloom. He was determined to be the one to bring this about.

His cock was burgeoning and he released it from confinement, cradling it in one hand and sliding the skin up and down the shaft. He was so absorbed in this and in spying on Maria that he did not realise there was someone else present until a voice spoke behind him.

'Your lordship, pray forgive me, but Madame has sent me to see if there is anything I can do for you. My name is Sally, and you've done me the honour of allowing me to satisfy you several times before.'

Damien glanced round and saw a dark-haired girl wearing the sprigged cotton dress, white apron and cap that was the uniform of the Descartes establishment. Accustomed to gratifying his lust wherever he willed, he vaguely remembered her, a lively trollop willing to fulfil every dirty fancy for money. Madame did well out of her girls, taking a percentage of whatever they earned through whoring for her. She prettifying the act by pretending she was simply obliging her gentlemen clients, but Damien knew she was no more than a bawd, no better or worse than Madame Flora, keeper of the bordello who organised his parties for him.

He did not hide his prick, letting it stand free from his breeches, proud of its virile dimensions. He reached for Sally's breasts, artfully displayed by her low cleavage. 'I remember you, girl,' he muttered hoarsely. 'Get on your knees and suck my cock.'

Sally needed no second bidding, sinking down gracefully, grasping his appendage in her fist and holding it to her mouth, then parting her lips and letting it slide between them. Damien kept his eyes on Maria who, far from showing an inclination to play with herself further, was slipping the gown over her head and adjusting it round her body. She looked sulky, as if not enjoying the task, something else preying on her mind.

He raised Sally up, needing to bury his prick in her slippery depths. She peered through the gap in the curtain and smiled mysteriously. 'What is it, wench?' he demanded, sotto voce.

'That's your lordship's ward, isn't it?' Sally replied, and her eyes sparked.

'It is. What is this to you?' He took little notice, busy parting her legs and bending slightly so he could insert his weapon into her.

'Funny thing... but I could have sworn I saw her last night, dressed in men's clothing.' Sally let him do what he wished with her, hardly heeding.

He stopped, grabbed her by the chin and made her look at him. 'What are you babbling about? Tell me.'

'It was in a gentleman's residence.'

'Whose?'

'Lord Charles Bradley's. I'm his mistress, sort of, when he fancies it, that is. I went round there and caught them in the parlour, and she was dressed as a man.'

'Why are you telling me this?' He removed himself from her. 'Charles Bradley, you say?'

'I'm telling you because I thought you should know, her being your ward and all.'

Not true, Damien thought. You have a grudge against Maria because your keeper fancies her. Women! They are all the same, whore or great lady! Sisters under the skin.

The thought of Maria bedding Charles went through him like a barb. He wanted to kill and if this could not happen right away then he longed to punish Maria. The jade, to slip off and enjoy herself with his foe! His palm itched to close round the handle of a whip and lay it on her, slash by cruel slash. How dare she flout him? He would make her suffer for it.

Was Sally telling the truth? He had no reason to doubt her and her very attitude spoke of jealousy and resentment.

He found coins in his pocket and pushed them into her eager palm. 'Keep watch on her and come to me if you have anything else to report.'

Sally dipped a curtsey. 'Yes, my lord. Is that all, sir?' She sounded almost regretful that he did not want her.

'That is all.' He dismissed her with a nod and turned back to studying Maria more intently than before.

She seemed abstracted, dropping the gown over her head and struggling with the buttons at the back, not bothering to fasten them all. It was a beautiful dress that would enhance her at any evening function, but she was not paying attention, scarcely studying her reflection.

Was she thinking of Charles? Had he robbed her of her maidenhead? The question buzzed in Damien's brain like a swarm of angry hornets. If the villain had helped himself to her virgin orifice, then he had poached on Damien's preserves and this could not be forgiven. There was one way to find out for sure and Damien would have to school his impetuosity and wait his chance to examine her. He slipped from Madame Descartes' establishment without Maria being aware of his presence, and set about putting his plans into action.

Arabella received a note from Damien, bidding her come to Strafford Hall without delay. With the prospect of nothing more exciting than a game of cards with her intimates, she decided to obey. There was always a whiff of danger in any communication from him. He expected her to comply and she was more than willing to do so.

She was well aware that he had been to the dressmaker's that morning, firing his lust by secretly watching Maria, and vaguely assumed that his summons might concern this, so the scowl that darkened his features as he greeted her in the Great Hall came as a surprise.

'What is the matter?' she enquired calmly, peeling off her gloves as she rustled towards him.

'You may well ask, my lady,' he growled, then seized her by the wrist, giving it a brutal twist.

'Release me, Damien.' She was indignant, having no notion of why he was so enraged. Not in the least afraid, though they were alone, her maid having been dismissed, a quiver of desire tingled through her as she wondered what he would do.

He flung her from him. 'You've been neglecting your duty. Word has reached me that Maria met Charles Bradley in secret last night, disguised as a man. What say you to that?'

'Who told you?'

'One of Madame Descartes' assistants, a girl named Sally. She caught them together in his house, apparently, and considered it her duty to tell me.'

'And what was this wench doing there?'

'She is Bradley's mistress.'

Arabella laughed lightly. 'Well then, my dear viscount, it's as plain as a pike staff. The girl is driven by jealousy and spite. And you believed her?'

'Why should she lie to me?'

'I've just told you. She wants to get Maria into trouble.'

'She has succeeded. By God, if he has deflowered her...!'

'What will you do? Call him out? You'll look like a fool... or a cuckold, and you're not yet her husband.' Arabella was deliberately goading him, aroused by his anger and inviting him to unleash his fury on her.

'Bitch!' he roared. 'This is your fault. If you had done your job properly she'd not have had the chance to wander around at night, meeting Bradley. Where were you? Whoring at some party or other? The earl should take a horsewhip to you. I'd not tolerate it in my wife! And I won't allow you to get away with it when we have joint responsibilities. Come with me!'

She knew his intentions but put up a mock fight, for he enjoyed resistance, and she anticipated at least an hour of decadent fornication. Pain would be mingled with sensual pleasure, resistance covering the desire to submit, all the joys of being owned and owning, the master as much enslaved by his submissive as she was to him.

Silently she followed him down to the vault. He lit the lanterns and the black and crimson decor sprang to life. A brazier already glowed crimson, throwing out heat. The heart of Damien's kingdom was once more immaculate, cleared from the debris of the orgy. He was a stickler for order, liking to be in control of everything and everyone.

'You have been careless. Admit it.' He pushed her towards the vaulting horse. 'You shall be punished.'

'Thank you,' she murmured, entering into the game.

He shook her. 'Thank you... what?'

'Thank you, master,' she replied meekly.

She was wearing a floor-length fitted coat, with long tight sleeves and a high waist, and her hat was pill-box shaped.

'Get undressed!' he commanded.

Arabella pretended to be frightened, fumbling with the buttons and then laying the garment across the back of a chair after baring her head. Her flimsy pastel gown offered little resistance to his rough hands as he stripped her of it, impatient of her fumbling. Now naked, save for her chemise and stockings, he made her stand on a stool and bend over the back of the wooden horse. In this position she was utterly vulnerable and rejoiced in her serfdom as he fastened her ankles and bound her wrists. Her posterior was fully exposed and she waited in trembling anticipation.

At first he did no more than run his hands over the soft skin of her rump and dip between her spread thighs, frigging her swelling bud. Arabella gasped and wriggled her hips. Though facing away from him, her head hanging over the contraption's side, she visualised his expression, such a handsome man with those steely eyes and fine features and that inky-black hair tumbling about his ears. He fulfilled her every dream of what a hero should look like, and yet he was so cruel, so heartless and mercenary. Once she had loved him, but he had broken her heart and she was glad to settle for the elderly but kind earl. Though she could never resist Damien, she no longer felt love or even a modicum of affection for him. She took from him in the same way he did from her. If she seemed heartless, it was because she had been taught by an expert.

He was silent now. Arabella wondered briefly if he had tied her up and left her, amusing himself by imagining her distress as time went by and no one came to free her. There was no sound except the settling of coals in the braziers. She considered calling out, but then felt his hand cupping her pudenda, the middle digit palpating her clit. It was infinitely pleasurable and she settled into the rhythm that would bring on her climax. He nibbled that tender spot where her neck joined her spine, and she moaned.

'You like that don't you, slave-slut?' he murmured. 'Poor little needy tart, who has been so disobedient. Do you deserve to come?'

'No, master.' Dear God, she thought, I'll say anything if he'll just bring me off.

'I shall decide when or even if I shall let you. Perhaps I won't, making you wait indefinitely. How would you like that, eh?' His words were supplemented by a hard slap on her left buttock.

'Whatever you say, master,' she whimpered.

Silence. Then a sudden rush of air and a biting pain that stung her bottom. He was using a whip. Involuntarily she cried out and jerked against her bonds. He leaned over her and touched her cheek with the smooth leather instrument he had just used to chastise her. He touched her lips with the handle and she wanted it in her mouth, like a penis, yearning for the taste of it. She lifted her head, but he moved it away and she could not reach it. Heat pricked where the lash had landed on her buttocks and her vagina was on fire.

'Not enough yet, slave,' he muttered, and the whip lightly touched the backs of her thighs, her spine, and the sides of her breasts, her shoulders and upper-arms. 'Tell me you want to be beaten. Go on. Say it!'

'I do... oh, yes... and make me come too!'

She heard his quickened breathing and felt the vibration in the air as he raised the whip and it cracked down across her skin. He was like an avenging angel meting out punishment for her sins. She knew she was guilty of many and absorbed the pain in retribution. Tears trickled down her cheeks and dripped on to the floor below. And all the time the tingling rush of pain added to her arousal. This was a well-trodden path. Both knew precisely what parts to play and how.

She wanted to scream, but kept it in. She was compounded of feelings; her thighs quivered in expectation of the lash, her anus clenched and her cunt ached for penetration. With each blow she absorbed the burning pain and it added to her desire for fulfilment. Lash after stinging lash blazed across her flesh until at last he flung down the whip and his hand slipped between her legs. She started to come, rising to the peak in a wild rush, the feeling so intense that she cried out, writhing on his fingers. Unchaining her, he pushed his cock into her from behind and thrust hard, exploding into orgasm.

He stroked her hair, almost tenderly, but his voice was harsh as he said, 'Tell your maids to pack. I'm leaving for the country and you and Maria are coming with me.'

When she had gone he sat at his desk and wrote a note addressed to Lord Charles Bradley, and had it delivered to White's Club.

Chapter 8

'I shall be taking you back to your mother later today, Jane,' Arabella announced as they sat at breakfast.

The sun streamed through tall French windows that gave access to the terrace, the staff were soft-footed and deferential, the atmosphere serene, and yet Maria sensed undercurrents.

'So soon?' she interrupted, giving her friend no chance to reply. 'May I ask the reason?'

'You may, though I was addressing Jane,' her aunt answered levelly, using a silver knife to spread orange conserve on a triangular slice of buttered toast. 'Miss Bailey has left her post, taking up another elsewhere, and a new duenna needs to be engaged, also your guardian has invited you and me to stay with him at Raven Towers, his manor house in the country.'

'For what reason?' Maria was devastated. It would rob her of any chance to see Charles. Not only that, she would be deprived of Jane's company. Agatha Bailey would be no loss, though it was said that the devil you know is better than the one you don't.

'What he and I decide is nothing to do with you. We are in charge, remember?' Though Arabella was usually amiable, when it came to Damien she closed ranks with him against all others.

It was two days since Maria had made love with Charles, and both she and Jane had begun to believe their escapade had gone unnoticed. Even her aunt's announcement did not indicate that they had been discovered. It could be mere coincidence that this journey was planned. It was the saddest news for both herself and Jane, making assignations with their lovers nearly impossible.

Jane was staring at her, trying to conceal her true feelings. 'Shall I not see Maria again, my lady?' she said unsteadily.

'Oh, dear me, don't be so dramatic. Of course you will, but not for some time I should imagine. But now I have one last treat planned for this morning. Get your wraps and we'll be off.' Arabella dabbed her lips, laid down her table napkin and a footman drew back her chair as she rose.

She gave him an arch smile and brushed her hand across the fork of his breeches as she passed. Maria pretended not to notice. At first her aunt's familiarity with the male servants had troubled her, but now she took it as a matter of course.

'What are we going to do?' Jane wailed once they were alone and on their way upstairs.

'Don't worry. I'll think of something. You are in a better position than me as you will be able to write to Robin at his lodgings.'

'Not for long. My parents are returning to Bath soon. And there will be a new chaperone to contend with. Though Miss Bailey was a bully, at least I knew where I stood with her.' Maria had never seen Jane so cast down and her own heart ached. She would so much miss this dear companion who had become like a sister to her, or probably something better as there was no sibling rivalry between them.

Her aunt had not given a time for departure to Raven Towers, and she wondered desperately if the wily Emily might be able to smuggle her out as she had done before. A hackney carriage would take her to Charles's house where she could tell him she was being taken away.

Now there was nothing else for it but to go along with Arabella's plans for an outing. Would it be shopping? A visit to friends as frivolous as herself or a drive through Hyde Park eyeing the beaux strolling there?

It turned out to be none of these, the coach weaving through the West End traffic and finally drawing up at an imposing house in a rank of others. Steps led to the entrance and there was a sign painted with a flourish that read, Signor Mancini's School of Fencing.

'Am I to take lessons?' Maria asked flippantly.

'Don't be pert,' Arabella chided. 'It is hardly an occupation for young ladies.'

Maria was in the mood to argue. 'I've always thought it a pity that girls can't take part in sport or learn the use of weapons.'

'There are enough gentlemen to follow these pursuits and, in my opinion, they are much more suited to it. Skirts would impede us.'

'Then perhaps we should wear trousers.' Maria was tetchy, weary of the restrictions that imprisoned her.

Arabella did not reply, sweeping towards an open door off the hallway and being greeted by the Italian himself, a charming man, swarthy and bright-eyed, wearing fencing apparel. He presented a dashing figure and Arabella smiled at him warmly.

'Welcome, milady,' he gushed, in heavily accented English. 'The viscount is already here.'

'So I should hope,' she replied, magnificent and commanding as she permitted him to escort her. 'I'm unaccustomed to being kept waiting.'

Damien was involved? Maria frowned, wondering what was going on but keeping quiet and waiting to see what took place.

There was no denying Arabella's aplomb and Maria was starting to copy her, finding it eased the way when it came to dealing with almost anyone. Glancing neither right nor left she followed her aunt into the large studio, aware of Jane and Sarah trailing behind her.

The room was spacious and light, stripped of furniture and carpet, with benches against the plain walls and racks holding foils, face-masks and protective clothing. Signor Mancini chattered as they walked across the bare wooden floor. 'My school is popular with the gentlemen who like to learn the finer points of the art. Though duelling has been outlawed, a nobleman might still have occasion to defend his honour. Pistols are in vogue for settling differences these days, though still forbidden, but rapiers have that certain flourish. Don't you agree, Madame?'

'Well, I don't make a habit of watching, but yes, I agree that a man can look mighty graceful when fencing. Take those for example,' and she nodded to where two combatants were hard at it.

The room echoed to the clash of steel and the stamping of feet. Both wore white quilted cotton jackets, nankeen breeches, stockings and pumps. It was difficult to know their identity for their masks were full ones with close-woven metal mesh to shield their faces. Signor Mancini watched them keenly, calling out instructions.

The ladies sat on the benches and Arabella said, 'The shorter of the two is Damien.'

'So it is. Do you know the other?' Maria was fascinated by the way Damien fought, as supple as a panther and as fearsome, giving his opponent little quarter.

'Yes, I do. It's Charles Bradley.'

Just for an instant the room darkened and all Maria could see were enemies striking at each other. Lunge! Parry! Riposte! And all she could hear were Damien's furious words when she met Charles at the soiree. Was he aiming to kill him? Not in public, surely? And could he succeed anyway? Charles seemed to be as experienced a swordsman, slightly taller and lightning swift. Desire and fear rushed through Maria in equal measure as she watched them wielding those flashing blades and realised they were not button-tipped. A hit would be for real, penetrating padding and then flesh.

'They are rapiers. Is this legal?' she demanded of Signor Mancini.

He shrugged, lynx-eyed as he observed the contestants. 'Sometimes the milords like to take a risk. It is more exciting for them. Don't worry. They won't go too far.'

Maria wished she was as confident, fearing for both of them, a pair of well-matched opponents. Charles appeared to be almost indolently relaxed yet parried with lightning speed, giving Damien no chance to pierce his guard. The tension was almost tangible and Maria's fear grew. Damien was an aggressive fighter, but unable to beat down Charles's blade. He fought like a soldier, full of courage and bravura.

Signor Mancini watched closely. No hint of scandal must be associated with his school. These hot-headed aristocrats were sometimes difficult to control. He gave vent to expletives in Italian, critical of their style. Damien appeared to lose his footing and fell, his left hand on the floor. A thrust upwards brought his sword under Charles's guard, the point at his throat. Charles leapt back, but before Damien could get to his feet Signor Mancini knocked up his weapon.

'Dishonourable play!' he shouted passionately. 'A stroke dessous! It is not en-regale!'

Damien leaned on his flexible rapier and looked down his nose at the enraged instructor. 'And why not, may I ask?'

'I follow the rules of the masters, and teach the ancient laws of fencing. You will abide by what I say.'

Maria knew Damien had intended to wound Charles and felt as if she was being torn asunder. She would be devastated if either man were seriously hurt; Damien with his domination or Charles with his love and tenderness. Who did she support? It was a question she prayed she would never have to answer.

Arabella was on the edge of her seat with excitement, her cheeks pink without the aid of rouge. 'Well done! I proclaim you my chivalrous knights and will give my scarf to the winner as a token.'

They both faced her and bowed, and then Charles turned to Damien and said, 'Let's get on with it. I can't think why you sent me a challenge, Strafford, but I'm happy to trounce you.'

They fell on guard again, fighting even more fiercely. Sweat was running from beneath the masks and dark patches spread up from their armpits and across their backs, soaking through the quilting. Charles used a sweeping parry that left him open to Damien's quick riposte, the blade slipping under his guard. The rapiers locked together and they were close as lovers, then gave a heave and broke away, the swords ringing as they met again.

Now they were losing their tempers and Signor Mancini looked worried. 'Gentlemen, please to desist.'

They ignored him. Damien was in pursuit of Charles, forcing him to defend himself and Charles did so fiercely, aware that this was no longer a game. Arabella was on her feet, white-knuckled fingers gripped around the handle of her parasol. 'My God! Damien intends to harm him!'

Maria clutched Jane's arm. 'Why doesn't the master stop them?'

He tried, leaping between them and attempting to block their strokes. Damien lunged at Charles, backed him against the wall, their sword hilts tangled and his opponent's went flying off across the studio. Charles was at his mercy and Damien directed the blade at his heart, leaning forward slightly, the point already cutting into the jacket.

'I could end your life in a trice,' he muttered grimly, eyes blazing. 'This should teach you to leave my possessions alone. Lady Maria is not easy meat for a cur like you!'

'Please, gentlemen, I beg of you! Whatever quarrel lies between you do not bring my school into disrepute,' Signor Mancini pleaded, his sword hitting Damien's and forcing him to drop it. 'Come now, be friends and we will have a glass of wine, eh?'

Charles and Damien did not move, their gaze locked. Then Arabella sauntered across to them, sensual and lovely, using her assets to stop the quarrel. 'You were magnificent! I declare I'm all of a quiver! Isn't there a less dangerous way in which you can work off that marvellous virility?' She slipped a hand into the arm of each and drew them towards Maria and Jane, adding, 'The girls were thrilled by it, too. Weren't you, my dears?'

Both men had removed their masks and Damien stood there stiffly, saying, 'This is not a social occasion, Arabella. I had a bone to pick with Lord Bradley and think I have now made the position clear.'

She knows! Maria thought. He told her to bring us here so that I might watch Charles being humiliated, though it has not quite worked out that way. She knows and will do anything he commands. I can't trust her!

Charles inclined his head towards Damien and smiled faintly at Maria. There was promise in that smile and her heart fluttered, but she was afraid for him. Her guardian was utterly ruthless.

'I'll take the matter no further if you promise that you won't approach her again.' Damien was speaking like a high court judge.

'Sir, I can't do that. I never break my oath and don't want to risk doing so.' Charles bowed again, signalled to Bates who had been waiting, his master's clothing over one arm, and made his way into the changing room.

'You may leave now. I will bring Maria back to Armitage House,' Damien informed Arabella in a tone that brooked no argument.

'But her chaperone?' Arabella glanced at Sarah, who was all agog, her large breasts rising and falling with excitement. Even the feathers in her hat were bobbing.

'Maria will be with me, her guardian, and there is no need of her chaperone.' He spoke with such authority that no one argued, though Maria wanted to. She disliked the way in which he organised her life, giving her no say in the matter, but at the same time a part of her enjoyed it. It relieved her of responsibility. Someone else was in charge, a strong man taking control and making her his willing slave.

'Very well, sir.' Arabella signalled to Sarah and Jane. 'I will see you later, Maria.'

'Will Jane be gone by then?' Maria rushed over and they embraced, clinging tightly as if they were never to see one another again.

'I have arranged for her to go back to her parents at three o'clock, so advise that you say goodbye now.'

'I'll write,' Maria promised. 'Don't fret. All will be well, dearest friend.' But she spoke with more certainty than she felt, watching them leave and then rounding on Damien. 'Why have you done this? I want to be with Jane.'

'And Bradley? Do you prefer his company to mine?' He spoke so softly that had she not known him better she might have fancied he was being pleasant.

'I can't say. We've spent little time together,' she lied.

'Really?' he said dubiously and, catching her under the chin, lifted her face to his. She could feel herself drowning in the blackness of his pupils. 'I hope you are speaking the truth, Maria.'

He released her abruptly as Charles left the changing room with Bates. He was attired in his outdoor clothing. He paused to exchange a few words with Signor Mancini, ignoring both Maria and Damien. Then he left and she had the awful feeling she might never see him again.

'Come with me,' Damien ordered, and addressed the fencing master. 'The young lady is my ward. She will be with me at all times. I don't wish to be disturbed,' and he gave him a look that spoke volumes. They understood each other well. Damien was an influential person who it would be unwise to offend.

He walked Maria towards a door. It was opened from inside by his valet. 'Leave us, Johnson. Wait by the carriage,' Damien said crisply.

The room was small, and furnished with a mirror, a washbasin, soap and towels, coat-hooks and a couch. Damien stripped rapidly. Naked, he seemed even more powerful. His body was muscular and tanned, with wide shoulders that tapered to a V at his narrow waist. His hips were slim, his buttocks tight and his thighs and legs could have graced a Grecian statue of a god. His chest was covered with a dark pelt that faded to a line crossing his navel and spreading out to join his pubic hair. There was pride in his stance and he was excited, too, his penis rising; a long, thick, sturdy weapon he delighted in displaying to Maria.

'Take up the sponge and wash me,' he commanded, standing spread-legged in front of her.

She wanted to avert her eyes but the sight of him was too compelling. She could not help comparing him to Charles, and both were prime examples. The cock was fascinating yet repulsive, so far removed from Jane's delicate mons and damp crack. Had Maria still been a virgin it might have proved too much for her, but she was experienced now - not fully, but enough to make her realise the pleasure this engorged object could bring her.

She rose and, going to the washbasin, tipped some warm water from the jug and soaped the sponge, then took up a towel and returned to where he stood. He was caressing his cock, making it larger and redder, more aggressive looking. She ran the sponge over his body, washing away the sweat, then went lower to his genitals. She cleansed his balls and inner thighs and he watched her, reacting to her touch, his nipples crimping within their circles of hair, his cock stretching and hardening even more.

Maria paused, rinsing the sponge and then soaking it in clean water. 'No, I like it slippery with soap,' he barked, and she followed his instructions.

The front of her dress was damp now and he pushed his penis in and out of her hands. Recognising his need she went to work on him, making him her slave, unable to control his frantic desire. His head was back, his throat stretched, his breath ragged.

'Ah, yes,' he hissed, and bucked towards her. She sensed he was coming by the way his body jerked and the force of energy sweeping through him.

He shot into the sponge and over her hands and she wiped him clean again. There was nothing left for her to say - not at that moment.

He withdrew and she sat on the couch as he dressed, his movements deft and precise, stepping into his linen shorts, then the hose and tight breeches, the shirt and waistcoat, the jacket with its trim waist and the high stock and frothing, lace-trimmed cravat. He smoothed a hand over his fashionably tousled hair, then picked up his feather-edge chapeau-bras and looked down at her.

'Time to go, my dear.'

'Where?' She was more than just apprehensive. When Damien was being reasonable he was usually at his most destructive.

'To my house. You see, I'm not satisfied and need to examine you intimately. Don't worry. You will be chaperoned. I have engaged the services of Agatha Bailey.'

'Jane's duenna? But why?'

'She is a very thorough woman, and will enjoy working for me.'

'Does this mean I shall be forced to dismiss Mrs Jenkins?' The idea of the stiff and starchy Agatha appalled her, though no doubt her absence would be better for Jane who had complained about her sternness and also said that the maids were in fear of her and her cane.

'Certainly not. Bailey will be in my employ, following my instructions. I

74

gather she has a bent for discipline. Jenkins will still perform her usual duties.' So saying, he escorted her out of the studio and through the front door to where his coach awaited.

Maria travelled alone with Damien. She was very aware of him lounging on the upholstered seat next to her, tapping his cane lightly against his lips and staring from the window as they left the centre of London and took the road to Hampstead. His body swayed towards her as they jolted over the ruts and he neither spoke nor touched her. This in itself was unnerving.

The idea of being incarcerated in Strafford Hall with him, even for a short duration, was anathema to her. She knotted her hands together in her lap as she brooded on his motives, tormented by guilt. If he decided to subject her to examination, then her secret would be out and all would know she had lost her virginity. The coach reached a hill and started to descend, careering wildly and coming to a jarring halt at the bottom when its wheels encountered a pothole. Maria yelped as she was flung from her seat, but Damien caught her and hauled her back.

The vehicle continued its bumpy journey, but Damien did not release her. With his free hand he pushed back her skirt, baring her legs and downy crack, his insistent fingers opening her thighs so he might gaze at her secrets. She made a feeble attempt to stop those predatory fingers, but the pleasure they evoked was too great to resist. Terrified lest he enter further and discover that there was no membrane to prevent penetration, she tried to push him away and close her knees.

He smiled grimly. 'Unwilling to have me explore you? Have you something to hide, Maria? Are you, perchance, bereft of the keeper of your treasure?'

She shook her head, trying to avoid his lips that were now moving seductively around the rim of her ear, tongue-tip darting inside, causing havoc with her resistance. He found her pleasure nodule and stroked it, keeping it wet and slippery from the dew seeping from her vagina. His touch was feather-light and she shivered, parting her legs for him, forgetful of anything except the pleasure he was bestowing on her.

No longer gentle he thrust a finger within her, then two, stretching her delicate interior. 'Ah, no hymen. You have been a wicked wanton, Maria, and I'm not pleased,' he muttered, his voice hardening as he poked in further, making her wince and try to draw back. He would not permit this, holding her tightly and filling her with his merciless fingers.

'Sir, please... have mercy,' she begged, while he continued to arouse her clitoris at the same time as plundering her love-channel, making her experience pain laced with pleasure.

Abandoning herself to him, forgetful of everything, even Charles, fired by their earlier encounter and needing his large phallus to fill her, she wound her arms round his neck, drawing him closer. He withdrew abruptly.

'You have disappointed me, Maria. I wanted to be the one to deflower you, not some strutting braggart like Bradley. If you find yourself with child by him

I shall have you sent to a convent and order the babe to be smothered at birth.'

'You no longer intend to marry me?' Maria asked, bewildered by his actions and willing to agree to anything if he would only satisfy the craving he had aroused.

He smile mockingly, sitting back and wiping his fingers fastidiously on a lawn handkerchief, then raising it to his nostrils as if a trace of her sexual fragrance lingered there. 'I am master,' he said. 'Of course I shall marry you. Your fortune will be mine, as will your person. I fully intend to enjoy both.'

'Very well, sir. I agree to anything as long as you don't leave me on the edge like this.' Maria could not believe she was saying such a degrading thing.

He laughed again, a chilling sound. 'Whatever I command you will do. Is this understood? As for bringing you off? I may, or then again I may not. The decision is mine. I could take you over and over and never give you relief. I could tie your hands in such a manner that you would be unable to masturbate. Think how that would feel? I don't give a damn how much you hate me, and it would be wise to fear me, too. Is this understood?'

'Yes,' she cried, able to deny him nothing in that fraught moment of desperate desire, losing sight of any principles she might have had.

His stare held a wealth of knowledge and depravity. He had seen and taken part in actions that she could not begin to comprehend. 'Say it again. Call me master.'

'Yes, master,' she repeated, welcoming his touch as he pushed aside her bodice and lowered his mouth to her nipples. At the same time he pressed down on her mound, his fingers parting the swollen lips and finding the hard nub between.

She sprawled on the seat for him, the carriage shaking as it bowled along, and Damien's fingers rubbed and stroked, his thumb entering her vagina, while he kept up that divine frottage on her clitoris. She could feel her orgasm rising as she strained towards the peak. Nothing mattered but this bliss. Nothing existed but Damien as he slowly, inexorably brought her to the brink. He kept her there for an instant and then toppled her over into a climax so intense that she lost consciousness for a second.

She came to herself to find that she was lying against Damien, trembling from head to foot. Now remorse took the place of desire and she hated her actions. What manner of woman was she that her lust took over, making her forget every other consideration? He sat up, freeing himself from her and straightening his cravat. The coach had stopped. Maria hurriedly rearranged her bodice and shrouded herself in her cloak, but was sure that everyone who saw her would know what she had been doing. They would be sniggering, gossiping, giving her side-long glances.

Nothing happened, however, and she was greeted at the top of the steps by the housekeeper and butler and ushered inside. Lordly and commanding, Damien ordered that refreshments were to be served in his private apartment and took Maria there without preamble.

Chapter 9

Maria was alone with Damien in his stronghold. She feared yet desired him, wished that Sarah or Jane were with her, would even have welcomed her aunt. Yet that reckless self that lay hidden in her psyche rejoiced that there was no one to come between them.

He took her upstairs to his private apartment. It was gloomy, though richly decorated and magnificent, the air heavy with the smell of the incense smouldering in elaborate wrought-iron burners. He had gathered treasures from every quarter of the globe to embellish his lair, a connoisseur of art and all things exotic and beautiful. He was proud of his skill, pointing out several objects as he poured himself a snifter of brandy from a cut-glass decanter.

He nodded towards a statue on a plinth. 'This is the goddess Kali from the Hindu pantheon. Isn't she amazing?'

Maria thought her hideous, with her many arms and fierce expression. 'I don't like her. She's frightening.'

'Ah, this is but one manifestation of her. She is the mother who defends her children, the vengeful woman who it is not wise to offend. One day you may come to understand her.'

She followed him as he toured the room, pausing before a life-sized painting of lovers in the throes of sexual abandon. 'How could models pose like that?' she exclaimed.

He chuckled, deep in his throat. 'People will do anything for money.'

'I wouldn't!' she averred stoutly.

'You're a pampered child. You know nothing of hardship, hunger and poverty.'

'Do you, my lord?' she shot back.

'Touché!' His smile deepened. 'You're a fiery little filly, aren't you? I like that.' He did not move from the painting, studying it closely. 'See how cleverly the artist has captured the woman's moment of bliss. The eyes half-closed, the mouth open languorously. Just as you looked when I brought you off, Maria. Were you equally carried away when Bradley penetrated your virgin hole?'

There was no longer any pleasantness in his voice. His eyes were cold, his face set in severe lines and his grip on her upper arm painful.

'How do you know it was him?'

'I have my informants. There is little that you do or say that doesn't come back to me. Half your worth has gone now you've been fucked. My fingers met no obstruction, and soon I shall use my cock to prove your wantonness. But first, come over here. I have something else to show you.'

He marched her across the floor to what looked like a curtained alcove. Holding back the drapes, he revealed a window giving access into the next room.

'It's Jane's chaperone,' Maria whispered, astonished by the sight of Agatha, wearing nothing but corsets and stockings, beating a cringing servant girl whose raised skirts revealed a plump posterior striped with scarlet weals.

'No longer a duenna. I told you, she now works for me, and revels in it,' he commented, one hand caressing Maria's buttocks, scrunching up her flimsy dress until he encountered bare flesh.

'How is it that we can see them and they are unaware of us?' Maria attempted to pull away, but he would have none of this, his grip tightening painfully.

'Ah, that is one of my little secrets. All they see is a mirror,' he murmured, inserting a finger into the crack between her bottom cheeks. 'It was through just such a one that I saw you with Bradley. Be careful in future, for you will never know if or when I am observing you.'

'You're a devil!' she hissed, gasping as the finger rimmed her anus.

'And you love it.'

'I don't. I hate you,' she flung back, but his touch was so knowledgeable and insidious, almost impossible to resist, and the sight of Agatha maltreating the girl reminiscent of scenes she had witnessed at school. Even in those days she had found it arousing and now, with the addition of Damien's skilful fondling, she was burning with desire.

'Watch the inestimable Agatha,' he answered, ignoring her protests as his middle digit entered her anal opening.

Fascinated, yet aware of the discomfort of his probing, she stared through the trick glass. The girl was strapped to a bench, facedown, and now Agatha stood in front of her, opened her legs wide and started to frig her prominent clitoris. The prone servant had no option but to watch her at close-quarters.

Sickened yet aching for orgasm, Maria could not avert her eyes. Agatha was skinny, her pubis covered with a black thatch, her cleft protruding between, the lips dark red and wet. Her fingers flew over her engorged nubbin and she moaned in a frenzy of lust, moving closer and closer to her victim. She pushed her slit against the girl's face, continuing to finger-fuck herself, but augmenting this with her victim's nose, mouth, cheeks and chin.

Damien bared his cock, thrusting it into Maria's hand. She toyed with it, hardly knowing what she was doing as she saw Agatha reaching a convulsive orgasm, then throwing herself across the helpless servant, delving into her intimate places, making her moan and shudder.

He let the curtain drop, hiding the scene, and then forced Maria down on the purple-draped bed. He rolled her on to her face, bared her behind and slapped her again and again. His palm was hard through sword-play and horse training and meted out severe punishment. She struggled, but he knelt above her, trapping her legs with his knees. She could hear his harsh breathing and the sharp impact of that hand on her skin. She started to cry, the tears wrenched from her in spite of her pride. She could hardly believe it when he suddenly ceased hitting her. There was a moment's respite and then she felt something else. He was pushing pillows beneath her to raise her hips, then stretching her legs wide and fastening cords to her ankles.

'Oh stop, please!' she pleaded. 'Haven't you punished me enough?'

'Bradley may have cheated me of your love-channel, but I imagine that your arsehole is still virgin, is it not?' His voice was crisp, but with underlying menace.

'I don't understand what you mean...'

'No? I promised you lessons in fucking, didn't I? You are about to learn an important one.'

She shivered with fear and anticipation, never sure what he intended to do next. He was an enigma, both in his lifestyle and lovemaking. She realised it was only experienced women, like Arabella, who could begin to understand him.

He was moving behind her, taking off his clothes. She heard him reach for something on the bedside table. 'What are you doing?' she quavered.

'I'm making the way easier for myself.'

She started as cold lotion was spread around her anus, a slippery sensation in a place that had never before experienced such a thing. Then she was aware of him between her legs, and felt the hugeness of his penis pressing against her most intimate area.

'Stop it!' she shouted, but Damien was not to be deterred. He continued to grind into her until the rim of his glans had penetrated, stretching her sphincter agonisingly.

He groaned, the effort costing him dear, and she rejoiced in his discomfort, wishing she could squeeze his cock with her inner muscles, mangle and damage it, so he would never again be able to enjoy sex. But she was helpless to do anything as he inexorably pushed in further and further, entering the dark recess Nature had not designed to receive the male appendage. Maria was convinced she would be ruined for life, stretched, split and wounded by that monstrous thing violating her rectum. It was not welcome there, as Charles's cock had been in her vagina, yet she could not dislodge it, though her muscles were striving to do so.

Damien was intent on his purpose, ignoring her pleas, determined to lodge himself fully inside her. She stopped moving, for this hurt even more, and lay there accepting the agony as, with a final effort, he distended her and the whole length and girth of him shot into her. She screamed as she was plumbed to her depths. He stilled then, obviously finding the opening restrictive and narrow and she was glad, hoping he was suffering too.

'Damn you!' she cried and, to cause him more pain, clenched around his tool. She shunted back and forth, her anus like a ring sliding up and down his shaft. The pain was diabolical, and yet that feeling of being stuffed to the very limits held an odd kind of pleasure.

Damien could not contain his groans of pain and delight, urging his cock in and out of that tight, restricting hole. And she yearned for revenge, longing to suck him into her bowels and absorb his prick, making it a part of herself and never letting him go, her prisoner forever. He came, and she felt the hot bursts of spunk exploding deep inside her and then he rolled away, swearing and clutching himself. She lay there experiencing a form of triumph, though her arse ached and she felt she would never recover from his assault.

He sat up, turning to look down on her. Then he freed her ankles and she raised herself, avoiding his eyes. His emission dribbled from her anus and she grabbed up a handful of sheet to staunch it. He pulled on his shirt, saying, 'You are too tight. I shall order Agatha to use butt-plugs on you.'

'And what, pray, are they?' She wanted to cry, to beg for a modicum of tenderness, but refused to grant herself that indulgence. If he could be icy, then so could she.

'Devices for stretching the rectum. She will start with small ones and gradually enlarge them until you can take me with ease.'

'You intend to repeat this atrocity?' Maria found her clothing and covered her bruised body.

'In time you will beg me to perform it.'

'I don't think so, sir.'

'Ask your aunt. Sodomy is one of her favourite forms of entertainment. We shall have plenty of opportunity for practice in the country.' Fully dressed, it was hard to credit that a short while ago he had been behaving like a rutting animal.

'May I return to Armitage House now?' She flung her wrap around her like a royal robe, head held high.

'You may, but make no attempt to contact Bradley if you wish him to live. My men are watching him, and you.'

'Oh, Robin, what are we going to do?' Jane tried to appear calm for they had arranged to meet in a coffeehouse, notes passed between them through her maid, Abigail. She was nothing like as reliable as Maria's servant, Emily. A stout, idle girl who, released from Agatha Bailey's domination, demanded money and privileges for her loyalty.

They were seated in the shadows, with Abigail at a table close by. A new chaperone had not yet been engaged and this afforded Jane a little more freedom, though such an arrangement could not continue for much longer. Robin touched the hand she had clenched in her lap.

'I will visit you in Bath,' he declared. 'There to see your father and ask him for permission to woo you.'

She shook her head sadly. 'He won't give it, determined that I shall wed Percy Tate. I am the last daughter, you see. My sisters have all been married in turn, I am the youngest and therefore the last.'

'If he turns me away we will run off to Gretna Green. Once the knot is tied he will be unable to part us. I shall take up my post in Burdock Village and we can reside with the vicar until a house is found for us.'

'I'm afraid,' she whispered, her fingers held in his as he worked them over her thigh and down between her legs.

'Don't be,' he insisted. 'Love will conquer all.'

They left the coffee-house and she sent Abigail on an errand and lingered in the shadowy stable with Robin, the coachman and grooms being in the tavern next-door. He pressed her against the white-washed wall, the air redolent with the sweet smell of hay, and she wished she could die and remain in that moment forever.

His arms tightened around her, and her breasts were pressed to his chest, their clothing chaffing her sensitive nipples. She rubbed her body against him, her lips opening under his as he kissed her, their tongues meeting. Now she recognised the hard object distorting his breeches, and pressed her pubis to it.

He groaned. 'Oh, God! I want you so much.' As he spoke he started to caress her breasts and her nipples peaked at his touch, pleasure darting down to set her clitoris on fire.

'And I want you,' she whispered. 'This can't be wrong, can it? We love one another, don't we?'

'Yes, yes, of course we do.' He was breathing quickly and there was increased force in the way he was caressing her. He thrust with his hips in a rhythmical movement and she responded, recognising his need.

The stable was fitted with stalls where lovers could hide away from prying eyes, and Robin took her to one of them, laying her down on a bed of straw. Time was of the essence. They had no idea when the grooms and Abigail would be returning. Robin lifted her skirt, opened her legs and sank down between them, his cock already exposed. He plunged into her without any foreplay and, although she was moist, she realised she could not climax that way. Robin seemed only aware of his own driving urge, bucking and plunging until reaching his peak, his tribute shooting into her. There was no way he could prevent it and she was fearful. Supposing he impregnated her?

He pulled out when it was over and sat there, looking shamefaced. 'I'm sorry, dearest. I couldn't wait,' he said

Her instinct was to comfort him, although she was disappointed at having failed to reach a conclusion and hoping against all hope that his flood of semen did not find its goal within her womb. She wanted children with him, but not yet. The obstacles were too great.

Rather crestfallen, they tidied themselves and prepared for the arrival of Abigail and the coachman. 'Best if you leave before they come,' she murmured, tears welling in her eyes.

'I will contact you in Bath,' he promised.

'Mama and I will be taking the waters at the Pump Room daily. Perhaps you could be there. She liked you when she met you at the school and I may be able to persuade her to speak with Papa.'

'I shall be staying at The Black Swan tavern in Southgate Street. Contact me there. This isn't the end, Jane, merely the beginning,' he promised, kissing her so tenderly that it nearly broke her heart.

Then he left and, within a few moments, Abigail and the others arrived.

'We're nearly there,' Arabella asserted. 'Thank God for that! I can't abide travelling. Dreary, boring, forced to stay in hostelries where the beds are lumpy and the privies stink.'

She was wearing a new carriage costume. The long coat was of military cut in tobacco-brown velvet, lined with white satin and trimmed with gold fogging. Beige kid half-boots encased her feet and her hat was like a soldier's kalpak, set at a jaunty angle and sporting a yellow plume. This was the latest vogue and Maria was similarly dressed, Madame Descartes doing very well out of these wealthy clients.

'Why did you consent to come?' Maria was tired of her aunt's constant complaints. For her own part, every mile that separated her from Charles was a torture.

'Damien ordered it.' Arabella was definitely tetchy.

'And you do everything he says?'

'Don't be pert!' She gave Maria a sharp glance and then continued to gaze out at the passing landscape. 'It should be fun. The hunting season is not yet over and he knows a number of jolly people. He's Master of the Hunt, you see.'

Of course, he would be, Maria thought glumly. Always the leader, ahead of everyone else. Did these rural friends indulge in the kind of perversions he enjoyed? Probably. And would she be forced to take part in them? Without any doubt. Agatha had not yet approached her with the butt-plugs and Damien had made no attempt to contact her. She had not seen him since the visit to Strafford Hall.

This was even more unnerving.

Arabella had kept her busy organising her apparel for the visit, but he could have appeared at any time. There had been no sign of him when they set out. They were travelling without him, using the earl's finest carriage and a train of more modest ones for the servants and luggage. James had been left in London in the care of his nurse and half a dozen nursery maids, with his father taking time out to play with him occasionally. Ali had also been left hind with Poppy. Both were fashion accessories, and there was no call to show off one's coloured page or lapdog in the country.

Now they were nearly at their destination, and Maria's curiosity got the better of her. She leaned forward and joined Arabella in staring out at the view. The scenery was rugged, the Dorset coast in all its glory. They were travelling along a road that edged a cliff, and the sea sparkled below them, grey-blue, topped with white horses. Seagulls wheeled and screamed overhead, and the bushes leaned away from the constant wind blowing from the open water. Maria was not accustomed to such an expanse of sea and sky, and longed to walk along the path, breathe in the salty tang and climb down the rocks to where golden sand spread out in secluded bays.

'Can we go there?' she asked Arabella.

'You're as excited as a child,' her aunt responded indulgently. 'Of course we shall visit the beach, with footmen carrying picnic baskets and our maids bearing rugs and towels. The sea is most refreshing and I shall take a dip, though I don't want to get burnt by the sun. You'll enjoy it here, and it will be most informative. Ah, can you hear the horns? What a thrilling sound. Damien must be leading the pack. Do you hunt?'

'I haven't done so since father died.' Maria's ears pricked at the distant clarion call, old memories and sensations rushing back.

'One never forgets. I'm looking forward to it. And there will be balls and parties and all sorts of entertainment.'

'Similar to those at Strafford Hall?' Maria gave her a straight stare.

Arabella flushed as she replied, 'Very possibly. It depends what your guardian has in mind.'

'And we all know what that is likely to be,' Maria returned boldly, no longer caring if she was angry with her. Matters had proceeded too far.

Arabella took no notice, leaning forward as the coach swung down a lane and then came out in a tree-shaded avenue. There, ahead of them stood an ancient mansion of great size. 'Raven Towers,' she said.

'It's like a castle!' Maria exclaimed.

Arabella nodded, saying with as much pride as if it belonged to her, 'Parts of it date from the Norman Conquest. Of course, there have been more recent additions, but much of it remains untouched. The turrets for example, from which it takes its name, the raven being on the family crest of its owners. Quaint, isn't it? Rather like something out of a fairy-tale.'

It lay amidst parklands, its long stone facade with regularly space diamond-paned windows surmounted by a red tiled roof, mellow with age. A series of fantastically ornamented chimney-pots reached towards the sky, and some of the walls were enveloped in masses of ivy, giving the impression that the house had evolved from the soil like some natural growing thing.

The coach rattled over the gravel at a spanking pace and soon the house loomed over it, dwarfing everything. Grooms and servants appeared and the passengers alighted, their baggage being off-loaded. There was no sign of Damien.

'His lordship is leading the hunt,' explained the dignified head butler, wearing a curling powdered wig. He was formally attired in a blue coat with gold epaulettes, white satin breeches, a lace cravat, pink stockings and black buckled shoes. 'He has instructed me to show you to your rooms so that you may refresh yourselves after the journey. He will be back shortly and a repast is being prepared on the terrace.'

The guestroom to which Maria was shown was spacious and finely furnished, with damask curtains at the windows and draping the four-poster bed. Sarah would be situated close at hand, and so would Emily, and they set to work helping her to wash and change, then busied themselves unpacking the valises and depositing her clothing in the armoire and tallboy. But, in spite of the apparently luxurious and comfortable surroundings, Maria could not still the quake of uneasiness that stirred in her gut. This increased as she finally joined her aunt at the top of the main staircase and they made their way down, guided towards the terrace by a liveried footman.

The hunt had returned in full force. She was aware of their loud, triumphant voices even before she passed through the open cedar-wood doors and stepped into the sunshine. She saw Damien at once. He was leaning against the marble balustrade, wearing a red coat and white breeches. His boots were muddy, his buckskins soiled and his lips curled in a smile, his eyes those of a hunter who has caught his prey and enjoyed the kill.

Arabella went straight to him, gazing up admiringly, a hand on his arm. The crowd of men, all in hunting pink, local squires, magistrates and landowners, were stamping about, leaving muddy footprints on the paving stones, talking, drinking champagne and indulging in the cold collation arranged on trestle tables spread with fine linen. There were ladies, too, hot from the chase, middle-aged and younger, excited by the bloodshed and the company of those virile males. A close-knit set, Maria guessed, recalling similar meets at Burrington Manor. They owned the villages around, and were still treated like feudal lords by the inhabitants. And none was more lordly than Damien.

He looked across and saw her, left Arabella and came straight for her. In a trice he had caught her by the arm and propelled her towards his friends. 'This is my ward, Lady Maria Granger.'

She was surrounded by gentlemen hunters, some tall, thin and aristocratic-looking, others sweaty and red-faced, bluff and stocky. They had one thing in common; a lecherous gleam in their eyes. The ladies looked her over, pretending to be welcoming but she guessed that beneath the show they were viewing her with suspicion. A new female in their midst was a threat, maybe intent on luring away their husbands or lovers. Running a critical eye over the men present, Maria could not imagine even bothering to try. Damien was the only one there who attracted her, and that was with very mixed feelings. Arabella was already known to them and they had her measure, it was the newcomer who posed a problem.

The terrace was a sun-trap and Arabella held her parasol aloft. The talk became louder, more boastful and bawdy as the wine flowed, and presently Damien said, 'Are you ready, friends? Shall we proceed to the training ring?'

What now? Maria wondered. Her head was swimming from too much champagne. Damien had kept her glass topped up. She had no idea what to expect, but his guests seemed to be enthusiastic and she had to go along with him, for he refused to release her arm.

They left the terrace, and walked towards one of the towers. It was surmounted by battlements where once bowmen had fired down on enemies. Inside it was large, with a lobby that led into an oval arena. The ceiling was high, the windows mere arrow-slits, but the sparse daylight was augmented by flares. It appeared to be used for putting horses through their paces. The floor was strewn with straw, and there were grooms in attendance, and a space at the far end that resembled stables wherein steeds could be housed. There were benches for spectators and Maria was guided to the opposite end to the stables, accompanied by Arabella. The hunters occupied some of the other seats, attended by footmen bearing trays of bottles and glasses, pies, canapes and beef in bread rolls. The party seemed set to continue.

Damien strode into the centre, acting like a Master of Ceremonies, holding up his hand for silence. 'And now, ladies and gentlemen, I have pleasure in presenting my pony girls!'

A door was opened at the stable end and, with a rumble of wheels and rattle of chains, four chariots appeared. The audience gasped simultaneously and Maria could not believe the evidence of her own eyes. Each was occupied by a groom, naked apart from straps that cradled his genitals and raised them, cock erect and balls bunched beneath. They were well-built, handsome young men and the ladies drooled as they rode the chariots into the middle of the ring. But the greatest surprise of all was the sight of women drawing the vehicles instead of horses.

They, too, were unclad, their faultless bodies displayed in nothing but a few strategically placed strips of black leather. These did nothing but emphasise their luscious breasts and shaven clefts, tight buttocks and long thighs. They were totally under the control of bridle and whip, the bit between their teeth. Adopting the attitude of the animals they represented, they tossed their long manes, stamped their feet in thick-soled boots and snapped their teeth at any who approached them. Croppers passed between their thighs, pressing into their cracks, and tails were rooted in their fundaments. The grooms flicked them with the tips of their bullwhips and the audience roared in approval.

Maria tried to catch the eye of one of the pony girls, but met nothing but a blank stare. However long they had been employed like this, it seemed to have killed their spirit. 'Where did they come from?' she asked Arabella, who simply shrugged.

'Who knows, my dear? And what does it matter? I imagine it is preferable to walking the streets. Damien has a vivid imagination, or else he has seen something similar during his travels. I, myself, have taken part and, believe me, becoming a mare can be quite fun.'

'You?' Maria was dumbfounded. Her elegant aunt transformed into a beast of burden, confined between the shafts while someone else controlled her by the pull on her mouth on that iron bit. It was unthinkable!

'Silly child!' Arabella cooed. 'There are more ways than one of skinning a cat! You have yet to learn the deep satisfaction of obeying your master to the letter. If Damien wants me to pull his chariot then I'll obey and so, my dear, will you.'

'Never!' Maria clenched her fists. 'I'd rather die!'

'La! How dramatic!'

There were no lack of takers, the hunters, men and women, forming a queue, awaiting their turn to take the reins. Damien was the first, leaping into the leading chariot, seizing the reins and flicking the whip. The ample-hipped brunette between the shafts broke into a trot, breasts bouncing.

He completed the course, then drew up and said, 'A race! Are you prepared to lay wagers on your steeds?'

The bidding was brisk, organised by his man, Johnson.

Four contenders lined up. Four ponies flirted their tails and fidgeted. The flag was dropped and they were off. Maria remembered the phaeton race vividly, but there was little resemblance. She found it utterly degrading to witness the girls straining between the shafts and to see scarlet marks appearing on their shoulders and upper arms as their drivers used the whip mercilessly. She rose from her seat and it was as much as she could do to stand there and watch this senseless spectacle, wanting to run out in the path of the racers and put a stop to it. Damien, the instigator of this barbaric performance, was in the lead, whipping his steed repeatedly until blood started to flow down her back. He reached the finishing post first and, leaping from the chariot, inserted himself between the front of it and the girl. Then he pulled the tail from her rectum, disposed of the crupper and mounted her from behind, while his fellow contestants cheered and hallooed.

Careless of being trampled, mobbed or reviled, Maria walked straight over to where he stood, pumping in and out of the exhausted woman, raised her arm and slapped him across the face. 'Monster!' she shouted while the arena grew quiet.

Damien withdrew, fastened his breeches and ducked under the shafts. A groom led his equipage away. He towered over Maria while the world seemed to hold its breath. 'Would you like to take her place?' he asked, loudly and clearly. 'This can be arranged.'

'You should be ashamed of yourself!' she stormed, losing all fear in her raging indignation. 'How dare you treat a woman like that?'

'They like it,' shouted several of his cronies. 'Makes 'em come off, don't-cher-know? Nothing a wench likes more than a good beating, followed by a good fucking.'

'They're right,' chorused the ladies. 'Keep out of it, and stop being such a spoil-sport.'

'You won that round. Let's have another,' urged his enthusiastic friends. 'Put her between the shafts. Give her a taste of your whip!'

'Not this time,' Damien said, and his eyes were steely as they gazed into hers. 'I have something better planned. Go to your room, Maria. Agatha will attend you.' He swung round, shouting, 'Another bout! Certainly, gentlemen, and raise your stakes this time.'

Chapter 10

Charles ducked his head under the lintel of the most disreputable tavern in Whitefriars. It was an area of winding alleys and tumbledown houses that made up the notorious 'Rookery', a thieves' hideout so notorious that even the Watch refused to go there, unless accompanied by the militia.

He had never quite become accustomed to seedy places such as this, but it was part and parcel of his job. Even though Maria seemed lost to him, there remained his duty to his country. It was to this end that he sought out an unshaven ruffian who wore tattered clothing, a battered three-cornered hat, a rat-tailed moustache and an eye-patch.

Charles bought two pints of ale, sat down and rested his elbows on a dirt-encrusted table, staring at his companion. The inn was noisy, for evening had brought out not only those who wanted to drink and gamble, but the hawkers as well, intent on making sales. These ranged from match-sellers to pimps, fortune-tellers, quack doctors and touts of every description. Charles had disguised himself well, as scruffy as the rest. No one would have guessed that he was a gentleman. He had learned his trade in the army and then on special consignments, apprehending those who sold information to the enemies of England.

'Viscount Strafford left three days ago,' said his confederate.

'I know that, Quint. What about Lady Maria?' Charles could hardly restrain his impatience for news of her.

'She went yesterday.' Quint drew a screw of paper from a broken-down pocket and stuffed some tobacco into the bowl of a clay pipe, then took a spill to the candle. Blue smoke arose to join the rest that polluted the atmosphere.

'Strafford's destination is as we thought?'

'It is, sir. Raven Towers in Dorset.'

'His country seat?'

'Aye. Within easy reach of the coast. A convenient spot for folk sneaking in and out, avoiding the customs officers.'

'Working for France.' Charles's eyes were keen beneath the battered brim of his felt hat.

'Exactly.'

'As we've suspected for some time.' It was satisfying to know they had been correct in their assumption that Damien was using his stately home for nefarious activities. 'But why did he want Lady Maria and Lady Arabella along?'

'As a diversion to conceal his real motive for being there. We're dealing with a wily character here.' Quint was an old hand at the game, and had been Charles's associate for months. Far from a vagabond, he was a respected member of the Government's band of undercover agents.

A woman in a tawdry, low-cut scarlet dress came across to wind her arms around Charles's neck. Her gin-tainted breath tickled his ear as she said, 'You're a fine cully, to be sure. Fancy a bit? Shall we go outside?' She hoisted her skirt high.

'Not now,' he replied, inhaling the salty smell of sexual congress wafting from between her legs. He was not the first man she had approached that night.

His body responded to her coarse invitation, although he had vowed to make his hand his mistress until he could find Maria again, eschewing whores and loose noblewomen alike. But, young and virile that he was, this was hard to do.

'Aw, come on, boy-oh,' she pleaded, painted lips pouting as she clasped his crotch. His cock began to swell in spite of his resolutions.

He pushed her hand away and thrust a coin into her grubby palm. 'I'm not in the mood. Have this. Buy yourself a tot of gin.'

'You're a real gent. I owe you one,' she said, hard exterior melting for a second before she moved on to the next prospective punter.

Unwilling to draw the slightest attention to himself he got up and nodded goodbye to Quint, then said in an undertone, 'I'll keep you informed. Be prepared to leave for Dorset.'

Though his thoughts were distracted as he walked back to his lodgings, a part of him was fully alert and he carried a cudgel under his jacket. As he paused at the front door, inserting the key in the lock, a figure darted from out of the darkness and he heard someone say, 'Charlie... no, don't turn me away!'

It was Sally, instantly recognisable by her voice and scent. 'What do you want?' He was brusque, still angry with her for betraying Maria.

'A moment of your time,' she begged, the lantern above the door shining down on her face, painting it with shadows.

'I told you that I never wanted to see you again.' He spoke more harshly than need be to protect himself. Memories of coupling with her tormented him and his cock surged in his breeches. 'Why did you tell me you had betrayed Lady Maria and myself to Viscount Strafford?'

'I don't know,' Sally sobbed. 'To be revenged, I supposed. I was jealous, and still am. Why do you prefer her to me? Anyway, you won't see her any more. She's gone away. She and her aunt have been to Madame Descartes' shop, spending a king's ransom on clothes.'

'I have nothing further to say to you.' Charles turned, but she flung herself at him, clinging fiercely.

'Don't abandon me. I love you!' she cried, the tears streaming down her cheeks.

Charles had never been able to endure seeing a women cry. 'Oh, very well. Come in, but only for a moment.'

Mrs Pritchard was going to visit her married daughter and the new baby, as she had told him when she brought in his supper. Bates had been dispatched with messages for one of Charles's colleagues, and he was anticipating an early night in view of the long ride tomorrow. The thought of glimpsing Maria again set him on fire, though he knew that discretion would be of the essence.

This was the only time he had seen Sally since she triumphantly announced telling the viscount that Maria had been to his house. This had resulted in his meeting with Damien at Signor Mancini's fencing school. It was apparent that Damien wanted to kill him and, to protect Maria from her guardian's rage, Charles had kept his distance ever since, though it cost him dear. Now the instigator of the trouble was with him, pleading for forgiveness.

He was disinclined to give this, furious with her, yet a part of him could understand her motives. He had seen enough of poverty and hopelessness during his travels to realise how an underprivileged girl such as Sally would seize any opportunity to better herself. Marriage would have been out of the question, but as his doxy she might have expected him to set her up in an apartment and give her a regular income. He had never intended to do this, using her selfishly, as he had used women before, never knowing love until he met Maria.

'I'm sorry, Charlie,' Sally said, slumping in a chair. Her nose was running and she wiped the snot on the back of her hand.

'You knew this would happen one day. We are worlds apart, but I thought I could trust you.' He stood looking down at her, then handed her a handkerchief.

The fire had been tended by Bates before he left, and coal glowed in the black iron grate behind the brass guard, giving the room a cosy intimacy. It reminded Charles of when he had introduced Maria to the mysteries of sexual congress. Not only that, he recalled many an hour spent there with the woman who was now begging him to pardon her. He was tired and downhearted and he could feel himself softening towards Sally. Life was short and he was about to risk his once again. Damien could be his Nemesis. He had seen brave men die in battle and since, fighting secretly against France. One sword thrust, one bullet and it was all over. He could feel himself on the edge. Any day it could happen to him.

Sally flung herself to her knees at his feet, clinging to the scuffed boots, her head back as she looked up at him. 'Charlie... please... I've never felt like this about a man. If this is love, then certainly I am in that state. I don't ask for much... don't expect you to take me into keeping... just want to see you sometimes.'

'You should be thinking of marrying, my girl. Find an honest tradesman to take you to wife.' Charles felt ashamed of his treatment of her and all the other women he had used for his pleasure. It was as if love had opened his eyes. 'Have you parents?'

'My father is dead and my mother is a washer-woman, with five young children to feed. I was lucky to get employment with Madame Descartes. At least I can help out at home, but I have nothing to offer as a dowry. There's the butcher who runs a shop not far from where I live. He has been giving me the eye, although he must be all of forty. A widower, so they say.'

'Then encourage him,' Charles advised, even while he responded to her hands running up and down his inner thighs, approaching ever closer to his cick. 'I'll give you a sum of money. It's the least I can do.' I must be moon-struck, he thought.

'I don't want him. I want you,' she moaned, her fingers tugging at the buttoned flap that concealed his penis.

'Do as I suggest,' he muttered. This was too much for his self-control. He could feel his balls tightening and his cock swelling, hard and hot and eager.

He grabbed her by the upper arms, jerked her to her feet and then backed her across the room until they reached the bed. There he flung her down, yanked up her skirt and inserted his erection into her warm and willing snatch. It was over in seconds, for him if not for her, and he regretted it as soon as he had discharged.

She knew this. Tears filled her eyes again and she gathered herself together, shoulders sagging. 'I guess this is goodbye, Charlie?' she whispered.

'I'm going away for a while, but will leave money with Mrs Pritchard and ask her to speak to the butcher on your behalf. Be happy, Sally.' He did not know what else to say, wanting nothing more than to see the back of her.

'Where is Mrs Jenkins?' Maria demanded when escorted back to her room by Agatha. She was furious because of the ignominious way she had been dismissed from the junketing, made to feel like a silly child in front of the huntsmen and their women.

Agatha stood with her hands folded at the waist of her plain black dress. 'The master has ordered me to attend you,' she replied in her harsh, aggressive voice.

'And Emily?' Maria had rarely been so angry, or so lonely and afraid.

'Only myself, Liza and the hairdresser have been given instructions regarding your toilette.'

'Why wasn't I consulted?' Maria felt like a prisoner.

'Never fear, my lady. The viscount has your welfare at heart. He knows what is best for you. Now, let me help you to bathe.' Agatha clapped her hands and a line of footmen entered through the door, each carrying a pail of steaming water. These were conveyed into the annex that contained a tub.

When they had finished and marched out Maria was unable to prevent Agatha and the maid, Liza, whom she recognised as the one she had seen being beaten, divesting her of her garments and enfolding her in a white towel. The good-looking coiffeur was too busy admiring himself in the pier-glass to take much heed of her nudity. The bathroom walls were covered in Islamic tiles, and the tub itself was large, squatting centre-stage on four clawed feet. It was three-quarters full of warm, scented water and Maria would have enjoyed it were it not for Agatha's intrusion.

What right had Damien to send Sarah and Emily away, even for a short while? She was appalled at the audacity of the man! None of her protests made a scrap of difference as she was soaped all over and her hair washed, then pinned to the top of her head. Helped out of the bath, the towel was wrapped around her once more and she was taken back to the bedroom. There it was removed and perfumed lotion applied all over her skin, including her breasts and bottom. It was very apparent that Agatha enjoyed this, lingering over Maria's nipples, crack and clitoris.

Liza rubbed her hair, removing most of the moisture, and then Agatha said, 'The master has decided you shall be shaved. It is his wish to view you without your pubic hair.'

'What?' Maria, who had started to relax, shot to her feet. 'I don't want this done. Go away.'

Agatha produced a slender cane, very much like the one Mrs Rossiter had used at school. 'I hope you aren't going to be defiant,' she said softly 'I have been told I can take what measures I think fit in order to make you obey.' The tip of the cane brushed across Maria's bare thigh, making her jump.

'How dare you?' she shouted. 'You're nothing but a servant!'

'I follow his lordship's instructions, and they are explicit. Join us, Russell.' Agatha gestured to the mincing young man.

He was exquisitely dressed in the very latest fashion, his plum-coloured jacket having a nipped-in waist, the sleeves straight with wide turned-back cuffs, and his lace jabot extra large. His breeches were exceedingly tight, his boots of the softest leather. He removed his coat, folded it fastidiously, rolled up his sleeves and donned a white apron. Maria had seen him before. He sometimes attended Arabella, a mine of gossipy information as he worked his magic with comb and scissors and razor.

Liza brought over a basin of warm water and a tray containing implements.

'Lie down, Lady Maria,' Agatha instructed, her bony hands gripping her by the shoulders and forcing her onto her back, the towel spread out beneath her.

The chill air made her nipples crimp, and she could do nothing but slither to the foot of the bed, her legs dangling over the edge and her pubis raised. Russell positioned himself between her thighs, lathered a brush with shaving soap and applied it to her mound. The sensation was far from unpleasant. She squirmed, but Liza and Agatha held her down. Her bush was coated with perfumed suds and Russell stropped his blade on a strip of oiled leather, and then used his left hand to hold back her pubis and apply his cutthroat razor to her foxy-hued floss.

He was deft, used to shaving the faces of tetchy gentlemen or the private parts of fussy ladies who wanted their pudendum swept clean. The experience was not painful, but strange nonetheless, and Maria stopped struggling, giving herself into his skilled hands. At first she was embarrassed because she was lying there with her sexual organs in full view. Then she realised he was not viewing her as a woman, only as a piece of flesh he had been instructed to improve. By his mannerisms and speech she guessed him to be more interested in members of his own sex. This brought a modicum of comfort, though the cooling water, the sharp razor and the removal of the hair made her feel vulnerable.

Russell worked quickly, his busy fingers parting her crack, opening the outer labia and making sure there were no wisps left around her arsehole. 'There, smooth as a baby,' he said proudly, dabbing her dry.

'You've made a fine job of it,' Agatha said, staring at the pink flesh where the slit was no longer hidden.

She flicked a finger over Maria's nubbin and it stirred. Oh God, Maria thought, it's even more sensitive! She stared down her body to where her mons veneris rose, smooth and hairless. She had not seen it like that for years!

'But it will grow again, be stubbly and itchy,' she grumbled, sitting up. 'Now will you all kindly leave? I've had enough.'

Agatha shook her grey-streaked head. 'I've not yet finished, but Russell can go. He will attend you regularly, my lady, in order to keep you clean-shaven.'

Maria was lost for words. What other indignities were about to be heaped on her?

Agatha had brought a carved box with her. This she now opened, revealing objects of various size, made of wood or ivory. Maria had never seen the like, though they were replicas of the penis. 'Lie on your side,' Agatha instructed, taking one of the smallest from its nest of red satin and applying lubricant to the tip.

'What are you going to do?' Maria asked, Damien's words coming back to her. He had spoken of butt-plugs to stretch her anus.

'The viscount wants the pathway made easier for him. This will help.' At a signal Liza restrained Maria, while Agatha inserted the slippery dildo into her cringing arse.

'Oh... that hurts!' Maria cried, but Agatha did not stop pushing it in.

'Don't struggle, my lady. It will be better if you don't. Let your muscle soften and accept it. This is a small dildo, but later I shall use larger ones.'

'How long do I have to keep it there?' The sensation reminded Maria of Damien's act of sodomy. She had not liked it then and certainly did not welcome such an impersonal tool, but tried to follow Agatha's advice and make it easier for herself.

'As long as it takes,' was the cryptic reply.

'You can't expect me to retain it for hours, surely?' Maria objected, hating the woman who was nothing more than Damien's creature, following his orders for gain and her own perverted satisfaction.

'We will try several.' Agatha selected more from the padded box. 'Thirty minutes each should suffice to begin with.'

'But this will take ages!'

'The time will quickly pass. If you need to void your bowels, then I will remove them temporarily.'

'This is degrading! What kind of a person are you to carry out his commands?'

Agatha shrugged, placing the mock phalli in a neat row on the nightstand. 'It takes all sorts,' she answered, a cynical smile lifting her narrow lips. 'One day you will thank me for showing you a different means of pleasure.'

'I don't think so. My arse is aching. Can't you take the thing out?'

Agatha looked at the ormolu clock standing between a dainty porcelain shepherd and shepherdess on the mantle-piece. 'Not for half an hour,' she pronounced.

'How am I expected to sleep?' Maria envisaged a night of cruel discomfort.

'I shall be finished with you before bedtime. We'll try again tomorrow.'

'Where is the viscount? Will he be visiting me?'

'Maybe. He is occupied with his guests.'

Nothing that man does appears to shock his staff, Maria fumed. They are either brow-beaten, well-trained, well-paid or as perverted as he! She decided on the latter. 'And Lady Arabella? Is she aware of this shameful treatment?' Oh, where are Charles and Jane? Maria mourned. There is no one to help me.

'No doubt milady has her own pleasures to pursue,' Agatha said briskly, covering her with the quilt and then tidying up. 'I shall leave you for a while.'

Maria heard her rustling about and the door closing behind her. Then the room fell into silence, apart from the logs settling in the grate. The evening was warm, but fires were maintained for the comfort of those in the bedchambers. It was too early to sleep and Maria moved uneasily, afraid to dislodge the butt-plug. She was tempted to release it from her rectum, but thought she might cause an injury. There was nothing she could do but await Agatha's return. The minutes dragged, and she could not see the clock from her position.

The plug was becoming increasingly uncomfortable. She considered reaching for the hand-bell and ringing it, but had the feeling that Agatha would not answer, determined to make her suffer. Then the outer door swung open and a crowd of drunken huntsmen followed Damien into the room. Maria propped herself up on one elbow and clutched the quilt around her.

'There she is!' Damien shouted, and his eyes had such a powerful glitter that she wondered if he had been mixing opium with his wine again. 'Isn't she a picture, gentlemen? My ward, completely in my charge.'

'You lucky dog!' shouted a beefy, red-faced squire. He had slopped ale down his shirt-front and there was a dark patch staining his breeches, as if he had lost control of his bladder.

'You are indeed, Strafford,' chorused the rest, leaning on each other's shoulders and ogling Maria. 'Always were and always will be! Let's have a look at her.'

Damien stepped forward and tugged at the quilt, but Maria hung on to it like grim death. 'No! No! Get away from me! Get off!' she yelled, unable to sit properly because of the dildo, and mortified that he wanted to show her to his drunken cronies.

This amused them hugely. 'A spitfire! What sport to tame her, eh, chaps? Come on, darling, don't be shy. Show us your pretty little minge!'

Damien gave an extra hard tug, wrenching the quilt from her hands. She wrapped her arms around her breasts and kept her legs close together, her every movement painful. He stared down at her, a satisfied smile lifting his lips. 'So... Agatha has followed my commands. How do you find the butt-plug? Is it to your liking or shall I insert a larger one? Maybe I'll remove it altogether and use my todger instead, eh?'

His friends almost collapsed with mirth at this witticism. 'Give me a go at her,' begged the fat huntsman, bending over and blowing his sour breath into her face.

Damien's mood changed like lightning. He thrust the man aside, glaring at him. 'Lay one dirty paw on her and I'll hang you up by your balls.' His voice was quiet, but held deadly menace.

'Beg pardon, old boy, but I thought you brought us here for sport,' his guest spluttered.

'I did. For my sport. The chit is wilful and needs correction, but I choose what form this takes.'

Maria, listening, was completely baffled. Was he protecting her? Had he brought them there to prove his supremacy? Whatever it was, it gave her breathing space. She was not to be turned over to these crude individuals, handled, abused and shamed. For this she could be grateful, though not for long.

Damien parted her bottom cheeks and pulled out the plug. She gasped and relief flooded her. She reached for the covering, but he stopped her. 'Ah, no, my dear. I'm about to test you.'

His companions edged closer. She breathed in the sweat of the chase, the alcohol they had consumed and their rampant lust. Damien tied a scarf around her eyes, whispering, 'You will be reduced to touch, sound and smell, and won't know which of us is pushing his cock into your hand or mouth.'

'But you said...'

'Don't worry. No man will enter you except myself.'

She felt hands on her arse. Damien's?

There were others cupping her breasts and pulling at the nipples. She heard the harsh breathing and inhaled the odour of lascivious males, and took a cock in each hand, closing her palm over the heated, wet members and hearing their owners groan. Damien was right. Denied sight her other senses sharpened. No one was hurting her, in fact the attention given to her breasts and delta was arousing. Responsibility for her actions had been taken from her. She was being encouraged to behave like a strumpet. There was no one to say her nay. It was her guardian's wish that she pleasured his friends and, in so doing, reached a climax herself. The fact that he was there, watching, excited her above all else and she wriggled her clit on playful fingers and moaned as others tweaked her nipples.

She felt hot come exploding over her right hand, while the penis in her left was jerking and starting to spew. Another moved against her mouth, prising her lips apart. It was large and tasted cheesy, making her gorge rise, but she could not move away. Someone was holding her head steady. The huge member worked in and out, its owner's large belly flopping against her face, nearly suffocating her. She felt spunk creaming her chin, her hands and buttocks and was floundering, trying to escape.

'Enough!' snapped Damien, and she was freed from their mauling. He took off the blindfold, sponged her face and hands and every part that they had fouled with their emissions. Then, after covering her with the quilt, he undid his breeches, took out his magnificent tool and stroked it to even greater size. His

94

cronies watched, those who had ejaculated turning their attention to the wine bottles, while the ones who had not been given the opportunity had their cocks in their hands.

Maria knew nothing but relief. Damien came to her, turning back the covering and saying, 'I shall see how the use of the plug has improved you.'

He turned her on her side away from the others, then slipped in beside her, lying against the curve of her spine, spoon-fashion. Maria was exhausted and wanted nothing more than to sleep cradled in his arms. Just for a moment it seemed that he, too, wanted this, but then his cock stirred and he pressed it into her, the helm nudging against her anus. It slipped into her easily, the opening lubricated and stretched. She backed into his lap, encouraging deeper penetration, finding that apart from feeling stuffed, the sensation was pleasant.

Damien inveigled a hand round her mound and found her clitoris. As he slowly pumped in and out so he rubbed the hard little pearl until she was aware of nothing except the need to reach orgasm. It was like a madness in her blood. She forgot the other men, her soreness and anger. Damien's dark hair brushed the nape of her neck, his lips trailed down her spine, his strong arms held her and his cock was in possession of her most intimate of places. His fingers never stopped, bringing her on and on. The feeling was blazing inside her, rising, rising till it broke in a firework display of stars. She yelled and he pumped, reaching his own apogee, gentle now, but not withdrawing.

Maria knew peace then, a feeling such as she had never had before. Even Charles's lovemaking was as nothing compared to this. And still Damien held her, till the fat huntsman tapped him on the shoulder. 'Well done. You arse-fucked her good and hard! Is there any more booze? We're running out.'

'Go to hell,' Damien muttered, making no move to leave her.

Maria could feel herself slipping into oblivion, grateful for the warmth of him, and the protective barrier he was forming. In the background she could hear the men grumbling and starting to leave and it was not until they had departed that Damien freed her and left the bed. She turned, wanting him to come back, but he was already dressing.

'That was much better,' he said, adjusting his cravat in the mirror. 'Agatha shall use a larger plug tomorrow.'

'You're leaving me?' She did not know whether to be glad or sorry.

'I am. Maybe I'll take you hunting in the morning. Goodnight, Maria.'

Then he was gone, like a revenant that had appeared out of the darkness. Maria thumped the pillow into a more comfortable shape and pulled the downy quilt up under her chin. She knew him no better than on their initial meeting, when he bested her at the phaeton race.

The curricle clopped sedately towards Gay Street, along the Paragon and down the hill to the Abbey Churchyard. There it stopped and Jane and her mother, Lady Rowena Dunn, plus a new chaperone and her ladyship's maid, alighted and crossed the broad piazza, then passed beneath the columns of the Pump

Room.

It was the place to see and be seen. This most popular out-of-town spa offered its famous mineral water as an effective medicine, while doctors recommended that the hot springs were used for bathing. The Romans had discovered this to be efficacious hundreds of years before, but now Bath had become the centre for high living, balls, routes and gambling. Beautiful houses had been built overlooking parks. Anyone of importance had a residence there, and this included Jane's parents, but all that concerned her was meeting Robin.

She had managed to bribe Bess into carrying a letter to the inn where he was staying. He had told Jane, through a fellow student who had smuggled a message to her, that he would be there that week, en-route to Burdock. Though Miss Carmichael had been engaged as a duenna she was a similar type of person to Maria's; kindly, forgetful and liking male attention. She presented little problem and Jane was sure she could wheedle her way around her. It was a blessed relief to have her after the flinty-eyed Agatha.

They had taken up residence in their Royal Crescent property yesterday, and Lady Rowena could not wait to make her presence felt at the Pump Room. It was mid-morning and crowded. There was a quite bewildering variety of silk or cotton gowns, feathered hats and flowered bonnets. The ladies were escorted by dandies in tight pantaloons and waisted jackets, flaunting walking-sticks and quizzing-glasses and snuff-boxes. Gouty old gentlemen in wheelchairs were being pushed along by harassed servants, while bedizened dowagers dominated the card tables. A string quartet played Mozart, occupying a small platform under a shell-shaped arch.

'La, such a crush!' exclaimed Lady Rowena, delightedly. 'And I know most of them! Bless my soul, if that ain't Baroness Selby over there! Could that pretty youth fawning on her be her latest beau? She must be all of fifty! Now then, Jane, stay here with Miss Carmichael and conduct yourself properly while I go and pay my respects to the baroness.'

And catch up on latest gossip, Jane thought. This is all they are interested in, gossip and tittle-tattle, tearing people's reputations to shreds, and yet my parents have the gall to forbid me to find happiness with a man of my own choosing. Her mother obviously wanted to be rid of her for a while, unable to conceal her relief when her husband had decided against coming. This left her free to chatter interminably with her female friends, flirt with the dandies and try her luck at the gaming tables.

Jane glanced around anxiously but could not see Robin. As soon as her mother was out of sight she tugged at Miss Carmichael's arm. 'I'm sure you must be thirsty. Why don't we go to the refreshment room where they will be serving syllabub?'

'If that is your wish, my lady,' Iris Carmichael answered readily, a pretty woman in her mid-twenties, the daughter of a schoolmaster and well educated. The position as chaperone to Jane was not her first. She had come highly recommended. Even so, Jane guessed she would have liked to be married and was keeping her options open for an eligible bachelor.

The corridor linking the reception room with the refreshment area was bustling. People were coming and going, laughing, chatting, flirting. Servants took their employers' outdoor garments to the cloakrooms or pushed their way through the throng to obtain wine or lemonade, and the biscuits and buns for which the city was famous.

It was then that Jane saw Robin. He was leaning against the wall and his eyes met hers over peoples' heads. Her heart seemed about to leave her chest with joy. How could she get away from Miss Carmichael?

'I have a great thirst,' she complained. 'Fetch me a drink.'

Fortunately the chaperone had been casting about her and had spotted a valet, very smartly dressed in dark livery who, having attended his master, seemed to be seeking more convivial company. 'Certainly, my lady. Wait here for me and don't talk to strangers,' she said and skipped off, heading in the valet's direction.

Jane made a beeline for Robin. 'Oh, my darling,' he whispered, while they pretended to be greeting one another as if they were casual acquaintances.

'Robin! Oh, Robin! I'm here with Mama. She's somewhere about and the chaperone will be on my trail. Where can we go?'

He seized her hand and they worked their way through the throng towards a doorway that led out on to a small balcony that overlooked a large bath that stood under the open sky. It was stone-built and surrounded by cloistered arches, so old that its origin had been lost in time. Arthritic suffers reclined on the steps surrounding the rectangular pool. They wore long white gowns and were assisted by bath attendants.

'Not only these seek help,' Robin murmured into Jane's ear, pressing her close to him. 'It's reputed to aid skin diseases and infertility.'

'It's not a very romantic place for a tryst,' she said.

'Don't you believe it. Many a frustrated woman has entered these waters in the hope of becoming pregnant. It has worked for some, but probably due to the stalwart services of the bathing staff rather than the magical properties of the spring.'

'I'm with you and that's all that matters.' She rested her head against his chest, desire blooming in her. It had been so long since he had entered her and her vagina ached, love-juice seeping out to wet her lower lips. She felt she would burst, run mad, scream and tear off her clothes if she did not have him soon.

'My dear girl, what are we to do?' He held her close and traced the outline of her breasts through her thin gown, and she ground her hips into his bulge and came to an abrupt decision.

For the first time she realised she was the strong one of the two. A woman, ready to fight for what she most desired. Maria had taught her a great deal, but she was not there and Jane must do it alone.

'Mama is here,' she said, pulling away from him and stiffening her spine, though retaining his hands in hers. 'I shall take you to meet her again. She hardly noticed you the first time. She is not so recalcitrant as Papa and may plead our cause. Come, don't be shy. Oh, God, I so much want to be your wife, Robin!'

Chapter 11

'Mama, do you remember Robin Claremont? I introduced you to him on the day I left school.' Jane had never felt more nervous.

Lady Rowena raised her lorgnette and quizzed Robin through it. Jane had chosen the moment when her mother had left her aristocratic friends, catching her on her way back from the powder room.

She waited for a reply, her heart pounding. 'Ah, yes.' Lady Rowena continued to study him as if he were a specimen in a laboratory. 'You were most helpful with Jane's luggage, if I remember rightly.'

'He's a curate, taking up a post as assistant to the vicar of Burdock,' Jane went on, while Robin stood there smiling uncertainly, hat in hand.

'How interesting,' Lady Rowena's tone indicated extreme boredom.

'We met in the refreshment room just now,' Jane struggled on. It was like rolling a boulder up hill.

'And where is Miss Carmichael?' Robin was subjected to another icy stare.

'Fetching me a glass of lemonade.'

'Well, we must find her and be on our way. Good day to you, Mr Claremont. Come along, Jane.'

She turned to leave, but Jane stopped her. 'Mama, please listen,' she said desperately. 'I love him and he loves me. We want to get married.'

Her mother turned, frowning at her. 'What? Have you taken leave of your senses, Jane? Apart from being already promised to Sir Percy, this would be a most unsuitable match.'

Robin cut in. 'Is it because I'm only a curate at the moment? I intend to rise in the ranks, I assure you.'

Lady Rowena stared at him down her nose. 'Were you an archbishop, it would make no difference, sir. Jane is already affianced. Is that clear? I'll thank you to leave her alone.'

'But Mama, we're in love,' Jane insisted.

'"Marry in haste, regret at leisure",' Lady Rowena quoted. 'The same applies to you. No one of standing marries for love. It leads to disaster. Forget this nonsense and you, young man, will not approach my daughter again. Is that clear? Churchman or no, my husband will not hesitate to set the dogs on you.'

She swept through the crowd, gathering up an apologetic Miss Carmichael on route. Jane hurried in pursuit of them, but Robin caught her up, saying urgently, 'Meet me in the garden tonight. We need to talk.'

The capricious English weather had changed by the time Maria and Damien went riding. When they reached open ground a wind had sprung up, huge clouds throwing their swift-moving shadows over an expanse of brown, gold and purple gorse. Occasional sunshine broke through, its radiance made even more dazzling in contrast.

He turned in his saddle, jammed his hat down on his head and shouted. 'I'll race you, Maria, staking a hundred guineas on the outcome. It will be like the phaeton race. Are you game?'

Now what's he up to? she wondered, as distrustful as ever. But never able to refuse a challenge she replied, 'Where's the finishing line?' Her mare was nervous, pawing the ground, straining to be off.

'Scratch Tump. The burial mound you can see in the distance.'

She jerked the reins and they exploded into action, two colourful streaks, one chestnut, one black. His horse was larger, but the mare was spirited and lively. Maria, absorbed, forgot all else, even the soreness of her butt for, although she sat side-saddle, her anus still caused her discomfort but not enough to detract from the enjoyment. She loved horses, respecting their moods, their great hearts and their bravery. She never used the spur or a cruelly tight bit that sawed at tender mouths, or the whip constantly. Having tasted it herself she had sworn not to inflict it on animals. Men perhaps, but that was different.

She loosened the rein and drummed her heel into the mare's side. The animal's neck was tense, her nostrils flared and her ears laid back. Maria glanced over her shoulder. Damien's pace was less of a gallop and more that of flight itself. Whatever his faults he was a superb horseman. The mare kept up with him, touching the ground only to leave it again with a single strike of her hooves.

Maria's hair was confined in a snood beneath a hard hat, but her face was whipped by the mare's flowing mane. She felt as if her body was weightless and that she had become one with her mount, wanting nothing but to gallop over the moor for ever, the earth, the grass and the mare mingling with her own soul.

Damien was gaining. His whip cracked down repeatedly and she remembered how it had slashed her during the phaeton race, and punished her since. This sent a thrill through her, and the pressure of the saddle's high pommel stimulated her clitoris with every movement. She had the absurd desire to rein in, throw herself on the grass and implore him to take her.

He was giving wild cries that were flung by the wind, tossed and echoed. His mount neighed in response, ebony hide flecked with foam. Maria cried encouragement and the mare responded. The barrow was coming nearer, huge on the skyline and, with a final supreme effort, she reached there first.

She slowed to a walk, leaning over and patting her mare's steaming neck, murmuring, 'Well done, girl.'

Damien drew up alongside. 'Congratulations! This makes us even. One all.' He was breathing fast, sweat running down his face. 'I'll give you the money when we reach the house, unless you want another race?'

'No, thanks. I'll take the cash.'

'Why do you need it? I supply you with everything.'

'Believe it or not I like to have some measure of independence, and whatever you give me comes from my estate, does it not?'

'Your father trusted me to manage your affairs.'

More fool him, she thought as she dismounted, petting her animal who was recovering her wind. The warmth of her breath wafted over Maria's skin. Her head, hot and moist, nuzzled into her shoulder. 'This is a fine beast,' she said, glancing up at Damien and then looking away. There was something in his eyes that she did not like. 'We must find water for them, they have both done well.'

'Not yet.' He cocked a foot out of the stirrup and swung down. 'I want to talk to you.'

The barrow loomed above them and the sun had gone. The clouds were piling up, black and threatening. 'We should go back,' she said. 'It's going to rain.'

He seemed not to hear her, coming so close that she could see the texture of his skin and the long lashes shading his eyes. His arm snaked out, winding around her waist. She could feel his heat, engendered by the gallop and his own pulse. It was as if his gaze was hypnotic, making her forget everything except him. His lips descended on hers and once again wove their magic. He had not approached her for days after her introduction to the butt-plug. She had spent them attempting to act normally, accompanying Arabella on a round of social visits in the parish, taking tea or playing cards.

Arabella's aplomb astonished her. She was well respected for being the wife of an earl, and played on this. Though Maria recognised a few of the ladies as being among those who had attended the hunt and the orgy that followed, on the whole they were of the old school, engaged in 'good works' about the village. Damien was a master of dissembling, too, when it suited him. What had once seemed a joyous escape from school and restrictions, had become clouded with doubt about her aunt and guardian.

The wind had an edge to it, and rain started to strike across from the sea. 'Stay there,' Damien commanded, and tethered the horses near Scratch Tump. He returned to Maria and took her hand, leading her into the shelter of the stones supporting the entrance where a Stone Age builder had inserted the fossil of an ammonite as decoration.

'Inside,' Damien said abruptly. It was pitch dark, the uneven ground sloping downwards. He seemed to know his way, as sure-footed as a cat. Maria stumbled after him, more terrified of being left alone than of what he might do to her.

He stopped and she nearly cannoned into him, chilled to the marrow, her riding habit offering little protection against the dankness. She heard the scrape of a tinderbox, followed by the glow from a lantern. Damien was no stranger to this ancient tomb.

'What a gloomy spot,' she said, trying to lighten the mood. 'Of interest only to those who study ancient monuments.'

'You think so?' His smile was demonic in the lantern-light. 'I'll admit that I have professors of archaeology begging permission to view it, and have permitted a few of the skulls and bones and artefacts to be taken to the nearest museum. It has been suggested that some of the dead may have been human sacrifices. Whatever it was, it belongs to me, situated on my land. No one comes here unless I allow them. The locals avoid it anyway, saying it is haunted. That's where it got its name. Old Scratch means the devil in these remote parts.'

Maria shivered. 'I'm cold. I want to go.'

'So soon?' He set the lantern on a ledge. 'Aren't you curious? There are still human remains in some of the alcoves. Wouldn't you like to meet your ancestors?'

He was amused by the situation and she determined not to be the victim of his macabre sense of humour. 'Another time, perhaps. I would rather return to Raven Towers,' she replied lightly.

He ignored this, lifting a skull from a stone shelf. '"Alas, poor Yorick",' he quoted. 'The Bard of Avon had something apt to say about almost every situation. Don't you agree?'

'You didn't bring me here to discuss antiquities or Shakespeare. Get to the point, Damien.'

'Hasty one! I always find anticipation hones the edge of appetite. But if you insist... take off your clothes.'

'You must be jesting! I shall freeze to death.'

He raised his crop and trailed it down the side of her face. 'Strip.'

'And if I refuse?'

'I would hate to mark that pretty face, but you know that I insist on obedience.'

Her hands trembled as she removed her gloves, then the hat, jacket, blouse and chemise. He rested against the wall, legs crossed at the ankles, watching her every movement. When she was bare to the waist he reached out and tickled her nipples with the tip of the crop. They puckered and she turned away, ashamed that he should see how much he excited her.

Unbuttoning the waistband of her skirt she let it fall, then laid it with the rest of her clothes on a slab that might once have contained a corpse. Breeches, hose and riding boots came next and at last she stood there, shivering with cold, as naked as the day she was born.

'That's more like it,' he remarked, stalking round her, absorbing her from every angle. 'No need for pretence here. There is no one to see us, only the dead. You enjoy the fear you feel when I'm near you. Before meeting me you never confessed, even to your dearest friend, that you wanted to be dominated. Isn't this true?' He spoke with an intensity that riveted her, and made her feel she was being interrogated by a judge. He raised the crop and brought it down across her bare thighs. 'Answer, damn you!'

Shocks rippled through her, her skin stinging where the whip had struck. 'I don't know,' she whimpered. 'I can't remember.'

'Liar!'

He taunted her with the crop, circling her breasts then letting it strike her skin, leaving red marks. He tapped her belly and thighs, and though she squirmed and tried to avoid that fast-moving whip, each stroke made her vagina wetter, slippery with love-juice.

'Stop!' she cried.

'Really?' he sneered. 'Surely not? I've only just begun.' He pushed her back. A few steps and she felt uneven stone. He prodded her but she could go no further. 'Face the wall.'

He poked her with the crop, forcing her to obey. The stone was cold and damp, chilling her breasts, belly and thighs. She kept remembering that for centuries the tomb had been untouched, sealed and filled with cadavers. The atmosphere was rank with the smell of decay.

'Don't make me do this,' she begged, though hating herself for whimpering.

'Spread your legs wide,' he ordered. 'And lift your arms over your head. That's right. Can you feel the rings? Stay like that while I bind you.'

Her fingers found the metal and hung on. He wrapped ropes round her wrists and tied them to the rings, then did the same to her ankles, attaching them to lower ones. 'Are these ancient trappings?' she asked sarcastically, still finding the courage to defy him.

He chuckled. 'My own additions. Friends enjoy coming here as a diversion. There's nothing like a touch of fear and horror to enliven one's lovemaking.'

She found this disgusting. 'How can you call it that, debasing a noble emotion?'

'Sentimental nonsense! We are all animals under the facade of respectability. And you, my dear, are no better than the rest. You like this, don't you? You look so lovely, strung up there.'

'Let me go. Free me, please. You are wrong to say I enjoy it. Give me the chance to love you in the normal way... romantic, if you like, mock it though you may.'

She could not see his expression, but caught a hint of regret in his reply. 'I renounced love many years ago. I gave my heart to someone who betrayed me, and I swore that never again would I allow myself to weaken. This is my way of loving now.'

The crop came down with full force, catching her lower back. Maria jerked in her restraints, steeling herself to endure the savage attack. He struck again and again, varying the spots on which the crop landed. She wept, feeling utterly worthless, a slave of no use but to bring pleasure to her cruel master. She was no longer conscious of the cold, her whole body suffused with a heat that concentrated in her loins. Every involuntary spasm when the crop stuck chaffed her nipples and caused her pubis to rub the stone. Her wrists were sore, her ankles too, but now she was sinking into a state where all she could think about was the next blow, and the next agony and the next thrilling stimulation.

Damien came close to her, pressing against her spine, grinding his prick into her open crack. She could feel it, that hard, engorged tool. It was bare, solid, the helm leaking fluid. Was the ordeal over? Could he be about to take her? Desire ripped through her and she moaned her longing.

'Damien, set me free. Do with me as you will, but don't beat me any more.'

'You want me, don't you, my poor little slave-slut? Say it.' His voice was a purr close to her ear, his arms around her, one hand clasping her mound, the other squeezing her breasts.

'Yes, yes... I want you.' She was willing to confess to anything if he would stop punishing her and give her what she craved.

He withdrew his hands, leaving her bereft. The air rustled as the crop cracked through it. Damien focused on her buttocks. Her emotions were engulfed by pain, her thighs quivering, her backside clenching and her sex wet with arousal. It was as if she was someone else observing this enslaved woman, seeing how her anger was dissipating. She was absorbing the pain, going beyond it, filled with desire for intimate contact with Damien.

Then, with almost cruel finality, her ordeal was over. He freed her wrists and ankles and supported her as she fell into his arms, weakened and disoriented. He held her cleft in his broad hand and frigged her clitoris. She was so close that she came within a few strokes, rubbing against his fingers. Convulsing and writhing she gasped out foolish phrases. Thinking about it later in the clear light of day, she feared she had told him she loved him.

He turned her, held her punished bottom in his hands and entered her vagina from the rear. He pumped frantically. A few strokes and he spurted, and she was completely satisfied, though wishing it could go on for eternity. He rested against her for a moment, then broke away.

'May I dress now?' she whispered.

'Of course, and hurry, we shall be late for luncheon.'

Charles, concealed among the gorse on the headland, saw Damien and Maria race towards the barrow out of the storm. With the aid of his telescope he was able to watch at close hand as they dismounted and disappeared inside the mound. He lowered it slowly, pulling his hat down and his collar up, braving the elements, every nerve taut as he speculated on what they would be doing there.

He had been in the area for several days, staying at an inn. He told the landlord he was a student of architecture, exploring the local monuments. Quint had been transformed into another scholar and Bates went along, too. They had secretly linked up with others who kept an eye on the coast, ready to track any suspicious looking vessels that anchored in one of the numerous remote bays in which the county abounded.

He speculated as to whether he should inform Maria of her guardian's involvement with the enemy. Not yet, common sense insisted. The last thing he wanted was for Damien to suspect he was on to him. But the situation needed to be closely monitored. He and his confederates were hoping to make arrests soon and bring the viscount to justice.

His every instinct was to rush into Scratch Tump and wrest her from Damien's arms. The thought of her yielding to him was abhorrent and yet he had to admit that he had fucked Sally before leaving London. Many men would have stoutly declared that this was different, but Charles was too honest and enlightened to cling to this outmoded creed. Even so, he longed to claim her as his own, dreaming of marriage and remaining with her till death parted them. While Damien was at liberty this was unlikely to happen, yet it was tricky. The last thing he wanted was for Maria to sympathise with her guardian. She must see for herself that he was a traitorous villain.

Closing the telescope Charles left the hideout, picking up Quint on the way so they could compare notes on what they had discovered that morning. Information had come in about a sailing boat expected to land by night very soon. They needed to be extra vigilant.

'Go and find Maria,' Jane insisted, clasped tightly in Robin's arms at the end of the garden. It was dark, and her attendants were asleep. She had slipped out in her nightgown and over-robe.

Robin had appeared from the shadows and she had been able to do nothing but yield to his kisses and ardent caresses. This joy was so new to her, every aspect of lovemaking thrilling her to the marrow, the secrecy, the fact that it was forbidden, all adding to her excitement.

He had refused to talk of anything sensible, and she felt his body heat through her thin attire, nipples peaking and pubis lifted to contact his bulge. The leaves were thick, hiding them from sight, and the only sound was the rustle of night hunting creatures. The hazardous nature of their meeting added an extra spark. It was a hurried mating, with her pressed against a tree-bole and him lifting her, hands clasped about her bare bottom, as he slid his erection into her. She raised herself up and down on his penis and then, unable to make contact with her clitoris, pushed a hand between them and massaged it, reaching a speedy climax. He groaned and jerked and discharged. Jane felt it, warm and wet inside her. Then he gently lowered her till her feet touched the ground.

'Will you go seek Maria?' she said. 'You've told me that it will cost a great deal for us to take the stagecoach to Scotland and Gretna Green. I have no money and neither have you; only the stipend your father gives you. Maria may be able to assist us.'

'It shames me to ask her, but there is little alternative. Where is she?' He stroked Jane's hair.

'At the viscount's home in Dorset. It is called Raven Towers, near the fishing village of Parnham Combe.' Jane rested her head on his chest and listened to the beat of his heart and felt quite sick with love. 'You must get in touch with her somehow and meet her secretly. No one knows you there, do they? You haven't met the viscount?'

'I've seen her maidservant and the chaperone, but only briefly. Leave it to me, darling. I'll do anything as long as we can be together eventually.'

'I must go before I'm discovered.' She broke away from him, though it was hard to do. Her thighs were wet with his tribute and her own juice. It seemed so natural and she longed for the time when they could sleep in each other's arms.

He kissed her once more, and then disappeared into the darkness. Jane slipped back to the house, tears coursing down her face. Why did love hurt? she wondered. Yet she would not have missed such an experience for the world. She did not doubt that Maria would come to their aid, were it humanly possible. She added these comments to her journal, though half afraid to write in it these days, lest it be discovered and herself compromised.

'This resembles a sultan's harem,' Arabella remarked, reclining on a divan in Damien's apartment.

'Have you ever been in one, my dear?' He lifted the mouthpiece of the hookah from his lips to reply. The rosewater in the bowl bubbled and the air was scented with herbs.

'No, but I've seen paintings and it looks most frightfully exotic.' She gave him an alluring glance from under heavy-lidded eyes. It was early evening and the ambience was that of lazing and lovemaking, reading poetry, smoking opium and whiling away the time.

In other circumstances he would have been happy to oblige, but he had important issues enquiring urgent attention. He rose, set aside the pipe and leaned over her. 'You will have to amuse yourself with someone else,' he said flatly. 'I'm busy.'

'How boring,' she pouted, silk robe outlining her limbs. Lifting her skirt she played with the gold rings in her labia. 'Have that young groom sent up. You know, the one who is caring for my horse that's gone lame. I think his name is Thomas. These country lads can be a pleasant diversion. They are so strong, and simple in their needs. It is amusing to teach them the refinements of fucking. Most of them don't know where a woman's pleasure spot lies.'

He slapped her backside. 'You have all the instincts of a strumpet!'

'I know. Isn't it fun?'

'Where's Maria?' His brows swooped down as he thought of her. She had not yet become entirely submissive. There was a haughty part of her that still defied him.

'In the conservatory, I think, with her chaperone.'

'Best place for her,' he grunted, picking up his hat and riding crop. 'I shall be out for a while and will see you later.'

'Another woman?'

'Mind your own business.'

'Very well, but don't forget to send Thomas to me.'

'I won't. Don't exhaust the poor lad, he'll be needed in the stable later.'

Sarah Jenkins was asleep. Maria watched her nodding off from where she sat, sketchbook and pencils to hand. It was warm, one of those days that summer drops into the lap of autumn. She had been there all afternoon with Emily in attendance.

Maria had learned to draw at school. It was considered a suitable accomplishment for a young lady, like playing the pianoforte, singing or needlework. Nothing too strenuous and all very proper. It was supposed to impress prospective bridegrooms. Maria was restless. She flung down the pencil and laid aside the pad. Emily looked up from her sewing.

'Milady?'

'I shall die if I have to stay here much longer. I need to get out... ride my mare... anything but sit here.'

'But it will be dusk soon.'

'So much the better.'

'Very well. I'll wake Mrs Jenkins.'

Maria went to her bedroom, changing into her riding habit. Sarah was too drowsy to argue and Emily ran to the stable and ordered Tranter to saddle the mare. Their affair was still going strong and Maria found her an able ally, ready to collude in any scheme she wanted to put into operation. Agatha was mostly engaged elsewhere, obeying Damien and keeping the servants under control. Maria was called to her aunt's room whenever Russell arrived, combining hairdressing and the offices of barber at one and the same time. Arabella's pubis was regularly shaved, and Maria was expected to keep hers equally smooth.

Tranter was in the stable and the mare was ready. 'The viscount left not long ago,' he said. 'You should be able to catch up with him.'

'In which direction?' she asked as he bent, cupped his hands to receive her foot, then hoisted her into the saddle.

'Past the spinney and headed towards the ruined chapel. Shall I come with you, miss?'

'No,' she flung back over her shoulder, already trotting from the stable.

Darkness was deepening, a soft velvety darkness made up of trees and the breathing earth. Maria glimpsed the moon, which she likened to an empress driving her chariot across the star-spangled sky. She rode towards the spinney, listening for the sound of hoof-beats. They came, but far ahead of her. She clicked her tongue and the mare moved off again.

She passed Scratch Tump, tingling as she remembered Damien punishing her and then taking her. Perhaps, if she caught up with him, he might do something similar amidst the ruins of the chapel. She admitted it was this ache in her loins that had prompted her to take a ride. Since experiencing sexual intercourse she was no longer content with pleasuring herself, and doubted that even Jane would be able to satisfy her. She needed a lusty cock inside her.

'Come on, girl,' she said to the mare, whose ears twitched in response.

It was a very different aspect to the one seen in daylight. An alien landscape filled with indistinct shapes and eerie sounds. She understood why the villagers kept away between dusk and dawn. It was even darker when she reached the woods and she almost gave up and returned to the house. Then a sound ahead drew her on. If she could find Damien her journey would not have been wasted. There were many things about him that mystified her and she wanted to know more.

The trees thinned and she entered a glade, seeing the outline of broken walls, then she nearly died of fright as an owl suddenly swooped past, hooting, disturbed by a party of men who now approached the ruin. The light of a single lamp fell on Damien's face.

Quieting the mare and hardly daring to breathe, Maria hid among the trees. The men disappeared through the chapel entrance and she dropped from the saddle and tied the rein to a branch. Skirting the edge of the clearing and keeping to the shadows she slipped across the threshold. Moonlight pierced the centre of the church were once there had been a roof.

Damien and the other men were gathered there, deep in conversation. Maria crept closer.

'I need to check on the crypt,' growled one, who seemed to be the ringleader. He had a black-stubbled jaw, a slouch hat that partly obscured his face, and a long ragged coat. 'Haven't been down there since the last shipment.'

'It went well, Towser. No hitches and the cargo slipped away across country to London, Bristol and Taunton.' Damien was at his most haughty.

'A fine load, to be sure. I like giving the coastguards a run for their money. And when shall we be paid?' Towser's eyes flashed and he flexed his hands.

'Same as before. After the job is done.' Damien gave a slow, menacing smile. 'Have no thought of betrayal or it will be the worse for you. I have friends who are magistrates and will see to it that they catch you and hang you high. I'll even enjoy watching you swing.'

'And I could squeal on you, my lord,' Towser threatened, and his companions muttered and rattled their weapons.

'You won't. Not while you're making money. This may be the last venture for a while. We don't want the authorities getting suspicious.'

'Then it'll be back to smuggling tobacco, wine and silk,' Towser grunted. 'Not Frenchies who are spies, eh?'

'Don't tell me you're developing a conscience?' Damien sneered.

'No need to take that tone, cully. Your word's good enough for me. If you say you're going to pay us, then pay us you will.'

'You accept the word of a gentleman? What a buffle-headed clown to be sure.' This came from a man who was wearing soldierly gear. He had a sword at his hip and a pistol stuck in his belt. A cocked hat was tucked under one arm and his hair was plaited, like a hussar's.

Maria knew that if she was discovered her chances of survival were slim. These men were utterly ruthless, including Damien. Traitors to their country? She could well believe it.

'You trust no one because no one trusts you, Captain Chesney. I believe that's what you call yourself, though I swear you're no more an officer than I'm a Dutchman.' Not for an instant did Damien lose control of the smugglers and

Maria was forced to admire him.

'We're in this together, and you'd best not forget it,' Chesney growled, a chilling smile lifting the scar at the side of his mouth. 'Birds of a feather, my lord. We'd sell our own grandmothers for a penny. Gent you may be, but you're one of us at heart.'

Damien did not reply. He picked up the lantern, walked to a door and produced an iron key. There was a grinding clunk and then the hinges squealed as he pushed it open. The men crowded behind him and disappeared inside. Maria gave them a moment, then followed.

Her heart was pounding so hard she feared they might hear it, but they had already gone down the steps that wound below ground. Holding her skirt about her so it would not rustle, she began to descend. The steps were slippery and the walls encrusted with lichen, and there was that musty smell of a place that has been shut away from air and sunshine.

Maria stopped when she reached the bottom, hidden behind a buttress. Stone tombs occupied the centre of the crypt. Some of them were draped in mouldy pennants. Damien's henchmen glanced round uneasily.

'This is a cheerless place,' Chesney remarked, gripping the hilt of his sword.

Towser brazened it out. 'What are you afraid of, cap'n? Ghouls and ghosties?' He gave a loud laugh that bounced back from the walls.

Damien ignored them, went to one of the tombs and heaved at the heavy lid. It slid back revealing a dark aperture. The men gathered round, familiar with the secret passage. 'This is damned useful,' Towser commented. 'Wish I'd known about it years back. Would have made my life a bloody sight easier, bringing goods up this way from the cove.'

'Not without my permission,' Damien reminded. 'It's my property. Remember?'

'You're a cool customer, my lord.' Chesney looked at him with reluctant admiration. 'Betraying your country without a bat of the eyelid.'

Maria was finding it difficult to accept that Damien organised the entrance of spies into England and helped them to leave once their work was done. For this he must be receiving a large sum of money from the French. By now she had learned that he loved money and power above all else, but even so, his betrayal was hard to believe.

He disappeared into the tomb with the others following. They took the light with them and Maria fumbled her way back to where she had left her mare. Just as she got there she was seized from behind and a hand clapped over her mouth.

'Don't make a sound!' growled a masculine voice.

Chapter 12

'Oh my God! Charles!'

It really was him holding her. Incredible, wonderful, true! Maria didn't know whether to faint, burst into tears or both.

'Hush!' he whispered, gripping her even tighter. Slowly and carefully he led her and the mare back along the path, then took another turning. Disoriented, she had no idea where they were. All she could do was trust him, and this took a lot of doing after what she had just heard. Damien a traitor! Was anyone trustworthy?

Charles took her to a clearing where a woodsman's hut stood. It was dark and dilapidated but offered shelter. Once inside he was kissing her as if there was no tomorrow.

No time for explanations. He found a bed of hay in one corner and they were on it instantly, clothing tugged out of the way, limbs entwined. She parted her mouth for him, sobbing between the kisses, her tongue tangling with his. She pushed back his hair, wanting to see his face, but it was no more than a blur. Touch took the place of sight - touch and smell and hearing.

'My darling,' he murmured, cupping her breasts in his hands and lowering his head to suck the nipples.

'Don't talk. Just love me,' she entreated.

She got rid of her skirt and breeches and opened her body to him gratefully. Whatever game the gods were playing, at least they had granted her this moment of bliss. He stroked over her belly, hesitating when he discovered her shaven pubis. 'Who did this to you?' He sounded angry.

'Damien ordered it.'

'You were in agreement?'

'I was helpless to refuse.'

He spread himself over her as if he would possess her entirely and have no other man even look at her. She was hot for completion, but he took his time, parting her cleft and anointing her bud, and while his fingers worked their magic he licked her nipples, sending shocks all the way down her spine into her groin. The dried grass pricked her bare skin, the hut was a poor place for lovemaking, and yet to her it was more beautiful than a palace. She was with Charles and this was all that mattered.

He took her to the peak of pleasure, hovering there for a second and then rubbing her nubbin swiftly so that she tumbled over the brink, gasping and crying out with the joy of it. Then he spread her thighs, positioned himself above her and thrust. Maria clasped her arms round his neck and enfolded his waist with her legs. There was nothing she would keep from him, wanting to give him her entire self.

How could she ever have imagined that she was in love with Damien? And yet as Charles pumped into her his action put pressure on her anus, a sharp reminder of her guardian.

Then even his memory was blotted out by the surge of physical pleasure and tearful emotion that flooded her as Charles made her his. Her inner muscles were still convulsing from orgasm, and they clenched around his penis as he worked it in and out. He was beyond control now, chasing his release and

Maria wanted to give it to him, to pleasure him as he had just done her. Faster and faster he went, weight supported on his braced arms, head back, neck strained. Then, with a harsh cry, he spilled his libation into Maria. She felt it jet strongly, and then he sighed and collapsed on her, his face buried in her hair.

It was some minutes before he recovered and sat up, rearranging his breeches. Then, 'What are you doing here?' he asked.

'I was riding, and came across the chapel. Curious, I followed Damien inside and heard him plotting. I was making my escape when you found me. I thought you were in London. Were you looking for me?' Maria fumbled with the buttons of her upper garments.

'No. I have business in this neck of the woods.'

She was disappointed, hoping he had come for her sake. 'What business is that?'

He hesitated, then found her hand, smoothing the fingers. 'I shouldn't tell you. But maybe you're in danger. A warning won't go amiss.'

'Is it to do with what I overheard in the crypt? I don't understand,' and she recounted everything said between Damien and the others.

He sat beside her and held her hand and listened attentively, then, 'I've been on to Damien for some time, but have only lately discovered the ways and means by which he carries out his operations.'

'What is your part in all this? I thought you to be a rich young man about town.' She nestled her head into his shoulder, breathing in the scent of his hair.

He gave her a squeeze. 'Capital! That's what you were meant to believe, your aunt, too. I have studied art and intend to go on doing so, but I also served in the army, Maria. When I left, friends in governmental circles let it be known that they needed people like me to try and break the spy ring. They had suspicions that there were members of the elite involved.'

'Oh, it must be so dangerous!' she exclaimed, clinging to him.

'Not if you keep your wits about you. I have a first-class team working with me. I've been putting together a dossier concerning the viscount, but needed final proof. That's why I am here, having received information that he is planning a landing by night very soon.'

'Let me help,' she implored, sitting up and trying to be level-headed, pushing away thoughts of further sexual congress, although she was more than ready for a second bout.

He stiffened. 'I hesitate to involve you. It could put you in danger.'

'Damien won't suspect me. He's far too sure of my compliance. I can follow him, perhaps, eavesdrop again and convey his movements to you. Tranter will help me. You know him. He's a groom and my maid's suitor. They are both completely loyal, too.'

'I'm not sure...' He sounded doubtful. 'How would you feel if Damien was apprehended and convicted?'

'I don't want him hurt, but if he could be persuaded to hand over my affairs to my banker and leave the country, then I should be free to do as I liked.' The more she thought about it, the more convinced Maria became that what she truly wanted was her freedom.

'This might be possible. He has plantations in the West Indies, has he not? He could go into exile until the war with France is over. Very well, my brave girl, see what more you can find out, but don't put yourself in jeopardy. You are too precious to me for that.'

His words inspired her, and the thought of adventure was exhilarating. Had she been born a boy she was certain that she, too, would have been a soldier, performing deeds of derring-do. Now she had the opportunity to take part in a hazardous enterprise.

This excitement added to that already aroused by his presence, and she turned, put her arms round him, and urged him onto the hay again. Her breeches came down and his were unbuttoned and their bodies were united. Maria enjoyed it even more, for the edge had been taken from her appetite and she could relax and go slowly. She was the leader now, kneeling above him and impaling herself on his upright prick. Bumping and grinding she used a finger on her clit, adding to the powerful feeling of riding such a stallion. She came before him, and let him roll her over and finish on top.

It was time to go and she wanted to cry, but Charles said, 'Don't fret. I shall be in touch with you. If I can't come then Bates will bring a message, or my colleague, Quint. I don't think we shall have to wait a lot longer, but it depends on the weather. If the Channel is too rough, then the boat won't be able to sail.'

He helped her mount and walked with her to the stables, where she bent from the saddle to kiss him before he vanished into the darkness.

Though Maria was convinced she would not snatch a wink of sleep, her head had barely touched the pillow before she was plunged into dreams that were wild and disjointed. Then someone was shaking her by the shoulder.

She was in her bed at Raven Towers. Emily was bending over her, the sunshine streaming in at the mullioned windows. Maria had never been more thankful to see her.

'Milady, wake up. Goodness, what a noise you were making! And look at the bedclothes! Have you been fighting in your sleep?'

'Oh, Emily, good morning,' she muttered drowsily. It was a good morning - a good-to-be-alive morning. Charles had found her and fucked her and all was well with the world, until she remembered Damien's treachery and her own promise to spy on him.

Emily plumped the pillows at Maria's back, and set a silver tray on her knees. The fragrant smell of hot chocolate wafted up. 'Thank you, Emily,' Maria said, with a smile.

'All this gallivanting about at night,' Emily sniffed, but with a twinkle in her eye. 'What were you up to? The hem of your riding habit is muddy. It'll take me ages to get it clean.' Her expression said, 'Do you want to tell me about it?' But Maria thought it best to keep what she knew to herself.

She sipped the chocolate while Emily moved about, tidying the room. Maria knew she had to act normally. Damien must have no idea she suspected him. She was certain that Arabella knew nothing of his schemes and was engrossed in enjoying herself with country squires, grooms, farmhands, or whoever took her wayward fancy. Maria had no illusions about her aunt's morals.

She astonished herself by her calmness at breakfast. Damien was at the sideboard when she entered, helping himself to bacon, eggs and kedgeree. They were alone. Arabella was not an early riser.

A mist hung over the meadows. The large bay window had been opened wide and the scent of roses and honeysuckle was almost overpowering. Such a vision of peace, where the ambience was one of easy-going elegance. The great rooms, with their writing tables, armchairs and glass-fronted bookcases, seemed designed for gracious living, for leisure and lounging, for light chat and lazy days.

It was a charade!

The idea struck Maria vividly. Up until yesterday she had given him the benefit of the doubt, but was unable to avoid the truth any longer. Damien lived a lie. He was no more interested in country life than the man on the moon! It was a clever cover for his nefarious activities. And there he stood, forking sausages onto his plate as if he had never had a disloyal thought in his head.

As if aware of her concentration he turned and smiled, coming across and seating himself beside her. 'You're not eating. Can I offer you something?'

'I'm not hungry.' A footman paused behind her and she nodded. He tilted the steaming coffeepot and poured the pungent liquid into her cup. The cream jug and sugar bowl appeared at her elbow.

Maria found it hard to pretend. She stirred the coffee, watching the cream transform its blackness into beige, and wondered how she was going to find the strength to do as Charles had asked. It was all very well to talk of it when Damien was not there, but once in his presence she found herself overwhelmed by his charisma.

'How much longer are we to remain here?' she asked, lightly.

'Are you missing the shops and theatres and balls?' He answered her question with another.

'Perhaps. There is little to do in the country.' She deliberately made herself sound like a peevish child.

He snapped his fingers at the footman, who stepped forward and filled his cup. 'You think so? I find it mighty entertaining. But we can't have you dying of ennui. That would never do. I promised to take you hunting, didn't I? Let us do it this morning.'

Maria was startled. Damien always seemed to catch her unawares. 'But I shall need to go to my room and change,' she prevaricated, laying her napkin on the table.

'Don't bother about that. Come as you are. It's a fine day and such a flimsy gown will make me think you are a nymph fleeing from me.'

'What do you mean?' Maria had risen, but now she hesitated, her hand resting on the back of the chair.

He stood too, taller by several inches, a lean, dark, masterful man. 'I mean, sweetheart, that we are about to play a game in which you will be my quarry. I shall give you a head start and then pursue you, my hounds picking up your scent. We sometimes indulge in this sport, the hunt and I, and there are several ladies who just adore being our prey. When they are caught, and believe me they always are, then they receive suitable punishment. Are you ready for this, Maria?'

Several excuses flashed through her head; she had a migraine or stomach ache, her aunt wanted her to go calling with her, but she was aware he would accept none of these. 'All right, I'm ready,' she said, with impressive hauteur.

Damien bowed, smiled and saluted her. 'Then let us go.'

She followed him to the stable where Tranter cast a worried eye over her as he helped her into the saddle. She was in no way dressed for the outdoors, her muslin gown and kid leather slippers unsuitable for riding. Damien was wearing buckskin breeches, a black cloth coat and a three-cornered hat. He led the way after whistling up two of his hounds. They were big animals, with slavering jaws and noses that twitched as if already scenting a fox or a deer - or a human being.

Maria watched them dubiously, cursing her impetuosity that had agreed to this rash venture.

They rode to the spinney and there he halted and told her to dismount. She did so, watching as he tethered her mount, then took her shawl and held it out to the dogs who sniffed it eagerly. He handed it back to her, and said as he took out his pocket-watch, 'Get you gone, Maria. Run as fast as you can and put distance between myself and the hounds. I will give you fifteen minutes start.'

I must be mad, she thought as she broke into a quick walk. What do I hope to achieve? Maybe I can lull him into a false sense of security, so that he is convinced I am his creature, willing to do anything he desires and never, ever question his actions.

The spinney was peaceful, sunlight pouring between the branches, making patterns on the grass. She quickened her pace, dodging and twisting as she reached open ground. In the distance came the clarion call of a hunting horn and the baying of hounds. Maria was possessed with terror, though trying desperately to keep calm. This is how an animal must feel when it is being chased, she thought, and remembered reading somewhere about escaped slaves or convicts being hunted by bloodhounds.

She picked up her skirt and started to run. Coming out on the open moor she found nowhere to hide. Over her shoulder she could see Damien, but he was a long way off. A copse presented itself on her right and she plunged towards it, even though there was boggy land between herself and shelter. Carefully skirting the marsh she managed to avoid being sucked in, sweating and panting, hearing the horn and the hounds, stumbling through bracken, with brambles tearing at her clothes and her feet sore with no protection save the thin leather slippers.

If the dogs get me I shall be savaged! She panicked, sure that those nightmare beasts would soon be on her. Damien would not let them bite her, would he? Spurred on by the idea that he might, she was running as fast as the uneven terrain allowed. No longer a pleasant spot, the moor had become a thing that seemed intent on hindering her, tripping her feet, snagging her skirt, delaying her like some malignant spirit. She reached the spinney, rushing along the path that wound through it, hoping to conceal herself in the shrubs and trees.

Crouching in the undergrowth she kept very still, though her heart was hammering and her breathing was rapid. The horn was closer and so were the voices of the dogs and the thud of hooves. Maria reached for a stick that lay close by. It was solid and heavy, a branch broken from a tree during a storm. At least she would give the hounds a fight before they overpowered her.

They were in the spinney, crashing and snuffling, following her trail. She glanced above her, but there was no way in which she could scale one of the trees. Instead she rose, put her back against the bole and lifted the stick. With a crashing of undergrowth and triumphal barking the largest of the hounds hurled himself on her. Maria hit him hard on the muzzle, drawing blood. He yelped and backed off, snarling ferociously. The second dog launched himself into the attack and Maria caught him a blow on the side of the head, but he was not to be deterred, his jaws fastening round a fold of her skirt, tugging and drawing her closer to those hideous teeth and salivating jaws.

She struck out at him again, but he seized the stick in his teeth and wrenched it from her grasp, then sprang at her, bringing her to the ground. The other dog recovered his courage and joined in. Maria was rolled beneath their smelly bodies, arms in front of her face, striving to protect herself from those murderous fangs. Her clothing was being ripped from her, their claws and teeth damaging her skin. She screamed and shouted and cursed, but could feel resistance draining from her.

Then a hand reached down and grabbed her arm, pulling her to her feet and away from the dogs who cowed back as Damian shouted, 'Leave it! Rex! Rufus! To heel!' They retreated, still growling, but his upraised crop was enough to silence them, and a couple of swift blows had them whimpering and shrinking back.

Maria was shaking from head to foot, the ordeal robbing her of strength but not courage. 'How could you?' she stormed, a wild-eyed termagant.

'Tut! Tut! It was but a jest!' he protested, touching the tip of her breast, bared where the bodice had been torn.

'A jest! Are you mad? I could have been killed by those brutes.'

'No, no. They are harmless as babes,' he said, patting their heads where they lay on the grass, gazing up at him with soulful eyes. 'Aren't you, my boys? Faithful Rufus and brave Rex. Come, stroke them my dear Maria.'

'Go to hell!' she grated, and started to march off the way she had come.

He was beside her in a flash, jerking her round to face him. 'Where do you think you're going?'

She tore her arm free. 'To find my horse.'

'Oh, no you're not. You have to be chastised first.'

'Why? I haven't done anything deserving of punishment.'

'It's part of the game, Maria.'

'For you, maybe.' She stood her ground, glaring up at him. Her green eyes and fiery hair seemed to be sparking with it.

Damien permitted himself a quirky smile. 'Come, come. Admit that this has your blood racing and set your cunt aflame. I'm about to administer a suitable reprimand.'

She fought him like a feral cat, but he was too strong for her, dragging her towards a tree stump. 'Damn you!' she swore as he pushed her down and, with one hand on her neck and a knee at the back of her legs, forced her to bend over it.

He held her arms behind her and slipped a noose around her wrists. She was on her knees, the stump's roots digging in painfully as Damien made her lie across it, breasts pressed into the knobbly surface. Her skirt had been torn by the dogs, but he lifted what remained of it and she felt cold air on her bare buttocks. He exchanged his crop for a many-thonged taws.

Looking across she could see the horse cropping the turf and the hounds scratching at fleas or licking their genitals. Then all her attention was focused on the eruption of agony as Damien's taws struck her backside. She cried out, but there was no one to come to her aid, the hounds and the horse busy about their own concerns, no Charles there to save her this time. As when Damien had whipped her before she tried to absorb the pain, waiting in fearful anticipation for the next blow, not one lash but several, working in harmony to inflict as much distress as possible.

And it came, as sure as night follows day. Damien wielded the implement with masterly skill, never striking the same place twice, hitting her right buttock, then her left, the backs of her thighs, her waist and tethered arms. A multitude of red stripes fanned out. She was pressed into the stump's rough bark, seeing a cluster of fungi at its base and a little pool of dew in a crevice, trying to fix her attention on anything except the awful anticipation of the next lightning strike.

This was the worst part, this tense waiting. She was never sure when it would come. Sometimes seconds went by in silence, the clearing almost normal, filled with birdsong and sunlight and she began to hope he had finished. Then she would hear the swish, the rush of air, and feel the blow that numbed her before breaking into a hellish agony.

Urine escaped her, trickling down her inner thighs to nourish the stump's root, but she was beyond caring. He came closer, running a hand over her welts. She was too numb to feel anything. He reached round and jabbed the handle of the taws into her mouth. 'Suck it, my beauty. Suck your master's toy as you will soon suck his cock!'

It tasted of leather and she soaked it with her spit. When Damien's organ took its place she sucked that too, inhaling the salty smell of him, and the tartness of his jism on her tongue, and the feel his hairy balls jiggling against her chin as she performed fellatio. He withdrew before he climaxed, going behind her, freeing her arms and inserting his erection into her vagina.

The pain faded, swallowed up in the delirious pleasure of feeling him inside her. She knew she was betraying Charles, but desire overwhelmed scruples. It was as if Damien and she were the only man and woman on earth, like Adam and Eve in The Garden of Eden. And where was the serpent? Damien must be him, as well as portraying Adam. The glade was like a golden bowl, brimming with sunshine, and Damien's rhythmical strokes were soothing and arousing, the pain subsiding. He knew what she wanted, a hand cradling her crotch, his middle digit masturbating her nubbin. She held her breasts, thumbs revolving on the nipples and her moans changed to urgent cries of need as the pathway to climax opened before her.

Damien pumped and lunged and frigged her organ until they were both ready and, as she came, so did he, and they were united in bliss. He sighed, slowed, but held her against him, and his lips caressed that erotic spot at the top of her spine. If only things were different, she mourned. If he was more like Charles and less of a reprobate, but then he would not be so fascinating. It is his very badness that is so attractive.

He withdrew his cock without a word and, as she had received no further instructions, Maria got up from her sore knees and tried to wrap her torn dress around her. Silently Damien handed her his jacket. He swung her onto the front of his saddle and mounted behind her, and then he whistled to the dogs that got lazily to their feet, and followed his horse as it clopped from the spinney and headed for home.

Arabella was luxuriating in a bath of warm water. It was all very well dallying with sons of the soil, but although she enjoyed the smell of sweat and raw sex while they were fucking, she needed to get rid of it as soon as they had discharged into her. The groom had been entertaining, a handsome lad who thought himself a fine, randy stud, until he came up against her sophistication and expertise. He left before dawn, dazed and worshipping at her shrine, and fully equipped to pleasure the village maidens and most of their mothers too.

She had sent her calling card, via the post-boy, to the rectory, announcing her intention of taking tea with the rector's wife that afternoon. She envisaged a leisurely hour or so dressing for the occasion. Maria should come with her, learning how to comport herself among the lower orders. Her maid, Kitty, was hovering in attendance. They understood one another very well, Arabella receiving unquestioning obedience and giving the maid numerous benefits in return.

Arabella ran her soapy hands over the length of her body, rousing the nipples into crests, and following the line of her rounded belly and dimpled navel to the dark groove that split her shaven mound. She rested her head on the rim of the bath, gazing down as she parted her thighs and played with the rings piercing her labial wings. The sensation quickly communicated with that most sensitive of organs, her clitoris. With her other hand she parted her labia and stretched it open. Her swollen bud stood out proud and she tickled it into even greater stiffness and prominence.

More soap was needed to make it silky smooth. She applied the scented bar to her slit, moving her hips against it, the water sloshing slightly, a moan escaping her lips at the spasm of pleasure that made her ache. Consumed with perfect delight she closed her eyes and became one with her sturdy little organ that always provided her with immense satisfaction whether she was with a man, a woman or alone.

'Ah,' she sighed, so close to orgasm that she held off for a moment, wanting the feeling to die back so that she might have the pleasure of bringing it on again. She guessed Kitty was watching with a hand up under her skirt, frigging her love-bud. This image heated Arabella's blood so much that she had to take her finger away, lest she come.

A knock on the boudoir door roused her from her sensual musings and she heard Kitty leave the bathroom and answer it. This was followed by the murmur of voices, Kitty's and a man's, and then the maid returned, saying, 'There's a Mr Robin Claremont wishing to see Lady Maria. He claims to be a friend of Lady Jane Dunn.'

Arabella opened her eyes. They sparkled with mischief. 'Does he, indeed? What sort of person is he, Kitty? Young, old, ugly or personable?'

Kitty pulled a thoughtful face. 'Mid-twenties, I could say, milady. Tall, with brown hair and eyes and most pleasant features. But the thing is, he's a cleric, or so he said.'

Arabella stood up, the water cascading over her voluptuous curves. 'Indeed. A person of principle, no doubt. Ask him to step inside. I can resist anything but temptation, Kitty, and a man of the cloth is a challenge.'

Robin waited in an elaborately draped, very feminine room. It was redolent of perfume, face-paints, hair pomade, and woman. He remained standing, nervously turning his hat round and round in his hands. The maid who had let him in was pert, pink-cheeked and confident. She had made him feel inadequate, and done nothing to raise his confidence in the outcome of his mission. Only love for Jane buoyed him up and kept him going during the journey by stagecoach from Bath to Dorset, and the sojourn in a tavern at Parnham Combe, where he had hired a horse to ride to Raven Towers.

The supercilious butler had looked down his nose and told him that Lady Maria and Viscount Strafford were out, but that Lady Arabella would see him. He had been conducted up the grand staircase by a uniformed flunky.

The very last thing he had expected was for this beautiful woman to sweep through from the bathroom wearing nothing but a white towel. Utterly confused, he bowed, 'Your ladyship.' He kept his eyes anywhere but on her person. Sirens from the Scriptures sashayed in front of his mind's eye - The Queen of Sheba - Delilah - Jezebel!

His cock responded to these images. It was embarrassing and he held his hat before him. Arabella gave him a radiant smile, and held out her hand for him to kiss. 'I apologise for being dishabille,' she said with a winsome smile, her voice low and mellifluous. 'I was taking a bath.'

Robin could feel his cheeks burning. He had never been in such intimate surroundings with a woman before. 'It is I who must ask your pardon for disturbing you at your ablutions.'

She disposed herself on a rose-pink brocade daybed, hair loosened about her bare shoulder, the towel slipping and displaying more of her than was perhaps seemly. But her manner was so casual and she gave the impression of being perfectly at ease, that when she suggested he sit by her, it sounded like the most natural thing in the world.

'Now then, Mr Claremont, and why are you here?' she asked, signalling to Kitty, who brought forward two glasses of sherry.

'I have a message for Lady Maria, from her friend, Lady Jane.' This was true enough, but when Robin thought of the contents of the letter his uneasiness increased. No doubt Lady Arabella would be as shocked as Jane's mother by his temerity in asking her to marry him.

'I haven't seen her this morning, but understand she has gone riding with her guardian. You can leave the letter with me,' Arabella suggested, and the tip of her pink tongue crept out to lick the sherry from her lips.

Robin's discomfort increased. This was the first time he had entered the bower of a highborn, fashionable lady, the glimpse of creamy skin and the honey-sweet tone of her voice seducing him from his purpose. He loved Jane with all his heart, but this was a situation the like of which he had never experienced and was totally unprepared.

'Thank you, my lady. You are very kind. Lady Jane will be so pleased,' he stammered. 'But she did charge me to place it in her hands myself.'

'Oh dear, don't you trust me?' Arabella's eyes widened and her lips pouted.

'Of course! I am just doing as Lady Jane instructed,' he replied, his colour heightening even more.

'Your loyalty is very commendable,' she said, leaning against his shoulder, the towel slipping lower, almost baring one nipple. Robin found it impossible to avert his eyes. She touched the side of his cheek. 'Why are you staring at me?'

'I'm sorry, my lady, but you are so beautiful, like a Greek statue... Aphrodite, perhaps.'

'Flatterer! My word, you should be at Court, your talents are wasted on the church. I grow weary of the beaux who spend so much time on their appearances that they forget the ladies they are trying to impress.'

'I have already given my life to God,' he answered seriously. 'But I would do anything to help a friend.'

'Very commendable.' She gave a sultry smile. 'Do you mean anything?'

'As long as it was within the law.' Robin felt a gutless fool, but Arabella was like no one he had ever met. She was behaving like a slut but with the air of an empress. He jumped when her hand rested on his thigh, but could not prevent the thickening of his penis.

'So, you are member of the clergy?' Her fingers were creeping closer and closer to his crotch.

He cleared his throat. 'That is correct. I'm about to take up my first post as a curate.'

'I'm sure you'll not stop there. I can see you rising...'

'You can?' Robin cursed his wayward cock for betraying him.

'Oh, yes.' She glanced down meaningfully, and then added, 'To the rank of vicar, or rector, even bishop. Would you like your own manse? Perhaps you have ambitions to marry.'

This brought him up sharply. Jane! Oh, God, he was forgetting Jane! But he hardly dared move, his weapon so primed it was likely to explode at any second. Arabella rubbed against him sinuously, her smile indicating that she was well aware of his discomfort.

Robin tore himself away with a supreme effort. He stood doubled over, clutching himself, willing that unsightly protuberance to subside. Arabella arched her back and the towel slid down, baring her to the fork. Robin came in his breeches. She watched his spasms and the wet stain that spread across the front of the black cloth. As she did so she licked her finger and caressed her clitoris, a musing smile curving her poppy-red lips.

Kitty, who had been observing the drive from her position in the window embrasure, suddenly said, 'They have returned, milady. The viscount and Lady Maria are heading for the stables.'

'Emily must tell her that she has a visitor,' Arabella instructed, then arched a slender eyebrow at Robin. 'You may use my bathroom to freshen up. It wouldn't be proper for you to meet my niece in that state, now would it?

Chapter 13

When Maria arrived in the stable she was greeted by Emily who said, 'My lady, Mr Claremont is here to see you.'

Damien dismounted and Maria slid from the saddle into his arms. 'Robin Claremont?'

'Yes, my lady.'

Damien gave Maria an intent stare. 'He's a friend of Jane's,' she explained rapidly, freeing herself from him and wrapping her shawl closely around her to hide the torn dress.

Damian scowled. 'What does he want?'

'I shan't know that until I've seen him, shall I? Where is he, Emily?'

'With her ladyship.'

The notion of Robin left to Arabella's tender mercies was a worrying one. He would be like a lamb led to the slaughter. Emily looked flushed and agitated, but Maria could not question her further with Damien looking on. All she wanted was to creep to her room, bathe and change. She felt soiled, her juices and Damien's wetting the insides of her thighs. She was also deeply ashamed of herself, feeling that she had betrayed Charles. More than anyone else she needed Jane, and hoped that Robin had brought good news from her.

'Go and tell him I will be with him shortly, Emily,' she said, and turned on her heel, left the stable and ran up the backstairs to the part of the house where her bedchamber was situated.

Sarah was waiting anxiously. 'Oh, my dear soul! Look at the state of you,' she cried, as agitated as a hen over her one chick. 'What have you been doing?'

'Hunting with the viscount.' Maria wanted to avoid too close an inspection.

'Dressed like that? Whatever possessed you?'

'We went on impulse.'

'Well, it's not right or proper,' Sarah continued to complain. 'Viscount or no, he has some very strange ideas, I must say.'

Maria changed the subject. 'I need to cleanse myself.'

'I'll summons the footmen to fill the tub.'

'There isn't time. Mr Claremont is waiting to see me. I hope he has news of Lady lane. I'll make do with a wash. Leave me. I'd rather manage alone.' Maria succeeded in shaking her off, only permitting her to enter the bathroom briefly to bring in a jug of hot water.

It was rare for her to wish for privacy and she knew that Sarah was suspicious. Examining her naked body in the mirror, she was glad she had insisted. There were blue bruises, long scratches and scarlet weals. Her stockings were torn and the dainty slippers ruined, their thin soles offering little protection for her feet. Damien had had his will of her and no mistake. Why then, didn't she hate him?

She washed herself all over, paying particular attention to her cleft. The pubic hair was stubbly and uncomfortable and she would need Russell's razor again soon. In some ways she yearned to be an innocent girl again, and yet the lessons she had learned at her master's hands, and those of his enemy, Charles, were ones she would not have missed for anything.

Returning to the bedroom wrapped in a towel, she succeeded in slipping into her chemise while Sarah was otherwise occupied. A leaf-green muslin dress followed, and Sarah fastened the ball buttons at the back. Still chilled by her recent experiences, Maria slipped her arms into a velvet jacket in a deeper shade. It fitted closely and was short-waisted. Sarah attended to her hair, coiling it high at the back and pulling out little curling tendrils to cover her ears and nape. Pendant pearl earrings followed, and a matching necklace.

'Don't fuss,' Maria snapped impatiently. 'I must go down. It is important that I see Mr Claremont.'

The butler led her to the solar, a pleasant, airy room where once ladies of the family would have gathered to sew and gossip and pass idle hours. Maria was accompanied by Sarah, who occupied a window seat with a book on her lap in which she appeared to be absorbed. Robin rose to meet Maria when she entered and she led him to the far side so they could talk without her chaperone overhearing.

'Is Jane well?' This was Maria's first concern.

'Oh, yes. Don't worry on that score.' Robin was fresh-faced and boyish, and Maria took comfort from this. Surely Arabella would have been unable to seduce him? In his black frock-coat and white collar, he looked every inch a clergyman.

'Tell me all that has been taking place,' she insisted as they sat on a chaise-longue by a low, brass-inlaid table, and she poured tea from a silver pot into bone china-cups. He glanced towards Sarah, but Maria put his mind at rest. 'Don't be alarmed, she won't hear us and even if she does, she is loyal to me.'

'I have spoken with Lady Rowena, and she absolutely forbids me to court Jane. This means it is no use approaching her Papa, so we are planning to elope to Gretna Green.' He sounded angry, but not despairing, his voice firm and resolute.

Maria clapped her hands. 'How romantic! Once the deed is done, then they can no longer keep you apart.'

'This is true, and I have a post where I can take my wife. Read what Jane has to say,' and he drew a letter from an inside pocket and passed it to her.

Maria broke the seal, tore open the envelope and unfolded the single sheet of paper. Jane had written in her elegant copper-plate hand, *My dearest Friend, I am dispatching Robin with this, and hope it finds you in good health, as am I. Mama has refused to allow us to marry and we have planned to run away together. Alas, neither of us have money to finance this venture. I hope you won't think it presumptuous if I ask you for help. I have no one else to whom I can turn. Of course, this will be a loan and we shall pay you back as soon as we are able. Any amount, no matter how small, will be greatly appreciated. With much love, from your obedient servant, Jane.*

Tears welled up in Maria's eyes and her heart bled for her friend's distress. How could parents be so blind? Robin was such a sincere, upright man and they were so obviously well suited. She remembered the hundred guineas she had won from Damien.

'I will gladly help you, Robin,' she said, folding the letter. 'Fortunately I have money in the house. Emily shall fetch it.'

She dispatched Sarah to the door to call Emily, who waited outside. It took but a minute for her to receive her instructions and, within a short while, she returned with Maria's reticule. It was simple for Maria to draw Robin into the bay window and there, out of sight of Sarah, pass over a purse. He kissed her hand.

'I don't know how to thank you,' he muttered, his eyes moist with tears.

'Think nothing of it,' she returned. 'One day, when Burrington Manor is once more in my control, perhaps I can arrange for you to be appointed vicar of the village church. It would be so nice to have Jane living close to me.'

'You are too good, and we shall be forever in your debt.'

'Will you return to Bath now?' There was a worry nibbling at the edge of Maria's mind.

'That is my intention. Why? Can I do something for you?'

It occurred to her to tell him about Charles and the foiling of Damien's unlawful intentions, but then thought better of it. The least number of people who knew about it the better. Even so, 'It would help me if you could stay for a few more days,' she said. 'Let me know where you are and if I need you, as well I may, I shall send Tranter.'

'I'll be honoured. He can reach me at the Blue Boar tavern in Parnham Combe, some three miles hence.' He bowed and she walked with him to the door, unwilling to let him go, a link with Jane and the world outside of Raven Towers.

'Who is this fellow who came a-calling on Maria?' Damien demanded as he stalked into Arabella's chamber.

'Oh, stop fretting! You remember Lady Jane?'

'I do. An innocent, who needed a thorough rogering.' Damien flashed her a wicked smile.

'You're incorrigible,' she scolded, reclining on the couch. 'I think this Robin Claremont is wooing her, or hopes to. He's a member of the clergy, an attractive man who could not contain his ardour when with me and spurted in his breeches.'

Damien threw back his head and laughed loudly. 'And you call me incorrigible! I swear you'd make a saint spill his seed! What did you do? Did you kiss him, toy with his prick? What?'

'I did next to nothing, my dear. He was ripe for it, and is no doubt suffering the torments of the damned and doing penance at this very moment. But enough of me. What have you been up to? Sit, and tell me all about it.' She patted the space beside her.

He accepted this invitation, aware that it would probably lead to intercourse, but wary of her. Arabella knew nothing of his association with the French. He firmly believed she would never betray him, but was not prepared to take the risk. Therefore he assumed a bored air, shrugging as he answered, 'Oh, this and that. Whenever I come here there is my estate manager to consult, my tenants to see, quarrels among them to be placated, as well as catching up with old friends.'

'You prefer to be in London or abroad?' Arabella's slim fingers ruffled the curls at the back of his neck.

He reached out and caressed her breasts. 'Each has its own particular interest, and wherever I am I enjoy the pleasures on offer.' He bared her nipples, which grew hard under his clever fingers.

'Oh, Damien, if only you could be faithful to one woman. I'd be yours for the rest of my days,' she sighed, body quivering.

He chuckled and bent to suck those ardent teats. 'You are a charming liar, my love. You know damn fine that you're as inconstant as myself.' And though he was enjoying the banter and foreplay, his main intention was to divert her from questioning him.

It was almost time, the tide right, the weather calm and the fishing boat sailing from Calais. If all went without a hitch then soon the passengers would land and be dispersed about the country, the boat returning whence it came, and Damien's part carried out successfully.

He warmed as he thought of it. It was a lucrative side-line. The French paid well for the privilege of smuggling their agents in and out of the country. He knew he was playing with fire, but had arrangements in place for a quick exit to a bolthole in the Caribbean where he owned a flourishing sugar plantation, manned by slaves. If need be he could reside there for years, as that particular piece of paradise was under Spanish rule and was beholden to neither England nor France.

Arabella drew his attention back to the present. She was kneeling between his spread knees and had his breeches undone. He looked down and saw the pleasing spectacle of his cock rising towards her face. She was studying it, stretching back the foreskin, admiring its size and the blue veins that knotted the stem. With a deep-throated purr she opened her mouth and took the helm between her lips. Damien forgot the French, his island, and every other consideration, lost in sensation as she brought him to a thunderous climax.

'I hope you had a wash before entertaining me,' he said breathlessly, as his heart slowed and the pleasure spasms passed. 'I know you've been spending time with common louts.'

'And you have, no doubt, been consorting with trollops,' she answered acidly. 'At least the louts were man enough to satisfy me, which you haven't bothered to do.'

'I want to see you play with yourself,' he said, making no attempt to touch her but, his own lust appeased, watching as she opened her thighs, exposed her slit and stroked her clitoris till she moaned and yelped and brought herself off.

They sat together in the afterglow, and he was prepared to indulge her and let her believe that he cared for her, when in reality it was far from the truth. Damien cared for no one but himself. Even as they sipped sherry wine and chatted lightly, so his mind was already streaking ahead to the evening s events. He was expecting a message from Captain Chesney. If all went according to plan he would be joining him and the rest of the gang at the ruined chapel after dark.

Maria was walking in the garden. She had arranged for Sarah to be with her, but had left her in the summerhouse and slipped away on her own. In her heart she was hoping that Charles might be somewhere about. The heat was going from the sun now and soon it would be autumn. Damien was talking of returning to London soon, and by this she guessed he was expecting his task to be completed before long.

He was a secretive individual and she had not been able to worm any information out of him, but by his preoccupied demeanour she assumed there was more than the mere running of the estate on his mind. Hopefully matters would come to a head for then, if necessary, she would send Tranter to Robin and enlist his aid.

She paused at a stile that led into a meadow, drinking in the sight of the lush green grass, the patient liver and white cows, and the trees that were beginning to shed their leaves. They lay like an amber, rust and yellow carpet on the path. Maria was lost in contemplation, and then became aware that she was not alone. Arms came around her from behind.

She recognised the man who held her. 'What are you doing here?'

Charles turned her to face him and she had never been more pleased to see anyone. 'Keep your voice low, sweetheart,' he cautioned, and then kissed her, the touch of his lips, the feel of his strong body intoxicating her.

He raised his head and looked down at her. 'I had to see you. To know that you were so near and yet so far tormented me and kept me from my duty.'

'Have you any news? When will this be over?'

'Very soon, beloved. Has Strafford divulged anything?'

'No. He is close as a clam, and I'm sure Lady Arabella knows nothing.' Maria's guilt was ruining this encounter. Supposing he had come upon her and Damien when they were coupling in the glade yesterday?

'We are confident that there will be a landing tonight. Our informants have picked up on it. The conditions are right. We shall be waiting.'

'Is there anything I can do to help?' Maria gripped him tightly, the thought of him going into danger terrifying her. 'I have a friend staying at Parnham Combe. You remember Robin Claremont, who we met in London? He came to me with a letter from Jane. I asked him to stay for a day or so in case we needed his help. I could send Tranter to him.'

'There is no need. My men are ready. Just stay safe and don't take any risks, Maria.'

He pressed her back against the stile and she was like putty in his hands, her flesh forgetting Damien and its recent union with him. Though afraid that someone might see them she urged Charles on, her mouth opening under his. He clasped her round the buttocks, pulling her to him, and she wrinkled up her skirt, baring her sex, and then slipped down the front of her bodice. She could feel the roughness of his coat chaffing her nipples and sending shockwaves of delight through her. He freed the hard bough of his cock from the restriction of his breeches and lifted Maria to the first railing where she opened her legs, enabling him to penetrate her.

She wriggled her pubis on the base of his penis, but could not reach completion until he inserted a hand between them and stimulated her nubbin. Grinding against his fingers, she was distracted by their exposure but fell into the rhythm of his regular penetration, her passion rising until she reached an explosive orgasm.

'My sweet girl,' he muttered and increased his thrusts, arriving at fulfilment shortly after her.

Maria was flustered, pushing him away and sliding from her perch, wanting nothing so much as to cover herself. 'I must go. My chaperone will come looking for me.'

He grinned at her, confining his prick in his breeches once more. 'Soon, my love, we shall dispense with a duenna. I want to marry you, Maria. What do you say?'

Her heart leaped, but there was something holding her back and she did not know what. 'How dear of you to ask me,' she said, kissing his smooth-shaven cheek. 'We must talk of this when the danger is over. There is the problem of Damien. He will never give his consent.'

'Damien will not be here, if my plans come to fruition.' Charles's face was stern, and Maria saw another side of him - the soldier and man of action who could be ruthless.

It thrilled her, yet made her afraid. Does one ever really know another human being? she wondered. Aren't there always unplumbed depths? Charles must have killed men during the course of his military career. She had seen him fencing with Damien when both of them wanted to slaughter the other. And yet they could walk, talk and comport themselves as gentlemen. It was a mystery, but looking into her own soul, she admitted that she was capable of avoiding the truth and deceiving; witness her behaviour with Damien and Charles.

His hands on her were tender and he kissed her gently in farewell. 'Keep safe, Maria, and I will contact you when tonight is over. Farewell, beloved.'

Dusk came and the dinner hour passed, with Arabella, Damien and Maria seated formally at table, waited on by a fleet of footmen. When the last course had been served he rose and pushed back his chair. 'Excuse me, ladies, but I have business this evening. My agent needs to discuss the harvest supper with me,' he told them.

'That's too tedious of you, Damien,' Arabella pouted, tossing her napkin aside and reaching for her wine glass. 'What am I supposed to do?'

'I've thought of that, my dear, and have arranged for Squire Longbridge, his lady wife and several friends to drive over and play cards. Does that suit you?'

'Indeed it does. Can you lend me money? Cards are no fun without gambling,' she responded, all smiles again. 'Will you join us, Maria?'

She shook her head. 'I think I'll go to bed early.'

She was highly suspicious of Damien's actions, more and more convinced that he was expecting the boat to arrive in the cove. If she went to her room, knowing that Arabella was fully engaged in gambling, once Sarah was asleep or engaged with a lover, she could go to the chapel and join in the excitement. Charles had forbidden her, but she was unwilling to miss any action, almost deciding to send Tranter to Robin, yet not quite sure if this was a false alarm.

Instead of going upstairs she decided to follow Damien. There was a crowd in the hall, the squire and his friends arriving, all loud voices, laughter and bonhomie. He greeted them warmly, apologizing because he could not stay, and she succeeded in slipping out of the hall and down the stairs to the servants' domain and there reaching the yard. It was filled with those attending to the visitors' carriages and horses. Maria hid behind a stable door. Soon the coachmen and postilions, who were in for a long wait, were invited into the kitchen. It was then that she caught sight of Captain Chesney sneaking through a side gate. A moment later he was joined by Damien.

She stood as if rooted to the spot, straining to hear what they were saying, but their voices were muffled. Then Damien led Chesney towards the stable and she shrank back into the gloom. 'Come inside,' she heard him say. 'Tell me your news.'

They were so close to Maria that she could see the scar that distorted the mercenary's face, and Damien's dark, handsome features illumined by a lantern.

'It's all coming together as sweet as a nut,' Chesney growled. 'We've had word from our fishermen that La Rondine will be anchoring in the cove about ten. There will be a rowing boat ready.'

'Splendid!' Damien clapped him on the shoulder. 'Go back now and I'll follow you. My horse is already saddled and waiting.'

They disappeared into the darkness.

Maria climbed the ladder leading to the rooms above usually occupied by those who cared for the horses, maintained the vehicles and drove their employers from place to place. She found Tranter there in his shirtsleeves. He leapt up on seeing her, reaching for his jacket.

She put a finger to her lips. 'I'm going out, Tranter,' she said. 'If I'm not back by midnight find Mr Claremont at the Blue Boar, say that I need him and then both of you ride to the ruined chapel.'

'But, my lady...' Tranter blurted out.

'Just do as I say, and don't tell Emily. Now saddle my mare.'

Once again she was not suitably attired for riding but could think of no excuse for changing at this late hour. Sarah would be sure to ask questions. As it was there would be a hue and cry once she was missed, and this would happen when her duenna realised she was not with Lady Arabella.

She had grabbed a cloak on the way out and slung it around her shoulders. Tranter gave her a leg up into the saddle. She had decided to ride astride, hitching her skirt high and tucking it between her knees. He was looking anxious, shaking his head at her daring and she smiled at him, trying to be reassuring.

'It's all right, Tranter. Just do as I ask.'

She jerked the rein, clicked her tongue and the mare moved off at a walk. Once beyond the boundaries of the house Maria urged her into a trot, mindful that she must keep a safe distance between herself and Damien. A gibbous moon hung in the sky and the pathway was shadowed, but the mare was sure-footed and Maria knew the way. She slowed, listening intently for any sounds ahead, but the only stirrings were those of creatures using the cover of darkness to find food.

So far so good, she thought, hardly daring to believe her luck. She had reached the trail that led to the chapel and realised that she had no plan formulated. What had seemed an adventure became a risky operation. It was all very well wanting to bring Damien to book, but she should have left it to those better equipped to do so. For the first time fear gripped her and she almost turned back.

Then she heard the jingle of harness ahead and curiosity overcame caution. She dismounted and tethered her horse, then moved forward stealthily, wishing she had been able to arm herself. Where was Charles? Could it be that Damien had been misinformed and the fishing boat carrying its illicit cargo delayed? There were so many variables and all she could do was follow her instincts and track the gang.

The chapel's ruined spire pointed to the moon like an accusing finger, but all was dark and still. Maria entered the nave and found the door to the crypt. In was unlocked. She almost turned and ran, but that inquisitive streak that had ever been her bane made her go on. She knew the way down the spiral staircase and caught the murmur of voices, recognising Damien's among them. Then they grew fainter and she guessed they were entering the tomb and descending to the cave, there to greet imports that were as illegal as brandy, silks, tobacco and wine. More so, for the smugglers were performing a traitorous act that threatened their country.

Maria climbed into the tomb and followed the tiny glow coming up from far below. The steps were uneven and it was as if she was descending into a desolate pit of hell. She followed the light like a moth to a flame. The voices grew louder. Concentrating on trying to catch what was being said Maria lost her footing, tripping down the last few steps and landing at the feet of a man who was guarding the entrance to a large cave.

There was an uproar as he dragged her forward, shouting, 'What have we here?'

Immediately Damien grabbed and shook her, his face thunderous. 'Maria! How did you get here?'

'I followed you,' she stammered, saying the first thing that came into her mind.

'Why?'

She had never seen such fury on a man's face. He was capable of killing her!

'I thought you were going to meet a woman.'

The men who had gathered round laughed loudly. 'A jealous little tart, eh?' said Chesney, looking her over lustfully. 'Is she one of your whores, my lord?'

'Never mind who she is,' he retorted, eyes blazing, fingers tightening painfully on her arm. 'She needs to be punished.'

'It won't take us long to teach her a lesson and take our fill of her,' Towser broke in eagerly.

Every man there was scruffy, villainous and ugly. The thought of Damien turning her over to them was abhorrent. Would he do so? He was furious and might well decide she deserved such a fate. There was a split second's silence and in that instant she knew he wanted her for himself.

'First she must be tied up and beaten,' he ordered.

Maria was manhandled, her dress ripped off, her naked body caressed, pinched, nipples and pubis examined. 'Someone's shaved her pussy,' Chesney shouted, lowering his face and licking her slit with a wet, fleshy tongue. 'I want first go at her, boys. Never had a hairless cunt before.'

In the midst of the pain, fear and confusion, Maria caught Damien's eye, and it was he who stretched her out, face-down on the sandy floor, tethered her wrists and spread her legs, attaching the ropes to pegs driven into the rock.

'Stand back!' he ordered his excited men.

They did so, forming a circle around her. Some had already bared their cocks, rubbing them to full erection, anticipating driving into Maria. Chesney's was huge, a great brown monster, curved like a sabre, standing proud from a nest of black curls. It was already bedewed with clear jism and he held it in his hand, licking his lips and grinning at her. Towser took second place, his prick rather less spectacular, and half a dozen other men were egging one another on with crude jests.

Maria was naked, helpless and angry. How dare Damien treat her thus? She was a titled lady and his ward! Did he guess she had been spying on him? Probably, and this was her punishment, this exposure to a gang of ruffians. If, as she feared, he had finished with her, then she would be delivered into their hands to be ravished. The idea made her stomach rise, for they were dirty, smelly and probably disease-ridden. She might become pregnant by one of them!

Damien flexed his riding whip. Maria heard the swish as it raced towards her. She felt the numbness as it landed on her buttocks and the rush of fire that flowed. The men guffawed and massaged their pricks. The whip struck again. Maria started to cry, her pride ground into the dust. Damien was so crafty, never striking the same place twice, making sure stripe was laid next to stripe. She could feel her sense of reality slipping away, the heat from her backside spreading to her cunt, her need for a male member penetrating her growing more urgent with every fresh cut of the lash. She wanted Damien, Charles and, even more shameful, anyone of those disgusting rogues who surrounded her. She was a suffering animal, but one, moreover, who needed to be mated.

She heard the clatter of the whip landing on the rocky floor. The smugglers were quiet now, only their rapid breathing reaching her ears. Then a man spread himself over her, and she clenched her inner muscles, expecting the violence of rape. But her body remembered and her nostrils recognised his smell as she felt the hardness of his cock entering her.

'Damien!' she sobbed, as he battered her furiously, releasing his rage in a far more potent way than with the whip. But this pain was one she welcomed, spearing herself on it, that deep, all-consuming thrusting that took her to the brink without giving her release.

She felt the surge as he discharged into her, and the emptiness as he withdrew. Then the full horror burst upon her as she heard him say, 'Your turn, Chesney.'

Chapter 14

'No!' Maria shouted, the denial coming from the depths of her heart and soul.

The horror was upon her, Chesney's big body knocking the breath from her as she was flattened under him. Her breasts were ground into the rock beneath her. With her face pressed to one side she could see little, but felt the enormous bar of his prick forcing its way into her entrance. She was still slippery from Damien's discharge.

Useless to struggle. She would only get hurt. But she vowed to kill Chesney if and when she got the chance. This insult could never be forgiven and neither would Damien's part in it. She wanted to scream at him to save her, but he was laughing with the others, watching Chesney rape her.

'Maybe the Frenchies would like a go at her,' bellowed Towser. 'What a welcome to England!'

Unable to resist he came forward, and so did the rest. While attempting to clench her buttocks and prevent Chesney's penetration she felt cocks in her bound hands and cocks stroking her back, leaving wet trails, while another was at her mouth.

She was suffocated, outraged, soiled by the men and deeply mortified because Damien was allowing them to besmirch her. She was aware he was watching, gaining satisfaction in seeing her used, and she cried out, 'Damien! Stop them! Please...!'

'Why should I? You've always defied me, and have the temerity to come here. What did you hope to find? Were you seeking to discredit me?'

'Whatever my reason you are my guardian and should protect me. Don't let them ravish me!'

He might have listened to her plea but she was never to know. There was a sudden outcry from the mouth of the cave. Men rushed in, shouting, 'We've been discovered! There's fighting going on out there!'

She was forgotten. Even Chesney left her, covered his cock and joined the rest. She tugged at her bonds and succeeded in yanking out the pegs, able to free her hands, though the ropes remained around her wrists. She found her cloak and huddled within it. Had Charles arrived? What was going on? She looked at her surroundings. A tunnel led from the tomb in the crypt to the cave. It had probably been used by escapees, refugees and smugglers for centuries, but now Damien had it for his own purposes.

Maria went to the entrance, coming out on a shelf set in the cliff. The sea would only reach it at high tide. Below her was a confused scene of men fighting, with a rowing boat half in, half out of the water, where others struggled to apprehend those who were trying to land. A ship was anchored in the bay, its sails filling as the breeze freshened, the helmsman waiting for the turn of the tide.

Flares were stuck in the sand, illuminating the turmoil. The clash of swords and pistol shots punctuated the cries of angry men. Then she saw Charles, face to face with Damien, the light dancing on their naked blades. Damien registered surprise on seeing Charles, followed by grim determination.

'You, Bradbury! I might have guessed you were up to something!' he shouted, and leapt forward.

'And you, milord, are a traitor! Meet me now, sword to sword, and I'll cut you down and send your black soul to hell!'

There was the ring of steel as the swords met. The duellists were old foes who knew each other's strengths and weaknesses. Maria's attention was riveted on them, though conscious of the skirmishes taking place all around her. The smugglers were fighting desperately, outnumbering Charles's men and giving them a hard time. The coastguards had not yet arrived. Some of the French, who had leapt from the boat into the water, had their swords out and were joining in the fray. One keeled over, clutching his chest, falling into the shallows where men splashed and fought and swore, blood turning the wavelets red. Powder flashed and the sound of shooting reverberated among the cliffs.

Damien and Charles circled each other, antagonists with an axe to grind. Maria knew this favoured neither. It was better to keep a cool head.

Crouching slightly Damien advanced in little leaps, while Charles avoided his blade and mocked him, 'Are you fighting, sir, or dancing a gavotte?'

Damien cursed and attacked with renewed vigour. The blades rang and Maria was terrified for both of them. This was real. No fencing bout, but a fight to the death. She edged closer, forgetting her own danger, seeing her lovers stamping backwards and forwards on the wet sand, admiring Charles's coolness and Damien's expertise.

He thrust high and Charles parried, the light running down the swords like blood. They were close now, glaring at each other, eye to eye. Damien broke free and leapt back. Charles followed, his blade whirling. Damien caught the point that was aimed straight at his heart. He knocked it up, but not before it had scratched his cheek.

This first hit enraged him and he started to lose control. He lunged at Charles, who pivoted slightly to one side, avoiding the strike. Damien recovered and beat down Charles's blade, attacking like a madman. Maria cried out and he backed towards her, grabbed her arm and retreated to the cave mouth with Charles after him. It was as if the fray on the beach was of no matter All that remained was the fight between two men over one woman. A story as old as time.

Damien kept his sword pressed to Maria's ribs as they entered the cave. 'If you don't let me go I'll kill her,' he ground out mercilessly. 'Call off your men.'

'I can't do that. Surrender and I'll put in a good word for you.' Charles kept cool.

'How magnanimous!' Damien sneered. 'And what proof do you have that I'm involved in this?'

'Plenty. I've been working on it for months.'

'Are you willing to sacrifice Maria's life?'

Damien's hold on her was strong, and pushed her against the damp rocky walls. Was this to be her tomb? Her last vision of life on earth? The tip of his sword nicked her skin just beneath her left breast; one thrust and it would penetrate her heart. Her cloak was open and she was naked beneath it, stripped by him a short while ago. She could see the spot on the ground where he had tied her and flogged her and permitted his hellions to abuse her. She ached in every limb from his treatment, and hurt inside because he cared so little for her.

Charles lowered his weapon. 'I'm willing to negotiate, but you'll have to be quick about it. From the sounds on the beach I would say that reinforcements have arrived. You don't stand a chance.'

Damien wiped the blood from his face on his jacket sleeve. He would carry the scar for life, his handsome features marred. He did not release his hold on Maria. 'I have a horse outside the chapel. Oh, don't worry, I've covered every contingency. I shall disappear and you'll not see me again.'

Charles paused. 'Does this mean you'll leave England?'

'Yes, until the war is over.'

'And what about me? Who will be in charge of my affairs?' Even at that fraught moment Maria kept her wits about her.

'Everything is taken care of.' Damien gave her a fleeting smile, and then turned to Charles again. 'Well? Do we have a bargain?'

Charles nodded. 'Do you give me your word as a gentleman that you have no more tricks up your sleeve and will disappear?'

'I agree.' Damien held out his hand and Charles took it. They shook solemnly, but Maria was not convinced of Damien's sincerity.

He looked at her, then reached out and touched one of her naked breasts and, even in that moment of peril, her body responded. 'Don't fret. We shall meet again, my dear little slave,' he murmured. 'Think of me when you're in your lonely bed, or even if you're sharing it with an inadequate lover. Think of me and remember that I was and always will be, your master.'

He let her go and she ran to Charles's side, his arm coming round her. Damien gave an ironic bow and vanished up the steps into the crypt. Maria hugged

Charles, unable to believe they were both alive.

Quint clattered into the cave, shouting, 'My lord, it's over. The coastguards have arrested all concerned. Except the ringleader who seems to have run off.'

'Don't worry. I'll come and sort it out.' Charles smiled at Maria and said, 'You're a disobedient hussy, aren't you? Didn't I tell you to stay out of trouble? Now what am I going to do with you?'

'We'll take care of her?' Robin spoke from the steps. He was backed by Tranter.

'And how many more people have you involved in this?' Charles said angrily, giving her a shake.

'None, but they have come in time and will take me back to the manor.'

'Stay there till I come. Make sure she does, will you, Robin? I've never known such a wayward chit!'

Although Charles was scolding her she could see he was relieved. He questioned Robin further, saying, 'Did you see a man leaving the crypt?'

'No, we were only concerned in finding her ladyship,' Robin replied, eyes wide as he listened to the clamour outside.

'Good man,' Charles said, and pushed Maria forward. 'I put her in your safe keeping. Maria, I shall call on you later, probably tomorrow morning. You'd better be there.'

He strode from the cave with Quint, and Maria gathered up her torn clothing and permitted Robin to help her climb up into the moonlight and find her horse. In the back of her mind was the disloyal thought that perhaps Damien might be lurking somewhere, ready to spirit her away. She hated herself for this. She loved Charles, didn't she?

Damien left his horse inside Scratch Tump, found a candle and tinderbox always kept to hand there, and then made his way down a long winding tunnel that led to the grounds of Raven Towers. He blessed his ancestors who, involved in religious strife and treachery towards the crown, had constructed it, and also the secret passages that riddled the old house.

He was furiously angry with Charles. He had lost money on this enterprise, having already laid out on expenses and been expecting a fat purse to arrive with one of the spies. Not only Charles roused his ire, but Maria too. He could have sworn he had succeeded in making her his own, an enslaved creature who would obey his every wish. He had several reasons for returning to the house; one was to collect money for his journey; another to leave letters for Arabella and his bank. These would be left in the care of his loyal manservant, Johnson. But the other, most pressing reason, was to remind Maria that she could never escape him.

He smiled grimly as he heaved at the bramble-covered grill set over the tunnel's entrance. It gave access to a disused folly at the far side of the garden. From there it would be easy to enter one of the hidden routes that would connect him to Maria's bedchamber.

Sarah had subjected Maria to a thorough scolding when Emily brought her in from the stable yard. 'Where have you been, my lady?' she ranted, though her voice was shaking.

'Riding,' Maria had answered shortly.

'At this hour? And what happened to your clothes?'

'She took them off to have a dip in the pool. Left them on the bank where an animal ripped them before she could stop it,' Emily lied convincingly, and Maria was glad of the quick-witted maid's support.

Sarah threw her hands in the air despairingly. 'I don't know what this world is coming to! Lady Arabella didn't seem all that bothered when I reported you missing. She said it was probably only a girlish prank. Well, into bed with you, before you catch your death of cold. I'll bring you some hot milk.'

Emily and Maria exchanged a relieved glance and before long she was installed in the four-poster, wearing a clean nightgown and tucked under the covers. She drank the milk, then begged Sarah to leave a candle burning on the side-table, the evening's events having frightened her more than she imagined. Courageous while they were happening, they now came back to haunt her in all their brutal vividness, and she trembled.

Trying to fix her thoughts on Charles and the rosy future she might share with him, she eventually drifted into a troubled sleep to be awakened abruptly by a hand clamping over her mouth. She struggled, unable to move, pinned down by a solid body. The room was dark. The candle had gone out.

'Be quiet,' hissed an imperious voice in her ear. She obeyed, recognising the tone. 'That's better,' said Damien. 'I'll take my hand away, if you promise not to scream.'

She nodded and the hand was removed, but not the body that was pinning her to the mattress. It was Damien all right, smelling of the night and damp air. His lips captured hers, stifling any protest and, despite everything, her mouth parted and her tongue met his and desire flared within her. But even so, he had some answers to give.

She twisted away from him. 'Why did you let your brutes make free with me?' she demanded, keeping her voice low. 'You objected to Charles touching me, yet would have stood by and watched me being raped.'

'You ask too many questions,' he said into the darkness. 'It was my choice to have my men enjoy you. Bradbury was another matter entirely. You were doing it of your own free will, forgetting that you belong to me.'

'I belong to no man!' Her indignation forced her to try to break free from him, but his arms tightened.

'That is not so. You may think you are free of me, and may have it in your mind to even marry Bradbury, but in your heart and in your cunt you will know that I am your master forever.'

'No! No!' she insisted, but weakening under his onslaught. 'You would have run me through with your sword, if Charles hadn't agreed to your bargain.'

'Yes, I would. You know I'm ruthless.'

He rose, pulled her to the edge of the mattress, rolled her onto her face, lifted her nightgown and brought the flat of his hand down on her sore buttocks. 'Don't cry out,' he ordered.

Maria buried her face in the sheet, muffling her sobs. He slapped her where she had already felt the scourge, his whip marking her earlier. He struck her again, and her flesh recognised her master's hand, though her mind denied it. No one owned her! No man should have domination over her! His blows flowed into one another, joining the dark stream of sensuality that lay inside her. He was right. Deny it though she might, he had tamed her, controlled her, and she would never be satisfied by a tender lover. Damien had taught her the mysteries of pain/pleasure and she would always hanker for it now.

She hated him for lifting the lid of this Pandora's Box, yet gloried in the riches he had shown her within it. Even now the pain was receding as his skilful fingers massaged her aching hinds. He pulled her close to him, turning her so he could caress her nipples and then replace his fingers with his lips, and cruise down her belly to her shaven mound. He parted her crack and found she was already dewy, spreading the fluid over her labia, folding back the lips and stroking her clitoris. His engorged cock pressed into her side, one thigh thrown over hers, holding her fast. She could not resist folding her fingers around it, feeling its heat and size as if to commit it to memory for all time.

He was an enigma; selfish, disloyal, concerned only with his own welfare, yet he intrigued her. Bad he undoubtedly was, but this in itself added to his fascination. And as his skilful fingers caressed her nubbin, circling it, rubbing it, holding off and tormenting it, then returning, so she forgot all his evil traits. She spread herself out in supplication, begging him to satisfy her, and he played her like a lute, bringing forth the sweetest music. Maria rose higher and higher, until her orgasm exploded in a firework display of awesome release. She buried her face in his chest, stifling her yelps of pleasure.

She felt his prick enter and fill her, battering and thrusting and the force of it was just what she needed, giving her something for her muscles to contract around. Damien was on his knees between her thighs, silhouetted against the window, a black, unearthly shape that could have been a demon, not a man. He hurt her, his fingers like claws, and his penis hammered into her repeatedly, gaining momentum until he discharged, filling her with his spunk.

He had barely finished when he withdrew completely. She grabbed at him, wanting tenderness and reassurance. He gave neither. 'I'm leaving now. You may never see me again. On the other hand, I shall probably survive. As they say, "the devil looks after his own".'

'Where are you going?' She sat up, staunching their combined fluids with the edge of her nightgown. Time stretched bleakly ahead with no Damien to tease, torment, and hurt her.

'Abroad.' He was gathering up his cloak, preparing to leave. 'I shall send for Johnson. No gentleman worth his salt can manage without his trusted valet.'

'You'll never return?' She wanted to light the candle and see his face.

'Not until this war is over. Don't worry, I've left your affairs in order. You can take over Burrington Manor now, if you wish. Your aunt and the bank will advise you. Marry whoever you wish, even that coxcomb Bradley, but one day you'll get a message and you'll drop everything and come to me.'

'Ha! You're very sure of yourself, my lord!' He still had the power to infuriate her.

He leaned over her and she felt his lips on her brow. 'Of course. You're my slave-slut and always will be.'

With that he vanished and she heard the gentle click of a secret door shutting, a door she did not know existed. Tears filled her eyes and her heat bled within her. Even though she knew Damien was rotten through and through, she would never tell anyone, especially Charles, that he had visited her in the dead of night.

Epilogue

Maria took over Burrington Manor and settled down there. With her help, Robin and Jane were forgiven by her parents for their flight to Gretna Green and he became the new vicar of Burrington. There was no word from Damien.

On the morning after the coastguards had arrested the French spies and those who were helping them, no one associated the disappearance of the viscount with these exciting events. It was his habit to come and go at short notice, and his agent had been primed to look after Raven Towers. Coutts Bank, in London, had instructions to manage his business affairs and Arabella already knew what to do about Maria's manor and property if he vanished for a long spell.

'Hey-ho, my dear. Don't worry your pretty head about anything,' Arabella had said, getting ready to return to the capital and all the delights of the Winter Season. 'I shall consult with the lawyers and the bank and they will follow his instructions.'

They did, and Maria returned to her home that had been cared for by a housekeeper and steward, opened it up and had a splendid Christmas gathering where everyone was invited. Charles enthused about the estate.

'It's an artist's paradise. Think of the landscapes I can paint, to say nothing of a formal portrait of yourself; mistress of all you survey. You can hang it in the Long Gallery, among those of your forebears.' She refused to give him the answer he craved, relishing her newfound freedom, but he was persistent.

'Will you marry me?' he asked again, as they lay in her bed in the master chamber. It was Boxing Day and she was to spend it taking presents and food round to all the villagers, as was the custom.

She had been expecting this and now pondered on it once again. For weeks she had heard nothing from Damien, who seemed to have disappeared from the face of the earth. Testing Charles, she had shown him that she liked him to be masterful in the bedroom. Nothing averse, he had become adept at putting her over his knee and spanking her or even taking a whip to her. She had soon discovered that this gave him a substantial erection.

'Do you want to beat an acceptance out of me?' she invited, pushing aside the coverlet and stretching voluptuously.

'You tantalising little witch,' he snarled, half amused, half irritated and, snatching her up, he spread her across his lap and slapped her bottom, not as hard as Damien would have done, but enough to satisfy her need to be aroused in such a manner.

After this he treated her roughly, pushing her down on the mattress and taking his pleasure of her. Responding fervently, her bottom stinging, she reached an almighty climax.

She rested in his arms, stroking his hair and purring like a contented cat, but all the time remembering the letter Damien had left for her in Johnson's care, and which he had delivered the morning after his master had fled. It had read, *Come to me in the Indies. You know you want to. No other can give you the pleasure that I can. You need controlling, and I'm the man to do it. Travel with Johnson, who will be leaving soon.*

There had been more in this vein, and she thought about it a great deal, but had now made up her mind. She would accept Charles's proposal and, if in the future Damien returned, she might permit him to be her lover. Whatever happened, he had taught her well and far from being his slave, she had grown into an independent woman who knew what she wanted. She was grateful for this, and could be his submissive or control him. Had he tamed her? Partly, she supposed, though it was impossible to entirely subdue someone as self-willed as herself.

www.ingramcontent.com/pod-product-compliance
Lightning Source LLC
Chambersburg PA
CBHW070752120626
46557CB00002B/556